First Contact

ESCAPE
TO
55 CANCRI

Kenneth E. Ingle

BooksForABuck.com

2009

Kenneth E. Ingle

First Contact:

Escape to 55 Cancri

BooksForABuck.com

May 2009

ISBN: 978-1-60215-098-0

Cognitive Dissonance
The mental torment that comes from being confronted by
two fundamentally opposed propositions

Dedication

This book is dedicated to my son Kevin
who often was a sounding
board for ideas.

Preface

This book became possible because some very intelligent people decided to help. Ideas from DNA research to quantum physics on the cutting edge of technology added the touch of realism.

Dr. Jordan Maclay, eminent in Quantum Electrodynamics or QED brought life to the Casimir engine. Without that idea, we would not have had a story.

Dr. Zdzislaw Musielak, Professor of Physics, University of Texas at Arlington, TX, besides being my friend, helped with encouragement and fielded many of the technical questions. He introduced me to Dr. Manfred Cuntz.

Dr. Manfred Cuntz, Associate Professor of Physics, Director of Astronomy Program, University of Texas at Arlington, wrote the definitive paper, et al, on 55 Cancri 'D'. This paper provided a realistic destination for the inhabitants of Orion.

Acknowledgements

Dr. Jordan Maclay
Senior Partner, Chief Scientist
Quantum Fields, LLC
Richland Center, WI
>   Dr. Maclay developed the engineering specifications for the Casimir
>   engines.

Dr. Zdzislaw E. Musielak
Professor of Physics
The University of Texas at Arlington, TX
>   Dr. Musielak provided counsel in many areas, interpreting physical
>   date. He introduced the author to Dr. Manfred Cuntz.

Dr. Manfred Cuntz
Associate Professor of Physics and Director of the Astronomy Program.
The University of Texas at Arlington, TX.
>   Hypothesis Paper: On the Possibility of Earth-Type Habitable Planets
>   in the 55 Cancri System
>   M. Cuntz, W. Von Bloh, S. Franck, and C. Bounama
>   Astrobiology, 3, 681 (2003)

Bert Rutan, President Scaled Composites, Inc.
With permission

DFW Writer's Workshop for their patience.

PREVIEW OF THINGS TO COME
Circa 1942

The Captain had moved his quarters directly behind the bridge shortly after the expedition cruise began. With a tendency to be impatient, he wanted immediate access to the nerve center of the ship. To waste time was more than slothfulness, it bordered on dereliction of duty.

Commissioned a research vessel, the ship had participated in a number of distinguished finds and the Captain intended to add to that record. Seven hundred meters long, and a crew of twelve, the vessel was an example of what a well designed ship and superbly trained crew could accomplish.

The Captain didn't suffer fools. He had personally selected all twelve crewmen. Each had graduated in their specialty at or near the top of their class. From propulsion engineer to cook, each crewmember was required to know at least two disciplines. The Captain's expectations were well known and never ignored. Aboard this ship, you provided information, the Captain made decisions. The only vice he permitted himself was a pipe.

Physical size made no difference. The shortest ever to graduate the military academy, he was the smallest at every officer's conference. But where he was concerned, size never equated to results. He excelled at martial arts. His small frame served him well in personal combat. He never lost a wrestling match at the academy. Academically, he graduated top of his class. Later, he was to serve as the academy director. His stint as head of the school, while marked by controversy, was acknowledged to be on a par with the school's founders. Now, he was realizing the second goal of his life. He had become an explorer.

The cruise, entering its eighth month, was shorter than most. Frequent stops had made the trek one to be envied. Some had offered to go as unpaid collegiate auditors. But the Captain selected as observers, two ensigns who had shown particular skills for such an expedition, namely fewer biases.

Two months earlier, out of visual range of the inhabitants, the ship had dispatched its spectators with orders to gather detailed data on what they saw. Now, it was time to present their findings to the Captain.

The two junior officers, both up for promotion to lieutenant, Junior Grade, made their way to the bridge.

The Executive and Science officers returned their salutes and accompanied them into the Captain's quarters. Everyone knew the remainder of these young officers careers would be determined by this meeting.

"Good morning, Captain. The detail assigned to make the exploration reporting," the Exec said. Despite the crew and ship being very small, adherence to naval etiquette was mandated and rigorously followed.

"At ease, gentlemen. Please be seated." The Captain motioned to the armless chairs fronting his desk.

Protocol required the explorers speak only after the Captain directed them to do so. The creases in their starched and pressed uniforms resisted their posture as they sat nervously waiting. In the next few minutes, their leader would judge everything they'd worked for over the last year. Indeed their careers were at stake.

The Captain leaned on his desk, elbows taking very little weight, and slowly filled his pipe. He picked up a small tamper and teased the filling to his satisfaction.

He studied the two junior officers for a moment. "I trust your opportunity to unobtrusively observe went well and brought appropriate results."

The senior of the two Ensigns said, "Sir, we attempted to gather the facts as they presented themselves. Every effort was made not to cloud the data with our opinions." Both young officers knew their job was to present facts not opinions. First in their minds was the admonition of the ships science officer—any judgment would be the Captain's. You gathered facts—he made decisions.

"Proceed." It was an order, not a request.

The Ensign cleared his throat and recited without looking at his notes. "Nation states are the rule here. Some are governed by elected officials, some by hereditary monarchs. Use of force to secure a position of leadership is common as well. Territorial integrity is consistent throughout this world. As with any grouping there are very successful nations and at the other extreme very poor countries. There is some sharing of wealth but usually tied to political objectives. Currently there are fourteen separate conflicts occurring, resulting in two significant wars. Some of the conflicts are over religion, some the result of grudges carried often for centuries. We found crime in every state and it was dealt with ignobly. Disparate groups are found trying to mend many of the social ills observed. However, they are often misused by whoever is governing. We could find no evidence of a universal moral code although many leaders talk as if one existed. That concludes the report of our findings."

Dismissing the junior officers, the Captain punched a button on the consol in front of him and said, "Set a course for home. We will bypass this place."

With that, the ship headed away from the third planet, the blue planet, the one called Earth.

Prologue
1967

Doctor Maria Presk, buoyed by the bustle and spectacle, allowed herself a moment of self-indulgence as she looked around the sterile one-room lab. At a time when many scientists were shunning the idea of DNA research, she had the vision to see far beyond them. And now, seven employees were hard at work, each the very best in some aspect of science that could help her seize the initiative in the new field of DNA research.

Plunked down on a less than desirable sprint of land amid a dismal setting in North Dallas with one bathroom, one specimen freezer vault, access to the fastest computer in the world, Control Data's CDC 6600, no office, and no windows, Advanced Bio-Yield, Inc. made its mark and worked tirelessly to stay ahead of the field. Maria made sure every cent possible had gone into salaries and the latest technology for these best minds. Just four years on their own in biochemical research marked them as an industry leader in the new untested science. Nineteen sixty-six had proven to be an excellent year. Her lab had discovered the genetic code that first deciphered the biochemical analysis of an amino acid.

With that discovery, Maria virtually ensured Bio-Yield remained light years ahead of others finally gearing up for serious DNA research. When many labs and investors doubted the wisdom of spending much time or money on speculative research she had gambled—and won.

David Rohm caught her piercing hazel eyes and smiled. She applauded her astuteness in hiring and foresight in making him a full partner in the lab. His doctoral work in nano electro-bio-mechanical engineering already had become a hallmark in academia and industry. His addition to the staff put the final touch to the lab's imposing résumé.

The deep muffled rumble was followed by a sharp crack before the blast swept across the room. The explosion, short lived, seemed far away. Gaseous clouds followed the force, whipping her skin and clothes.

The detonation moved across the granite countertops, shattering beakers, Petri dishes, flasks, tubes containing treacherous creations sending their contents into the air; some in streams others atomized into gas, boiling, mixing.

Involuntarily, as if on a pivot, her head turned, and arms swung, shielding her eyes and face. For a brief instant, the peculiar fine, grey, primordial smelling cloud enveloped the entire room touching everything and everyone. Then it dissipated under the steady downpour created by the automatic fire suppressants.

In spite of the fear, the terrible crashing noise, she would remember the cloud.

**PART
ONE**

CHAPTER ONE
Thirty-five years later

Maria Presk looked out over the small group—all people she had known for almost forty years. She never doubted this moment would test her leadership skills beyond anything she'd ever experienced. "Yes, Martin. That explosion did change us. We are aging at a much slower rate. And some of us," she looked with eyes that didn't flinch at those seated in front of her, "have been trying for the last ten or so years to find an answer." She made no effort to hide her contempt and asked, "Martin, why?"

Martin Grabel, genius mathematician, stood mute yet defiant before the group's leader. This was one of the few times his mercurial temper didn't lash out against anyone venturing close.

A grey cloudy sky filtered through thermo pane windows and stretched across the speckled white marble floor, adding to the stark chill that had settled over the group. Throw rugs spread before the chairs and sofas provided little relief to the cold that infected the room. Any semblance of coziness or camaraderie that might have existed a day earlier had disappeared.

Maria looked a youthful thirty, which belied her sixty-five years. The seven scientists seated before her were the first employees of Advanced Bio-Yield and shared the same anguish, now a curse. All carried wounds from that day—some physical and some mental. None had aged over the past thirty-five years and no one knew why. Only that whatever happened in that explosion changed their lives. Now, they could no longer move freely among people they had known for years.

For the last ten, Maria had prepared for the moment when they would have to disappear but now Martin's disclosure threatened everything.

Emotions ranged from anger to fear of what the future might hold. Hope and trust in each other remained all they had and now even that seemed betrayed.

She struggled to control the contempt, the impulse to strike out, even if only with words. Something threatening stirred inside her—anger deeper than anything she'd ever experienced. Her entire life had been one of quiet thought and exploration but in an instant, it had all changed—again.

Her eyes swept the gathering one by one: David Rohm, Erik Svern, Ann Bartlett, Bhani Patel, Gramina Flora and Roberto Macon, as if assuring each she would not fail them.

Roberto Macon, a calm, sober medical research doctor, sat resolute and unmoving. Gramina Fiora at his side as she had been since the two were married and left Bio-Yield together. She'd worked with Roberto ever since and some who knew them said she was his backbone. His brows drew together in an agonized expression. At a little over five foot seven, carrying a slight stoop, a legacy from spending hours perched over a microscope. Not particularly strong in personal relationships, it seemed he had the need to speak but in a defensive manner. "I think I can speak for the entire group." There seemed a touch of angst as his voice highlighted his Spanish heritage. He continued, "Maria, we joined Bio-Yield many years ago when you first put the lab together because it was *you*. And when you hired David, I knew I had joined a winner."

Maria felt the heat rise on her face.

"The problem was, so did the industry. Over the years, competitors proselytized us because you had singled each one out from the many. That made us special—a commodity ready for the headhunter's pickings."

Quietly, Macon ticked off the ironies as he saw them. "The lure of promotions, big salary increases and in his case both, plus a laboratory of his own, was too great to resist." But not before Bio-Yield had locked basic patents that made it the undisputed leader in DNA research. "We left for what appeared better opportunities." He didn't mention Grabel's temper tantrums. "You have what it takes to hold us together and the resources to help find a solution. I think I speak for all of us. We believe you're our only hope."

Maria was not at all sure of that, until her eyes reached Martin Grabel. She calmed the fury that boiled, wanting to explode in a tirade that would do more damage than good. To some it may have seemed more moral rage than anger but Maria knew better. Her voice, though quiet still carried a keenly honed edge. "Martin, why?"

Martin Grabel, arguably the most intelligent of the eight, had quit the lab after a run-in with Maria more than thirty years before over how to write some computer code. The two had not seen each other or spoken since. Over the years, he'd held any number of jobs—all only for short periods. Yet, companies, even the government, kept bringing him back to solve a problem or move their systems ahead. He was just that good. Even at that, opening old wounds brought them no closer to a resolution. It had taken Erik Svern almost six months, using every bit of guile he possessed, to locate the unpredictable, volatile mathematical genius. They couldn't afford to lose him again.

"Why, Martin? Of all people, why tell a reporter? And a tabloid at that." Maria struggled to soften her face. Yet the air of indignation permeating her voice conveyed anything but self-righteousness. She knew she sounded incredulous but letting that weakness show seemed better than the anger roil in her gut. Grabel's action had placed them all in great peril. What had been their secret, although frequently questioned by outsiders, now lay in the hands of someone who could threaten their very existence. If it became public, any hope the group might have to live some reasonable kind of life disappeared. Grabel had betrayed them all.

Within the room, the atmosphere seemed smothering, frigid with little or no hope of improving. Normally, the open lava rock fireplace gave the large family room a sense of welcome comfort. That it now lacked the warmth of a ranch style home and said volumes about the complexity of the situation the group faced.

Maria, dressed in dark blue slacks and a ruffled white high-necked blouse, glanced across the twenty feet or so through the doorway leading to her den, seeking solace from the goddess statuette Athena shelved in her Greek idol collection. Instead, her eyes focused on Thor and retribution. Even the exposed large overhead beams and an ornate west Texas chandelier, a gift from her father, brought little comfort.

Bald head perspiring, the diminutive man stood at the floor-level fireside's massive end, dwarfed by the room size. He tugged uncomfortably at his tan pullover cashmere sweater and faced his former colleagues, back turned toward Maria and David, manner defiant, belligerent.

Not a single voice rose to his defense.

A few inches shorter than his former boss, spectacles as thick as bulletproof glass hung on a nose large enough to handle the weight and made him look like the cartoon character, Ziggy. His volatile-as-nitro-glycerin personality meant everyone stayed on guard. People who knew him kept their contact at an absolute minimum and avoided confrontations as they always became fiery with no winners, only casualties.

Grabel hesitated, then the anticipated explosion came as his arms shot into the air. "What did you expect?" His body quivered as he contemptuously shouted back. "People laughed when I told them I was seventy-two. Called me crazy, delusional. I haven't aged a day, physically or mentally. I needed a friend and only Arlo made any effort to help me."

His disposition hadn't changed. Always bad. The man's hallmark. Current circumstances didn't help a bit. Being outnumbered and surrounded by people who knew him and were constantly on guard against his hostility only added to the isolation.

Maria paused to hide her real anguish. "Thank you for being honest. Let's hope with all of us facing the same situation, we can become that friend." Her voice was uncompromising, yet oddly gentle and, sincere.

She gestured to everyone. The doubt Maria saw in their faces came with experienced justification. These people knew the man, now the focus of their worry. In earlier times, each had faced his derisive and demeaning outbursts. Still they placed their hopes in Maria as they had years earlier.

Grabel flinched, his chin raised as if to defy the kindly response. Then, as if rethinking his actions, his manner changed and he seemed surprised that his own behavior, which usually elicited a volatile reaction in self-defense, had resulted in a kindly response. Fury dulled for the moment, the ripe strawberry-red face and neck faded to its normal pallid white.

Erik Svern, the deliberate yet adventurous former chemist-turned-CIA agent, had located Grabel and enticed him back. He interrupted the confrontation, the first to come to the man's defense. "Martin realized his mistake—that's why he lived on the street. New York's a good place to hide. If you're clever enough, you can do it in plain sight and Martin pulled it off." His focus, predatory, never strayed from Grabel.

Rigid, hands fisted in her lap, Maria sat almost at attention on the small two-seater, off-white leather divan. The strain of the day's events should have taken its toll but if they did, the effects hadn't shown. Yet, there seemed little reason to celebrate the reunion.

She caught David's glance but remained impassive, confident, determined her usual steely resolve would settle the issue without a further split. Quiet settled over the room despite the tension.

A gentle rushing air, no more than a whisper, echoed through the ventilators. Even though the frail Texas autumn pastel colors had tinged the trees and foliage, the cooled air and even the slight noise, made a welcome diversion and seemed to take the edge off the appalling conflict.

Erik put an end to the moment. "But, you can be sure, the reporter's name, Arlo Marik, will show up at Bio-Yield and that means he'll be at your door." He stared at their leader. "And sooner rather than later."

Erik had the ability to sound an alarm without being an alarmist, to make you aware without creating panic. "Here's a picture of the guy so at least he can't pass himself off without you knowing who you're dealing with."

Maria remained stoic but only she and David knew the depth of her resentment. Open hands moved from her lap to a contemplative steeple under her chin. Bit by bit, they slid down to form fists pressed against her stomach. Her round black eyes opened. Her oval face, framed in close-cropped raven hair, seemed apprehensive yet filled with determination.

Maria stood.

All eyes moved toward her.

In a voice almost a whisper, yet calm and steady that cut through the quiet like a razor shaving off any veneer of complacency. "Now that an outsider knows, or has strong suspicions, that our aging process has slowed, we can't afford any mistakes. I suggest we move up our time table."

Everyone there look the same as they did when they started at Bio-Yield forty years ago. Over the last few years, each had fended off comments about her or his appearance. That it had changed their lives beyond all comprehension also went unsaid. To a person, they had cut ties with their past, as much through necessity as choice. No believable response, no defense to their youthful appearance seemed to stem the curious glances or looks of disbelief.

Silence as unearthly as their circumstance settled over the room. For a moment, no one moved. Ten years of dedicated research had failed to disclose the reason for their slow aging. They had lost control over their lives.

Maria worked to hide the torment that churned her insides, and looked with anguish out over the group wishing their research over the last few years had given, at the least, a clue as to the cause. But that wasn't the case.

What went wrong? So many chemical combinations at varying conditions and stages of development existed and they'd tried every one that came to mind. Temperature variations, concoctions of every description, time—anything that could affect the outcome came under scrutiny. The blast destroyed all test sites and any one or all may have contributed to their dilemma. No effort to duplicate the conditions had shed light on their predicament.

Maria's eyes swept each person again searching for independent reactions, and she made no effort to stifle the mild sigh that escaped her.

She asked, "How do the rest of you feel?"

First Contact

Martin jumped to his feet and yelled before anyone else could answer. "What time table? I don't know about any plan. You've told me nothing."

Maria quelled her impulse to smack the little man. But deep down she knew he could be as important as anyone in carrying out her plan, maybe even more so. "Martin, please sit down. Of course, you're right. You don't know what we've been up to over the last few years. Before I go ahead, I must have your word that what I'm about to tell you will not be discussed with anyone outside this group."

Martin hesitated. He looked past Maria, staring, as if for the first time he wanted to confront the reality he'd steadfastly avoided. And then nodded. "You have my word."

A collective silent sigh swept the room.

Maria took a deep breath, stood, and said, "My calculations show we will all live up to four hundred years. The fact that someone outside the group knows, or at least suspects, confirms we can no longer continue to live as we have. Even the lifestyle changes we've made over the last few years are no longer sufficient. That hasn't been comfortable for any of us. And it's only going to get worse. I do not intend to become anyone's guinea pig, prodded and poked for the rest of my life. We must continue our research and yet avoid becoming lab rats. We've known this time would come. All of you, except Martin, know what I believe we must do. You also know that plan has been steadily moving forward."

No one moved except Grabel. Now seated at the rear, he jumped to his feet. "Your calculations? I want to see them. Along with your assumptions. All of them."

Quiet, as anxious as death, settled over the room after the boisterous outburst and for a few seconds, no one moved—waiting—not knowing for what.

Over the last few years, as each had become aware of their changes, they had returned to Maria's fold. All but the bespectacled man had the advantage of participating in the research and planning that had moved ahead over the last few years. Only Grabel's self-imposed isolation had kept him out of the information loop.

Maria opened her clenched hands, white from the tight-fisted strain, brushed them across the end table next to the divan as if clearing a place for the problem, picked up a manila folder, and handed it to her inquisitor. "Gladly, Martin. Here." She gave the documents to Bhani Patel, seated at the front of the group, who walked them back to where the mathematician stood and with a smile, handed them to him.

Martin's eyebrows rose in surprise—surprise that not so much as an argument got him what he had wanted.

Maria broke the silence. "The information cannot leave this house. I suggest we all take up residence here."

CHAPTER TWO
The Gathering

Maria Presk turned to face Martin Grabel;, the rest of the group seemingly dreading what they were sure would be a fiery confrontation. Her voice softened. "For the last ten years, we've planned to leave this planet. Over the last fifteen years, David and I sold our interest in Bio-Yield and put the money where we can readily get to it. We netted about forty Billion dollars."

That brought a gasp from the bespectacled man. "After taxes."

That got a laugh from the group, all except Grabel.

"For the last eight to nine years, David has had a design team preparing the specifications in detail for our spacecraft, a spaceship more accurately; one that will take us to our future home. Quantum Fields, a research company, has been designing the Casimir engines to drive the ship." She stopped for a moment, if for no other reason but to let what she'd said soak in and hopefully get some idea of how Grabel might handle it.

Martin jumped to his feet, arms waving. His voice more like a banshee than human, which ran the norm for him and not unexpected, "You had no right to do make such a decision without permission. *My permission.*"

Scattered around the room, the rest of the group in chairs or seated on the floor all winced at Grabel's tirade.

Fists clenched, Ann Bartlett stomped to face her fellow mathematician. Ann had worked for a number of labs involved in DNA research after leaving Bio-Yield. In *her* mind, her greatest achievement had been a successful marriage —, which ended when a plane accident made her a widow. She describes her married those years as the happiest of her life. Two years after returning to Maria's fold, she and Erik Svern married.

The steel in her voice matched her eyes. A head taller than the smallish man, she said, "Martin, why in the hell don't you grow up?" Her nose just inches from his, white knuckles jammed against her waist she growled, "No longer than you've been here, I've just about had it with you. All you ever do is bitch no matter what anyone does or says. And to top it all off, you never contribute shit. So why don't you shut your," her lips started for form an 'f' but changed, "damned mouth?"

Oh, no. Why did this have to happen? Maria wondered if she could salvage any kind of working deal between these two. Grabel had it right. She hadn't consulted many of them. Only David and Erik had full knowledge of what she'd planned. But the fight between these two didn't bode well at all.

Everyone except Ann stood quietly. At one time or another, they had all sampled her temper. Professionally, these two they had a high regard for each other's capabilities. The biggest difference; Ann had a firm grip on her social skills although at the moment anyone in their right mind would suggest that seemed in doubt.

David, the eternal mediator, had stepped between these two dozens of times in the small company's early life. He took a step forward but Maria casually touched his arm. Out of the corner of her eye, she saw Bhani Patel move toward the cornered man.

Martin's mouth had dropped open. He had tried to speak but no words came out. Only with an effort did he regain a bit of his innate combativeness. "Why are you talking to me this way? What right have you?"

Ann's eyes were like lightning. "*Every* right you inconsiderate bastard. Since you won't do it, it's about time someone else put a stop to your childish behavior."

Bhani closed on Grabel. "Martin," her touch on his arm distracted him but the smile allowed her to coax him away. "Could I see you for a moment?" Her soft singsong voice seemed to tranquilize the small man.

Bhani, a smallish figure that belied her dynamite personality, guided Martin toward the den. After serving as Bio-Yield's business agent, she had retired from a distinguished career in the same position at Johns Hopkins a few years ago.

Maria breathed a silent sigh of relief. A solution to her biggest concern could have just presented itself. Four men and four women—and without any matchmaking on her part, the last of the group may have paired off. Grabel may not realize it, but he had at least one admirer. Maria could not have been more satisfied, pleased. Out of the most explosive circumstance, a potential bomb looked like it had been defused. Now, if Bhani could only work her magic and smooth things over.

Small talk dominated the conversations as the group waited for the outcome of Bhani's intervention.

After a few minutes, Erik made his way to the den.

The group watched as Svern rapped on the door, and spoke to the two. They emerged arm in arm.

Maria hid the grin she felt and instead offered a pleased nod. Martin's face held a look she had never seen before and doubted anyone in the room had. She suspected the little man had never before experienced the strange emotions racking his body. Bhani, chin held high made no effort to hide her delight.

Neither Ann nor Martin gave an apology. Still, Martin seemed enrapt with Bhani's attention, maybe bewildered suited his demeanor better. *Whatever worked.*

Maria seized the moment and drove ahead. "A few years ago, I purchased land in Baja Mexico, more precisely, Bahia Los Angeles, on the Sea of Cortez, to be our construction and launch site. Erik has been very busy in Mexico," she nodded in his direction, "setting up four companies that control the day-to-day operation. Naturally, we control the companies."

Much to everyone's surprise Martin asked, absent the expected explosion, "Do you really think this can work?"

Erik spoke next in a benevolent, official manner, "Martin I won't kid you. There are many unknowns but the one I'm most concerned with is this tabloid guy. Something just doesn't smell right. Why haven't we seen something in print? This kind of story should churn the muckrakers into a frenzy. I have a gut feel that something else is at work here. Something that I don't like."

For over an hour, they debated ramifications of the plan in detail and filled in the many gaps for Martin, before finally breaking for dinner.

Two days later, Maria returned from what had become weekly errands to the neighborhood grocery. The change of pace gave her a little time alone. She parked her car in the garage. A sudden temperature drop and the blue autumn sky offered another hint that Texas had seen the last of its all-too-short fall season.

Instead of entering the house directly from the garage, she headed for the front lawn to pick up the newspaper lying near the walkway. On her way out, she turned to flip the switch closing the wooden overhead door but stopped abruptly at the sight of an approaching man.

"Doctor Presk…

"We have a mutual friend, one with a very interesting story." A robust bearded man with no tie and in a dark blue suit that looked more like an unmade bed strode forward. He stopped between Maria and the main door, hands relaxed at his side—a menace, but not a threatening pose.

"Do you have a moment?"

Maria recognized Arlo Marik from the picture Erik had provided but didn't acknowledge her awareness. Trying to hide her concern she answered, "It would seem I have little choice. Who are you and why are you blocking my way?"

Marik nodded. "I'm Arlo Marik. Sorry to intrude, but—"

Maria cut him short and said in a voice of dismissal, "Sir, I've retired from my scientific pursuits and public life. I don't give interviews. Now if you'll excuse me." She sidestepped the reporter and in deliberate strides moved toward the electric switch.

The overhead closer wailed and drowned out any attempt at conversation.

Quiet settled after the door closed.

Marik parried. "Doctor Martin Grabel worked for you and he says you've discovered the secret of long life; Ponce de Leon's fountain of youth." A chuckle followed his dry nasal Brooklyn accent.

Maria turned to face the intruder and forced a smile. "Really? How fortunate. And you mean Texas had the elixir all the time and not Florida?"

"How 'bout your laboratory?" Raised scraggly eyebrows accompanied the remark.

She gave a nonchalant shrug and decided to keep her response in the scientific realm. "I have no proof of that. I'm sure I would know if such existed." At least about that, she didn't lie. Beyond doubt, the scientist's world had changed forever.

CHAPTER THREE
Exposed

Maria, engrossed in the many problems facing them, walked with measured steps across the den that had become the office and focal point of the group's activities.

Shortly after she arrived, Erik Svern strode in still wearing his dark blue Prada jacket and light grey slacks. He shed his coat, laid it over the back of a chair, and in his usual casual habit announced, "We've got company." The former agent's southern voice, when quiet always seemed covered in velvet, and he always appeared to have his emotions under control. An asset CIA must have found to their liking.

Maria quizzically eyed him. "No need to be cryptic. What does that mean?"

"Arlo Marik has taken up residence in the Gillman place across the street. Rented it month to month. Makes a perfect spot to keep an eye on us. I think it helps explain why nothing has made the daily wipe. Got it through a third party. He doesn't know that we know."

"How's that?"

"He's on someone's payroll. Someone that's not in a hurry. They've got time and money."

Her look was more than a question.

"Our government. Probably CIA. But it could be someone else."

Erik didn't offer his source. He had the information and for Maria, that made the difference.

"Make sure all of our people know about the guy. Let them build their hide and seek skills. What about Martin?"

"He's the easiest identified of our group. Stands out. Those glasses look like the bottoms of a coke bottle. He's so short that in a crowd, it looks like a hole where he's standing."

David and Bhani stepped in, joining the two. The small Indian took the recliner next to the window, smoothed her beige slacks, but said nothing.

David leaned against the doorjamb. "What's up?" Dressed in jeans and sneakers he stretched, crossed legs at the ankles, and clasped his arms across his chest.

Erik told him about their inquisitive neighbor and concern about Martin.

"Resourceful fellow, isn't he?" Maria's hands unfolded and formed a steeple under her chin—a habit she'd developed while in graduate school.

Bhani said soberly, "I have an idea for Martin." Without further elaboration, she stood and left the room.

* * * *

Across the street and two houses east of Maria's twenty-room ranch style home, Arlo Marik prepared for a long stay. The old two-story pale brick house had been empty for some time, tied up by heirs in an intestate squabble. On the second floor, he adjusted the tripod and settings on the camera and telescopic lens. To complete his spying menagerie, he spread another tripod, tipped it with

19

a motion detector, aimed at the garage, then settled into a reclining chair a few feet back from the front window. That position, he'd learned, minimized accidental discovery.

The reporter came to wait, dressed in jeans, t-shirt, sneakers and with a large coffee thermos, snacks, a portable TV and an assortment of warm clothing. Using binoculars, he swept the area around the front entry and driveway plus that part of the back yard visible from his perch. Only the rear door and a bit of the immediate yard escaped his surveillance. A laptop for note taking and on which he would write his final report completed his clandestine spy nest.

Marik survailed only Maria's comings and goings convinced nothing would happen without her leading the pack. The one exception remained David Rohm's trips, mostly to the Addison Airport. Marik had learned the engineer had purchased a Gulfstream IV in Maria's name, qualified as first pilot, and had it sent off for electronic modifications. Nothing new or unusual about any of this or so he thought. Presk and Rohm did schedule an RV vacation but he figured little chance of tailing them for any time without being spotted so he decided to stay in his cubbyhole and monitor the others. Besides, Presk wasn't about to abandon the rest of her group.

* * * *

David steered the RV and the trailing Saturn into its assigned slot at the Valley Village Mobile Home Park in North Hollywood. The balmy afternoon breeze wafted through the palm trees.

The drive from Long Beach had been tense, they were unsure if their deception had worked. Erik, in charge of any emergency needs, hadn't made contact.

Ann Bartlett had developed a devilish method of communication using screen pixels. Martin Grabel came up with an algorithm to make her system virtually invisible to the knowing eye, and you could forget the unknowing.

On the way to LA, Maria and David detoured to Nevada just long enough to be married using their real names. Martin and Ann hacked the social security system and decided there was no need to use aliases. It was David's second marriage, his first wife having died a few years ago. Her first.

David let the RV manager know he and his wife would be sightseeing in the Saturn and should return in a few days. They headed north the fifty miles to Mojave.

"There it is, Scaled Composites." He pointed toward a structure facing north along the tarmac and parked the car in a visitor's slot. The fabricated office building fronted the factory and hangar. "I've admired these people for some time and am looking forward to meeting them."

Together, he and Maria entered the lobby. They had already decided to use their real names. This entire idea was too risky to sow any seeds of doubt that they might not be legitimate or legal.

Inside the lobby, many pictures depicted the myriad of exotically shaped airplanes including the White Knight. Space Ship One, which held center stage.

First Contact

The secretary escorted them into an office, pointed to chairs in front of the large wooden desk, and offered each coffee. "Someone will be with you in just a moment."

The amount of clutter piled about somehow seemed normal; about what you'd expect—organized chaos. "Just my type of guy," David quipped.

An oversized drafting table piled high with reams of papers, dominated the far end. A large picture of those key to Space Ship One, with White Knight in the background, occupied center stage behind the desk and over a credenza and computer.

Both turned at a slight rustle and Gunther Reinhardt in long urgent strides, entered through a side door. He introduced himself. His slender, large powerful hand shot out and grabbed David's and then Maria's.

Dressed in jeans, plaid shirt and leather jacket, the man noted for his genius aircraft designs seemed intense yet casual.

Maria had no hesitation about David leading the discussion. With his engineering background, he'd communicate with Reinhardt at a level she could never achieve. David had primed for this moment over the last ten years. Everything they'd prepared for rested on this meeting. He touched his briefcase as if to ensure himself it was there, knowing good and well he still had it. He'd checked it at least twice earlier.

The energy the engineer projected caught David off guard. Startled for a moment, he took a silent deep breath and introduced himself and Maria.

"It's a pleasure to meet you," he continued. "I've been a fan for years, read of your efforts, and applaud them."

Reinhardt didn't waste much effort acknowledging the compliment. He paused a second, gazed off into the distance, a slight furrow crossed his brow before returning a penetrating look at his guests. Again, he hesitated before taking his seat. David feared recognition had triggered the reaction.

The three settled into their chairs, Reinhardt, pepper colored sideburns that mimicked his boss's, in all their glory, scrunched down in his Naugahyde-covered executive chair. "We usually don't take calls like yours, but something you said sounded irresistible. How can I help you?"

David wondered, for a moment, how what he had to say would be received. "Mr. Reinhardt."

Chin resting on his chest, eyes looking past hairy eyebrows, the casual command came, "Gunther."

"Great, Gunther." David noticeably relaxed. "What I have to say is known only to a few people. It requires the utmost in confidentiality." He quietly added.

Reinhardt looked up, face stony; his light blue eyes swept the two. "We are used to that."

For a long moment, the engineer stared hard at Maria.

Once David started his presentation, you'd have thought they were the only two in the room. Nothing else seemed to matter. Reinhardt, head slightly cocked to one side, teeth clenched, lips open in a slight grimace appeared to take the measure of David. It fell something short of a stare down.

David waited; didn't flinch, tried to soften his countenance and kept his gaze steady.

"Okay," Reinhardt said. "But if this ride starts to get wild, I'll stop you and that will be it."

"Fair enough," David would have preferred the meeting start on a more cordial note. He adjusted himself in the chair. "I want you to build me a space ship."

The engineer grinned, eyes dancing. "That's what got my attention when you called. That's what we do for a living."

David relaxed and leaned forward adding emphasis with his body. "A big one." He waited in the chair, hands clasped together. "One that can support a number of people for a long time—years."

"We can do it—if you've got a billion or two dollars."

"In that case, you should be able to build me twenty or so." Seeing the expression of disbelief on Reinhardt's face goaded David on. "But one is all I want or can use. However, I do expect to use most of the money in building it." Again, he pressed on. "Actually, the idea I have in mind is to first build a factory in space. Once completed, it will become the hub, living quarters, galley, and machine shop to handle all work on the space ship. It *will* be incorporated into the ship. We have named the ship "Orion". Are you interested?"

Reinhardt sat with his mouth slightly open, silent. Not a muscle move on his face, only an occasional shirt button move gave any indication he had taken a breath. His mouth closed. "I have the feeling that I came in after the show started. Care to fill me in?"

David sat silent for a few moments, gave a long look down at his hands then up at his host. Once Maria made the decision to go into space, most of everything she had done pointed toward this moment. Everything hinged on David's answer and his host's acceptance or rejection. "I will if you can assure me that what is said here will go no further."

Reinhardt squinted at Maria, head cocked, the area around his eyes strained, he stared hard. A spark of recognition touched his face. He started to stand.

"Please," David said struggling to keep what had to sound like a plea from being too obvious. "Wait." The look on Reinhardt's face said it all; he'd put it together. He recognized Maria. But David's voice, husky with emotion and with an undertone of unmistakable sincerity, caused his host to stop.

"We've got plenty to do. We won't take on something that may place the company in jeopardy."

David sat mute. While the engineer had made no charge or indicated in any way that he recognized his guest, neither affirmation nor denial seemed required. If neither said anything, a tacit agreement existed and at the least David had not lied to the man he had decided to entrust their wellbeing. Reinhardt remained free to draw his own conclusion. His thoughts were no more than speculation.

Gunther, still on the edge of his chair, stared slowly at the picture of Space

Ship One and back at Maria, then David. "Once we start, the word will get out this place will be crawling with people. And that includes the federal government. There's no way to keep this quiet."

David let the words hang then said, "I have a plan. Our research shows that if we can get into space, no earth government will have jurisdiction over what we do. Our only concern is that we continue getting needed supplies to complete the ship. I'll admit *that* could be a problem although Mexico has no prohibition covering space launches. In fact, it has no viable space program. I plan to give it one.

"If you agree, since you will be a contractor only, your liability will be restricted. Both you and your company will be protected and should not be open to criminal or civil charges. However, should any occur, we will cover all legal costs. I think you'll find the monies escrowed are more than sufficient to handle any problems."

Reinhardt sat immobile, staring at his guests.

David had no way of knowing what concerns the impassive face hid, but they had to be myriad.

Lanky soft-spoken much like his boss, he half turned away, swung back, and said, "Forty billion dollars. You do have that kind of money. And you want us to design and build you a space ship. Is that it?" He paused, "I'm not saying we'll do it."

"Understood." David saw this as his opportunity to show the forward-thinking engineer considerable expense had already gone into the project. "I have a design concept to show you. If you agree to do it, you have only to provide the overall final design and dimensional drawings."

A nod moved the discussion into a rapid-fire exchange. David had no idea what motivated Reinhardt to further the discussion. Maybe his aim was to gather information and to call the authorities.

For twenty or so minutes, they debated, exchanged thoughts, ideas about the design and a host of attendant matters. Most of the discussion centered on ideas Reinhardt had been kicking around for Scaled Composites. Beyond that, the major concern remained where to put the design company. They would need some country that would not restrict their ability to launch and that appeared to be Mexico.

"I have property on the Baja peninsula," David explained. "We're prepared to built the necessary facilities to plan, purchase materials, assemble, and launch from there. You supply the *know-how*, and train the people to do the actual fabrication and assembly on orbit.

"Why do you want to build this spaceship?"

David considered his answer. "I'm prepared to answer every question you have. However, if I can persuade you to forgo the details, it relieves you of a host of legal problems. If you don't know, you can't be liable."

Reinhardt interrupted him, "What you say in this office stays here. You have my promise."

David reached into his briefcase, pulled out a dozen CD's, and handed them to Gunther. He had done extensive engineering over the last few years. "Look at the first one. It shows an overall view of how I envision the finished ship. If you agree it's a workable idea, then we're set to look at details."

Reinhardt slipped the first disc into his PC. The screened image seemed to catch him off guard, at the least peeked his interest. After a few minutes he said, "I'll be damned. I think it will work."

He paused; look fixed on David and asked again. "Why?"

* * * *

Maria gave a pensive and hopefully approving look at Grabel, eager to show her satisfaction. Standing in the den, she turned the man first one way and then the other.

He nodded. "Bhani, I think you may have created the newest version of Mickey Rooney, and just as handsome."

"Isn't he?" She beamed, and Grabel visibly relaxed.

"Well, Martin, how do you like it?" Maria asked.

The diminutive mathematician had always been nervous around Maria.

He spoke in a weak and tremulous voice and held Bhani's hand. The man had made a move he could never have pulled off alone. "Should have done it years ago."

"It wasn't available," Bhani said. "The FDA only approved Collamer Lens (ICL) about a year ago."

Martin mused, "You know, I don't miss those heavy glasses in the slightest. Everything seems normal. Amazing." He turned to Bhani, "Thank you for suggesting the operation and helping me through it. I could have only dreamed about this without you."

Before the eye surgery, with those glasses, Martin's appearance had been hard to ignore. Perhaps this change would minimize the danger from Arlo Marik.

* * * *

Three months later, from his perch, Arlo Marik kept a weary eye on the cartage van that backed into the driveway and loaded a number of crates. Rohm had filed a preliminary flight plan with FAA Addison to Hawaii with an RON (remain over night) refueling stop in Long Beach.

Marik watched as his charges got into a stretched limo, satisfied they were headed for Addison and the vacation their travel agent, encouraged by a few dollars, had told him about. He finished typing a report to National Security Agency, NSA, and Grady Moffitt, NSA's top spy.

Money the reporter had spread around the FBO operation bought him all the information available on the scientist's activities in and around Addison: flight plan filed for Long Beach, six people on board, pilot, David Rohm. Should be in Long Beach by noon local time. Everything seemed okay there— except the other two people? Just how wrong could his information be? It didn't make sense. Who were the missing two? He'd really screwed up. He should have paid more attention. Presk and Rohm he recognized, but the others, he just hadn't given it a thought.

First Contact

Almost four hours earlier, across town at DFW International, Eric Svern, and Ann Bartlett boarded an American Airlines flight for John Wayne Airport.

Four hours later, Svern confirmed with the FBO that the Cessna Citation II had arrived with the equipment as ordered. He then guided the rental car toward an RV storage lot not far from Long Beach Airport where three RVs equipped as no others had ever been waited. The RVs were to be their homes for a couple of years—and would help them disappear.

Ann patted his arm and relaxed beside him. "I can see how the spy stuff could have such an appeal."

Almost four hours after Erik Svern had left DFW the six boarded the sleek Gulfstream parked next to the hanger at Addison field. David seated himself in the pilot's seat while Maria made sure everyone was safely buckled into their seats.

David placed the map case next to the pilot's seat and strapped it down. They waited as the line crew loaded their luggage and worked through the ground check.

The handler signaled the completed inspection and okay.

David acknowledged with a hand wave.

He finished the cockpit preflight. Following the ground handler's clearance, he started the engines. At eight percent RPMs he flipped the fuel switch and the jets roared to life.

Ground control directed him to the active runway. A few minutes later, the control tower cleared the jet for taxi to the active runway.

He centered the Gulfstream on runway three-three, added ten degrees flap and eased the throttles to eighty-five percent power. At one hundred twenty knots indicated, he eased back on the yoke, and the plane lazily climbed into the clear light blue sky.

He contacted departure control, squawked the transponder, and within minutes was safely under IFR flight rules, on course for Long Beach.

Arlo Marik watched the plane leave. He drove from Addison field toward DFW not the least bit confident he had a clue what had happened.

* * * *

The Gulfstream leveled off at thirty-five thousand feet with the sun at its back. David set about testing the link between the aircraft's electronic command and control system, and those installed in Svern's RV. The installations in the RV, Gulfstream, and Cessna II Citation were essentially identical so he had no hesitation about a live system test. Twenty minutes later, he sent a signal to the Swede that everything had worked as planned and broke the connection.

Once the autopilot took over, Maria spoke, her tone strong yet almost a whisper. "David, I've been giving considerable thought to the premise that has driven the research to solve our problem. The answer must be in the telemeres, more specifically the telomeres." Over the next hour, she outlined her thinking for the next stage of their research. Their dilemma had never been far from her thoughts.

For the next two and a half hours, David's attention alternated between flying the airplane and digging deeper into Maria's thinking. More than once over the last forty years, she had planted a seed that led to success.

Long Beach approach control ended the discussion and vectored the Gulfstream onto the glide path for runway three zero.

* * * *

At six-thirty that evening, taking the first available space, Marik boarded American flight 617 for the California airport. At seven-thirty, the airliner approached its destination.

He began his search for the Gulfstream in the dimming daylight. Not having spotted it during the landing, he rushed from the terminal, caught a cab, and headed for the fixed based operators. Had they already given him the slip?

After three months of work, had he screwed up? His heart pounded. He brushed sweaty palms against his trousers. Both happened when he panicked, and he could feel a grand dread coming on.

It took almost twenty minutes to navigate the traffic and get to the first operator. Nothing. He ordered the driver to the next FBO.

As they passed through the chain link gate, avoiding the main entrance and rounded the corner onto the tarmac, he yelled the cab to a halt. There next to the hangar sat the white Gulfstream.

An audible sigh escaped his lips.

"Back up," he ordered the nervous driver, and the cab slipped around the building side.

He paid the cabbie, gave him on hundred dollars extra, and asked him to wait.

Shadows covered the north side of the building as he left the car and he hugged the wall.

Marik walked toward the huge hangar door, stopped, and, with extra caution, peered into the building much darker than the fading sunlight outside. It took a few minutes for him to separate and identify the hangar personnel and the people who were his main concern. Over the next three hours, he moved back and forth from his vantage to the cab having to fork over another hundred to keep the driver happy.

He satisfied himself the plane wasn't going anywhere that evening and retreated to the taxi as his cell phone buzzed. He answered and said thank you.

The cartage company had shipped the crates to Hawaii. Maybe they were going on a vacation, but that still didn't answer the question about the missing two people.

Dead tired, Marik got into the cab and headed toward the nearest motel.

At four-thirty that morning, David Rohm opened the flight plan for him and seven passengers to Honolulu, Hawaii. A few minutes later, he boarded the Gulfstream. With all the confusion mostly made by the pilot and passengers, only seven people ever boarded.

Parked about one hundred yards off the end of the runway behind a grove of palm trees an RV waited with Erik Svern behind the wheel.

In the dark and the tower's visibility hindered, Gulfstream *N408LM* stopped on the tarmac short of the runway, and seven people raced from the aircraft to the waiting RV. The last one out, David Rohm calmly threw a series of switches putting the Gulfstream under the control of Erik's RV electronics, left the plane, locked the door, and followed his cohorts.

From the RV's duplicate set of controls, David Rohm piloted the jet into the air. Erik had already headed the van away from Long Beach toward John Wayne Airport and the second airplane. Time was now their biggest enemy. The van's effective control distance over the Gulfstream was limited to a five hundred miles radius even with the jet at thirty thousand feet. The second Citation had to be in the air in less than one hour.

David called ahead and ordered the Cessna preflighted.

Arriving at the airport, he quickly boarded the airplane and got clearance to file his flight plan for Honolulu *en route*, refuel, and return the next day.

Forty-five minutes after the Gulfstream took off, the Citation's wheels cleared the runway and had control of its ward.

Two hours from Honolulu, David, in the Citation, threw a series of switches remotely cutting off Gulfstream *N408LM's* fuel to its engines—and the plane plunged to its watery grave.

Erik drove the remaining six vacationers to the RVs, their homes for the next few years, as David landed at Honolulu.

Almost seven hours later Arlo Marik awakened, still in his street clothes and in a panic. The almost thirty hours he'd been awake had overtaken him. Grabbing the phone, he called the Long Beach FAA office. Gulfstream N408LM had taken off at 04:30 that morning for Honolulu. They'd been in the air for almost two hours.

In less than ten minutes, unshaven, he checked out, hailed a cab for a nearby heliport, and boarded a helicopter for L.A. International and his flight to Honolulu.

Elbowing his way through the LAX lobby, he followed an inexplicable urge to again call Long Beach FAA.

Dumbfounded, he dropped the phone as the voice droned on: *N408LM disappeared from the in-flight radar a little over three hours after take-off and is presumed lost. Air and sea searches underway but the plane vanished over water fifteen thousand feet deep.*

Stunned, Marik slumped against the wall, gathered himself, retrieved the receiver, and hung it in the cradle.

Two days later, Arlo Marik read with trepidation of the crash of a Gulfstream carrying eight retired DNA scientists near the Murray Fracture Zone northeast of Hawaii. All passengers were presumed dead. The Navy started a massive search but offered little hope of any survivors. His government meal ticket had just run out.

* * * *

In Fort Meade, Maryland, three weeks would pass before Grady Moffitt returned from a clandestine operation and Arlo Marik's letter would be old news.

CHAPTER FOUR
The disappeared – Seven Years Later

Lt. General Wallace Verson watched the darkening autumn sky from his fourth floor window. Shadowy clouds like dirty cotton boles, drifted low over Fort Meade. The Maryland location, away from Washington, suited him fine. In twenty years in the Air Force and eight working his way up to his appointment as NSA director two years earlier, he'd had little time to smell the roses—not that he particularly wanted to. But that was beside the point. Grady Moffitt had asked for an unscheduled meeting.

His secretary's familiar knock helped settle him.

She stuck her head in. "Dr. Moffitt is here to see you, General."

Midge Foley was a free spirit. She'd been with the agency for over twenty years and knew everyone, and most important, how to screen out the complainers and those wanting to be seen with, by or near the director.

"Send him in. Then you go home," he ordered. It wasn't uncommon for her to stay late.

She nodded and without ceremony motioned the Deputy Director toward the entry.

Grady stopped in the doorway, conjured up his worst made-up glare, "Have you no respect for my position or who I am?"

"I understand you are related to Rodney Dangerfield. What do you expect? Besides, you should be used to it."

He laughed, "Yeah, I guess you're right." His use of humor belied the closely curried and feared make-up of this man.

"Of course." She closed the door. A quick pert smile crossed her lips.

Grady Moffitt, dressed in a dark blue double breasted and a thirty-year veteran of NSA, held the informal distinction of being a spy's spy and master covert strategist. Most of the major actions that had framed world events over the previous few years carried his imprint and were as much a part of his résumé as his birth date. Next to Verson, the one man not to cross was Moffitt. He blamed Erik Svern for his mangled leg that never healed properly after an AK-47 chewed it up during a mission billed as passive. He'd never allowed another joint NSA/CIA mission after that.

He limped to the director's oversized oak desk. His dark eyes bored like x-rays, dissecting ones' soul. The various canes he used had become hallmarks. Rumor had it they all carried a single shot twenty-five caliber hollow point bullet in the tip and whiskey in the handle, and he used both to devastating effect. "When you decide to fire her, let me know. I believe I could use that woman."

"You and a hundred more. Forget it." Slight of build, though Air Force, he had the spy's knack for being a loner but did have a streak of moral decency—an accusation never leveled at Grady Moffit. Some said those limits were beyond a mortal's reach. He lacked some of Grady's patience and his never-diminishing zeal, yet, anyone who dismissed Walter Verson as a lightweight did so at their own peril. He often said he could tell when something wasn't right—it had a smell all its own that he seemed to sense. His benign but deceptive grandfather face, just what a good spy needed, belied the unyielding attitude that made up his inner being. He asked no quarter and gave none.

He didn't press for the meetings' reason. If anything, Moffitt leaned toward too concise to require prodding. He nodded, about the only deference either showed.

"Need to go over something with you. May be nothing but I've got a feeling."

Verson motioned his deputy to a brown Naugahyde armchair as he settled into his oversized executive leather swivel. The long hours, constant interruptions even when away from the office, and maybe most of all the secrecy had done in his marriage. He knew himself and wasn't afraid to admit his work came before everything. If anything, he and Moffitt were two of a kind —except the deputy director had earned the reputation for never forgetting or forgiving.

Without fanfare, Moffitt moved the chair so he braced the desk corner, leaned forward, his stiff right leg shoved out to the side, a folder tucked under his left arm, elbows on the desk. "About seven years ago a plane went down, a private jet, en route to Hawaii. Eight scientists aboard, one of them a Nobel winner. All were retired. Worked for Advanced Bio-Yield when it first started. A laboratory doing DNA type work. Owned by Maria Presk, the Nobel winner. All were in their seventies. At one time or another, we had private contracts with that lab. For the most part—us trying to keep current with DNA technology." He laid the manila folder in front of Verson.

"So far, it doesn't listen." He did have some vague recall about the lost jet. Seldom did he get involved in details except where threats to NSA came into play. A dreaded fear nagged him that someone might compromise the organization. And it wasn't a foreign government that worried him most, but an employee or worse a former one. He eyed the folder.

"It gets better."

The General nodded, his hand gestured: "Go ahead."

"One of the people on board was a former employee at NSA. You may remember him, Martin Grabel."

An inward flinch zapped Verson but beyond that, he didn't acknowledge any awareness. People like Grabel cost him more sleep than he'd ever admit. The man's instability was a damned good example of what lay at the root of most secrecy concerns. He recalled the man had worked for NSA over the years and been the primary force in their computer system design, considered the best in the world. He couldn't remember how many tours the guy had. They kept bringing him back because no one could touch him in computer systems, *the best, not on the cutting edge, but he defined the cutting edge.* The scientist had a better grasp of NSA's computer potential than anyone else. Even though a genius, the mathematician fell into the unstable ranks. And Verson had to admit there were others as well and that only added to his concerns.

Moffitt continued. "The manifest showed Erik Svern, a retired CIA agent also onboard. Both worked for the Advanced Bio-Yield before joining NSA and the *Company*."

Light glistened off the General's chested ribbons. He didn't move. Moffitt had his attention.

Grady drew in a breath. "Svern left CIA the day he became eligible for early retirement. Didn't stay one minute longer even though the director asked him to. His service jacket indicated he had high marks for what he did—which pretty much ran the gamut."

Verson cleared his throat. "You must have a point. Why is this coming up now? You said seven years."

"One of our snoops, Arlo Marik, worked for a tabloid, got a phone call from Grabel. They had maybe a couple of meetings before Grabel disappeared. Anyhow, Marik's report says Grabel babbled that he hadn't aged a bit in the last forty years.

"And about Erik Svern, scribbled on the margin, not a part of the official record is a comment on his mustering out fitness report."

"And it says?" Verson fought the irritation in his gut.

"'*Svern doesn't look a day older than when I gave him his entry physical.*' This is the same doctor who examined him twenty years earlier." He paused, "A look at his chart shows the body of a man thirty to forty years old."

The General wanted to say, *so the guy stays in shape. How were we brought into this? And again, after this long?* But his instinct told him not to rush to judgment. Verson made no effort to hide his aggravation; his lips pursed, eyes squinted and brow furrowed. And from practice, his face reddened.

"We reran the computers and got a match on the company name, Advanced Bio-Yield, and spit it out. One agent took time to follow up but transferred and the standard separation comparison never finished. Just didn't rank high enough on the priority list."

The General started to get up. A clear unspoken statement he'd heard all he wanted.

"Wait, boss." That word always seemed to please Verson. "Marik made contact with Maria Presk. Got only a denial and brushed-off. He tailed them until they all boarded a Gulfstream. Flight plan called for Hawaii, Honolulu. It never made it. Crashed into the ocean, fifteen thousand feet of water. We dropped Marik a few weeks later. It wasn't until that crash that I found out Erik Svern had worked for Bio-Yield before joining the *Company*. A CIA type thinks he spotted Svern in Mexico. But now we have some other unusual activity and there's been this sighting. The CIA agent in Mexico Bassett, Harold Bassett, said the same thing; Svern hadn't aged. He remembered Svern and said he looked just like he'd remembered him. The guy did some investigating and thinks the thing stinks. If Erik Svern is still alive, what about the others? One thing the investigation did show is that no life insurance or casualty claims were ever paid or even applied for by anyone in the group. Not one."

"Why? Why in the hell would people with that kind of brainpower pull a crazy assed stunt like that? Nobel Prize? Sounds like it should have been the ding-a-ling prize." Verson, now standing, moved toward the door a clear signal the meeting had ended. He knew why he felt so irritated.

Moffitt, with surprising speed, hopped on his good left leg and blocked the officer's path. "General, you've got to hear the rest."

The director, face darkened with exasperation, gave his deputy a long stoic look his and took one of the armed vinyl side chairs. "It would seem I have little choice. Please hurry."

"If they're in Mexico, CIA will have to handle the *look*. We don't have jurisdiction."

Grady knew that. Also, knew that had never stopped the Agency before, his shot up leg was proof of that.

He made no further effort to hide his concern and with an air of reluctance acknowledged, he knew Svern. "I know him well—too well. Crossed swords with him more than once."

The General could sense a threat when others seemed complacent. His senses honed over years of putting himself in his enemies mind. He often framed his remarks to reflect the adversary, perceived or real. People sometimes took this for negativism, others as the devil's advocate but those who knew him best also knew better. It made it easier for him to get the core of a problem. It had gotten him where he was today. Yet, he hadn't picked up that Grady's animosity toward Erik Svern bordered on hatred. "And Grabel."

"Worked for us off and on over a number of years. The brainiest code writer and breaker we ever had. More importantly, he is responsible for our system design. Our computer also spit out the Advanced Bio-Yield—Grabel—Erik Svern connection."

A deep scowl formed on Verson's brow, and his hands fisted. The deputy looked passively up at his boss.

"Grabel told our snitch he hadn't aged a day since leaving Advanced Bio-Yield thirty-five years earlier. The guy is scared shitless. Worried something terrible had happened to him. The nutty guy disappeared but not before the reporter learned the company's name. Marik tried to talk to Presk, she's the group's leader, but got stiffed. Three months later, the plane crashed. As I said, seven years ago. Marik snooped around once in a while most likely to try to get his monthly stipend from us again. Never came up with anything."

"Maybe that's because they were dead. He looked in the wrong place." Verson's effort to control his temper failed.

"Wallace," the fact that he'd used the General's first name signaled a warning to Verson. "I'm serious about this. I think there's something going on here."

"I can see you are, Grady. Make a folder; classify it top secret; eyes only. I'll look into it."

"I'd like to handle this one myself."

Verson stopped as he neared the door. "Why? Don't you have enough to do?" A common complaint at any level of government.

"More than enough. But this rings for me. I think Marik was onto something."

"Okay. It's yours. Make the folder and keep it here in my office. Eyes only," he repeated.

NSA *eyes only* investigations did not allow copies of any documents. The director's safe remained a virtual guarantee no one would see the contents without permission. This he didn't want to see on the evening news, particularly the talking heads. He'd be laughed out of town if it amounted to nothing. He'd had a good career and had less than a year until retirement. He would not permit anything to screw his life up now. If they were onto something special, keeping it quiet remained paramount.

Grady Moffitt nodded, gathered up the manila folder, which Verson had never opened, hobbled to the door, opened it and walked with difficulty through the receptionist area.

Something about the information had tripped his trigger. Sometimes his gut misled him and that might be the case this here. Only time would tell.

Entering his office, he picked up the phone messages. Sitting to relieve the troublesome hip pain, he scanned them and decided they could wait.

Without anyone to keep unwanted intruders out, well after five p.m., he locked his office door. The corner office had a better view overlooking the campus than any other in the building. His oak desk was about half the size of Verson's, at his insistence. He could reach all its corners without the pain of standing to reach far-flung folders. One hour later, he'd completed the necessary paperwork to start the top-secret *Eyes-Only* file on the missing scientists. He placed the information into the folder and returned to Verson's office.

He handed the manila accordion file to the seated director.

Verson, his expression cast in stone, looked hard at him. "I had a nag that this didn't sound right when I heard about it. The crash." It was his first admission that he'd given more than a passing thought to the missing people.

Grady sensed he had a virtual a blank check to go after this one and said so.

"I want to stay in the loop on this one. Anything that has Erik Svern's odor on it, I want to see." Confrontations between NSA and CIA agents occurred more often than agency heads would admit publically, and Moffitt seemed to have trouble letting go of this one.

Verson motioned him into the chair still at the corner of the desk, opened a lower drawer, and pulled out a quart of Seagram's Crown Royal.

"I assume CIA is on this?"

Moffitt nodded and said, "I've set up a meeting with the Mexican CIA operative so I can talk to him. Away from here. I would like for you to issue a personal BOLO—on all eight."

A slight shiver of delight snaked down Verson's back. Like all NSA people, he knew what a *Be On the Look Out* diktat really meant when issued by the director. Something the book never envisaged.

CHAPTER FIVE
A Day Of Reckoning

Sitting in the oval office the six men steeled themselves. The President seemed agitated, already hammered, and embarrassed in the press. Jaw clinched, he appeared in no mood for excuses.

During the group's entry, he'd not left his chair to offer a handshake. Instead, his eyes swept from one to the next, leaving no doubt as to his displeasure.

State, Treasury, Defense secretaries sat to the right of the national emblem woven into the short pile rug, FBI, NSA and CIA Agency directors to the left— all equidistant from their leader. Their chairs arranged in a semicircle in front of the desk; a tactical placement, that sent a clear signal to Washington hill climbers.

The waiting game had started and each man tried to seem busy reading notes, thumbing through papers, politely coughing as they waited to see who would cave or be bold enough to answer first.

This President's reputation for lambasting what he considered slipshod work received more press than most other occurrences in Washington. Guessing the next to be skewered had become a favorite game and his hallmark. People, especially reporters, delighted when he tore into bureaucrats or political appointees with seeming relish.

It was a double-edged sword. A lot of good people refused to serve but those who did had to perform at a very high level. No one ever climbed above a raking over the coals except his inner circle and none of these assembled men shared in that luxury.

"No, Mr. President. I can't tell you how these people went undetected, especially considering the overwhelming size of their effort. Not to mention they'd done all this in plain sight over a seven year period." The very fear Wallace Verson, Lieutenant General, head of NSA, scheduled to retire, had harbored for the last two years had happened. He'd had premonitions something would come along screw up his record, and cost him his retirement.

The Secretary of Defense, Verson's boss, said, "They didn't fool just you Wallace, every one of us has to share this one. I'd like to know how they got forty billion dollars out of the country without Treasury's even having one clue what had happened." His voice had grown louder the longer he talked.

Everyone in the room knew the Secretary had just tried to shift the blame, with some justification. The movement of that much money should have set off sirens. Whatever maneuvers Maria Presk had used, she'd managed to snooker all of the safeguards Treasury had set up to alert the government in the fight against money laundering and detecting clandestined groups. The system, designed to identify when large sums of cash were about to move had failed utterly.

"We can stop them by shutting off the stuff that's on the ground waiting to

33

go up." said the CIA chief. "Shut that off, the whole program falls apart."

"True," Verson said. "But the Mexican Army moved over one thousand soldiers to Baja and the mainland's west coast on the Sea of Cortez, opposite the launch area." The General hesitated. *CIA should have known that* he mulled that thought for a moment and then left it. "It's obvious they're prepared to protect the installation."

The FBI head leaned forward in his chair, looked almost with hope, at Verson and said, "Maybe a better idea is to intercept any goods that are *en route* or even go after manufacturers of stuff not yet shipped. That shuts them down and we can do that without leaving a footprint."

State countered, "Mr. President, Mexico has already served notice that it will be an act of war if any nation makes a move or takes any action that will in any way jeopardize or interfere with their orbiter or space program."

The President threw the sheaf of papers onto his desk. The six men immediately froze, and then almost in unison leaned forward, straining to make sure they didn't miss a word the soft-spoken leader uttered.

"You people are full of crap. Haven't you read the papers? The entire nation is pulling for these guys to win. So's the rest of the world—when they stop laughing at us long enough to express themselves. And who do you think would get the blame if all of a sudden their suppliers were blown to hell? Me, you assholes."

People, particularly enemies, had mistaken his quiet voice for weakness. And that often was a fatal error. This man had the instincts of a killer and those who knew him went to whatever lengths necessary to avoid an assault. He'd learned to temper his anger with acute political skills that left few opponents standing. He'd earned his behind the back nickname, *bruiser*.

Not a large man, he had eyes any actor would kill to have. He seemed to look right through a person, see everything they were not, instantly recognizing what they were. *Vulnerable* didn't come close to describing the feeling his gaze could pin on you.

"What about the people still here?" the President asked. "Those that have yet to join Doctor Presk? Any idea how large that number is?"

Verson's look touched each one of his co-defendants. No one seemed willing to take the initiative. He shook his head and decided his career had turned to shit already, so what the hell. "Mr. President, of the original group of scientists, we're told six are still in Mexico. I personally know one is, Doctor Erik Svern. At least we think the rest are in Mexico. We believe it will take many more people to complete the crew, maybe as many as one hundred.

"Erik Svern is the brains behind the entire Mexican organization. He holds a Ph.D. in chemistry, and is former CIA."

That made the CIA chief shrink further into his chair. Verson got no satisfaction from seeing the man agonize but today, that was the way this part of the world turned.

"Also started a very successful security company after leaving the agency. This guy implemented Doctor Presk's plan. Presk handled the finance, scientific and Doctor David Rohm took care of the engineering development. Everything else, Svern organized and directed. The guy turned out to be a manager of the highest ability. He put together four Mexican companies that are the real strength behind the internal organization. In Mexico City, the heads of these companies are collectively called *Los Quatro Socios* or The Four Associates. Individually, they are above average, and under Svern's direction, collectively they have become one of Mexico's most ominous behind the scene's power brokers. Screw with one and you take them all on. They have to be reckoned with."

Verson paused cleared his throat, tried to swallow, and couldn't. "We now have reason to believe they may have penetrated out computers."

Everyone, including the President, froze. It would have taken a baseball bat to move anyone. The Secretary of Defense regained his equilibrium first and bolted upright in his chair. "Oh, my god," the President said. "Wallace. Compromised?" He let out enough air that he sank back in his chair and didn't move staring straight ahead, all color drained from his face.

"Possible," Verson said. "But not necessarily so."

"Explain." The President's eyes riveted the NSA director.

"They have his guy, Doctor Martin Grabel. Fucking math and computer genius. I don't know anybody that can come close to him in these skills. He's goofy as hell but also that smart. Anyway, he worked for us on five different occasions. Initially, he designed our computer system, then quit, came back a couple years later, added to the system, quit, came back a few years later, added to the system and so on. Well, we now believe that for the last six or so years, he's been inside our computers keeping track of what we were up to where it concerned the Presk group. Probably had a lot to do with their ability to keep below our radar. We see no evidence he looked anywhere else. So, we believe that to say the system has been compromised may overstate it a bit."

A smile touched the President's face. "The fate of the civilized world has on occasion rested in your hands, Wallace. And you have to gall to suggest that someone not under your control, crawling around in the most sensitive information known to mankind is not a threat?"

Verson's eyes fell to his hands. How he answered this question would set the stage for everything that followed. "Yes, Mr. President. I know the man. NSA has worked with Presk and her company over the years. If they had wanted to harm us, it would have already happened. And it hasn't."

The President's eyes bored into Verson and stayed fixed for a long moment as if reassessing the measure of this man. Finally, he relaxed, returned to his chair, sat, and leaned back. "Recommendations."

After the latest revelation, no one seemed ready to offer any suggestion without exchanging prepared situation papers. Hacking NSA computer system needed a completely new and different answer and clearly, no one had prepared for anything like this. For seconds that seemed more like minutes, not a word sounded. The President seemed prepared to give them whatever time they needed. He did have a liking for impromptu responses. He believed it got him closer to what the individual personally believed unfiltered through the bureaucracy. Also, if someone offered a dumb-assed comment, everyone could hear it. Took some of the load off him.

A puzzled look crossed the President face. "How in the hell did they get cash to live on during all this time? That should have triggered something, maybe even IRS."

CIA director said, "They used *hawala's*, Mr. President."

"What in the hell is a *hawala?*"

"That's an individual or group you can move money through. Been used in Asia Minor for four or five hundred years. If I give a dealer here in the US one thousand dollars, someone I designate can go to a *hawala* dealer in Pakistan and claim the one thousand."

"And it's safe? What keeps them from ripping someone off? Especially where the kind of money we're talking about is moving."

CIA kept the lead, "First, Mr. President, the really big money didn't' go through the *hawala's*. Second, even the terrorists don't cheat a *hawaldar* dealer. *Hawala's* are known for long memories and a very unforgiving nature."

The President seemed satisfied and Verson said, "Mr. President, I think we should not impede their leaving. In fact, we ought to help them. I spent six hours with Erik Svern yesterday." He ignored Secretary of Defense's admonishment that he should have arrested him. "To the best of my knowledge, he held back nothing to the questions I asked." Over the next few minutes, Verson touched on many of the unpleasant problems the group of eight would face if they stayed on earth—the guinea pig status they would inherit. Erik Svern had told him about blood transfusions extending some measure of life. And no one had a clear picture of what it did to life expectancy following a transfusion. That would take years. He then talked about the turmoil that would beset world governments if this longevity could readily be passed on to others. Before ending, he asked that the information about the blood maybe extending life be in the strictest confidence. Not even number two's to be told although Grady Moffit already knew.

The President nodded then held up his hand—a signal to stop. His first thought, "Do we know how many people have received this contaminated blood?"

"Yes sir. And according to Svern, all of them are now at the Mexican location."

Looking out the East window, the President said, "If the longevity can be passed this easily…how do we feed all these long-lived mouths? This presents a threat that could drive the world to self-destruction and a problem few nations, if any, could handle." He walked around the desk and stopped in front of Lieutenant General Wallace Verson and said, "You're due to retire in a little while, correct?"

"Yes, Sir. Eight months." The General could see thirty years disappear down the toilet but held the President's gaze.

He turned to the Defense Secretary and said, "Get this man's replacement recommendation to me ASAP." Still in front of Verson, he asked, "Want another job? Help these people get on their way?"

"How?" Mr. President.

"First by dumbing this down. We need to keep it quite until I can get some of my counterparts onboard."

"My number two may be a problem. He thinks we should put a stop to them now." Version brought the President current. Few in the room had illusions about Grady Moffitt, most having dealt with him over the years. "The CIA guy in Mexico and Moffitt have worked together on a number of occasions."

The President had political instincts Version would never understand. "Make Moffitt understand he has a better chance of getting his way if this remains black. Of course, we'll try to make sure he's wrong."

* * * *

Verson stood as Grady Moffitt struggled to his feet or more correctly his good leg and cane.

His voice higher than Verson had ever heard, Moffitt bellowed. "Goddamnit, Wallace, you had no right to do that. Let those bastards go? Don't you realize what you've done? You people didn't think this through."

He watched Verson's face grow a deep red. Something he'd seen before but at that moment, he could have cared less.

Verson leaned forward, hands on his desk. "What the hell's with you, Grady?" Moffitt had never before challenged him so directly. Thirty years of military service, dealing with every label from president, or senator or janitor to terrorist had honed his skills but the ferocity of this reaction caught him off guard. Despite his anger, he calmly asked, "What did we miss?"

"Miss? Grady fumed. "In a hundred years they will be aliens. No hell no, they're already aliens. Some of our most capable minds are among those people. Those bastards could be the one major threat to our civilization."

"Don't be dramatic, Grady. You're not making sense."

Moffitt shook his head in disbelief. Hooked his cane on the desk corner, fumbled for his chair, and sat, crippled leg pointed toward the window, his back to Verson.

"Maybe I'm overreacting but think about the future. If these people find a habitable planet, a few hundred years from now, they could dominate this part of the galaxy. Some of our most talented scientific brains are a part of that group, they live four hundred years or more. We don't know…" he hesitated. "Their scientific achievements could leave Earth in the dust. Let's just assume, for whatever reason, they become belligerent. I don't think we'd stand a chance against them."

Verson stared at his number two. "I can't put that into perspective. It's something I could never have conceived." He brushed his hand through the close-cropped graying hair. "Grady, the Presidents orders were very specific. And I will obey them."

Moffitt strained to stand but made it and said, "Wallace, in all good consciousness, I must resign."

Verson noted something strained in the response. "What are you going to do?"

"Stop them."

CHAPTER SIX
The gathering- Baja Mexico
Bahia Los Angeles

Maria Presk stood in the giant hangar tucked in at the base of a sandy Baja California foothill away from prying eyes. Huge sliding doors stood open a few inches. She watched as dusk made its brilliant offering over the mountain background. The golden orange setting sun brilliantly lit the billowy clouds and belied the anxiety that had built with the approaching launch. Everything had come down to this. Ten years in the planning and design and seven making it happen. Leading hidden lives, every move taken with the thought of secrecy paramount...all that was over now. Everyone who cared or followed world events would know. In two days, a specially modified Boeing 747-400 with the orbiter *Independence* bolted to its back would leave the airstrip at Bahia Los Angeles to launch the orbiter. She had no illusions about the media and political storm this would unleash around the world. Some people and groups would applaud—others would condemn the launch. Everyone with access to any kind of publication, paper, TV or internet, would have their say. The talking heads would have a field day.

Most of the credit for their survival hinged on the untiring work of Martin Grabel, Ann Bartlett, and Erik Svern.

Maria shook off the thought of what it would have been like without anyone of the three. Of course, the petite but strong willed Bhani had been miraculous keeping Martin under at least partial control.

In the dimming light, overhead steel girders spread like webs that spanned the opening providing cover to the shuttles from weather and prying eyes. She watched Erik Svern enter the cavernous building shadowed in dimmed sodium vapor lamps framing the two Scaled Composites-designed and built shuttles and the much larger *Independence*. The former spy and now CEO of TTC, S.A. (they had decided to name their group The Travel Company) motioned toward the quiet room, his normal easy gait quickened.

Maria's pulse accelerated. Already edgy with anticipation, she awaited the arrival of the stripped-down heavily modified transport that would carry the craft to the needed launch altitude.

Bahia Los Angeles, on the east coast of Baja Mexico, offered the privacy needed for multiple space launches. Barren and mountainous, the terrain surrounding the site necessitated a shortened airstrip. That had her nervous. Engineers had assured her landing should be no problem. Takeoff of the 747 with a fully loaded shuttle strapped to its back, remained problematic, and a concern. Her greatest fear—she suspected events were cascading out of control and time had become a problem.

She walked past the stacked items brought in over the last year by boats, planes from all over the world, to await their turn for loading onto a shuttle. Others like these were either already on board *Independence* or in adjacent warehouses. The designers had made sure the containers became part of the finished spaceship. Every item sent up had been designed to be in the finished assembly. Everything had to pay its way. The one exception, one shuttle would make a final return and become the property of Mexico.

Perhaps the most important items, heaviest and last to leave earth remained stored in cryogenic tanks along with the DNA of virtually every plant or animal they could lay their hands on—a virtual Noah's ark.

Even though the general pace of things had reached a fever pitch, Maria's calm demeanor had kept the schedule and behavior intact. Had chaos taken over, it wouldn't have surprised her.

Huge stacks of material stood racked against the warehouse walls represented a small fraction of what had yet to arrive at Baja and then go on into space. It wouldn't be long before she and her small band would know if their gamble to leave earth would succeed.

Maria worried she'd overlooked something that would tear the guts from their hopes. Yet, a vision of their spaceship orbiting one hundred sixty miles high, assembled, then moving to a geosynchronous orbit thirty five thousand seven hundred eighty six kilometers above earth remained clear in her mind.

With the spaceship design frozen, Erik and the four Mexican companies, *Los Quatro Socios*, handled virtually everything. Traveling between Bahia and Mojave *had* been a burden and tricky, but would be so no more. Ann Bartlett's programming and hacking efforts, designed to keep their aliases a step ahead of any questioning authority, had worked to perfection. Once they had all been approved for Mexican citizenship, many of their travel and currency exchange concerns disappeared. The problem of established friendships with locals never materialized; each of the eight had far too much work to do. All had spent a major part of their lives working alone for extended periods. So the needed isolation wasn't anything new. Maria reminded everyone that whatever they did, do it in such a way as to minimize suspicions.

Maria convened the group often to anticipate every contingency they might meet in space and to provide for some kind of response. Food, water, fuel, and breathable air came up in every discussion. There were a myriad of other concerns. Materials of every kind would be critical. Wherever possible, composites would be used. But in some instances, structural needs made that impossible, like the high strength, high temperature special alloys required for the engines. The gathering of special materials and exotic minerals necessary for advance electronics remained a constant concern and required the most deliberate, sometimes deceptive action to obtain.

Relying on the untested and unproven ZPV Casimir drive was beyond doubt a major risk. After a comprehensive review with scientists and engineers who developed the drives, David remained convinced the risk could be made acceptable. The best engineers money could hire had worked long hours modeling computer simulations testing every aspect of the concept as the design materialized. Getting the metallurgy right had proven a major problem but one finally resolved. David's intention never to operate the Casimirs over three-tenths c aided the solution and added a major safety factor.

So far, unwanted, prying, nosey types had been dealt with by the Mexican army and private security guards employed by *Los Quatro Socios*. Maria had feared the size of the operation would attract a lot of attention. In fact, she would have bet on it. Seventeen countries had contributed material, people, and services. The size awed even her.

Svern's four Mexican companies had also yielded some good people who helped solve political problems—local, state, and national. The Four Associates had become the public force guiding Erik through the maze of political intrigues that had brought them this far. He discovered a knack for counting political votes. Influential Mexicans, both in and out of government, knew that eventually all of the earth-bound assets would become the property of the Mexican government. The fact the Mexican Space Agency legitimized Maria's efforts didn't go unnoticed. To her surprise, the traditional space-faring nations showed little interest. Mexico did not measure up as a heavyweight in space exploration and so the newcomer agency remained largely ignored. Maria encouraged a sense of pride fostering a strong desire for a Mexican space program. She nudged every influential person she'd met since coming to the country.

Everything they'd work for lay before them. She turned and walked toward Svern.

Maria had long since learned Erik had few ego needs to satisfy, but one did matter—his commitment to his word. That was something Svern didn't hold as a badge or test—it was simply something he lived by.

Even the *hawaldar* money exchanges had few hitches. But compared to the amounts of money that moved through open legitimate business transactions, the *hawala's* were small change. However, they now served a different purpose than intended when handling *la mordida, the bite* payments. These small intrigues went unnoticed while the huge complex organization came together. Even though surrogate companies fronted the groups, insiders knew Scaled Composites and Quantum LLC were the design brains behind the scene. And these same insiders knew when someone spends this much money, time and effort designing, building three shuttles, one large space ship without ever alerting the press or other prying eyes, some serious money changed hands and minds. A sleight of hand she understood. It also had the potential to attract the nefarious.

Scaled Components kept their end of the bargain. All but the engines lay packed in containers, some already stowed on Independence and the other shuttles awaiting launch onto orbit. One of the perks, lessons learned in designing or building the shuttles and spaceship, quickly made its way into Space Composites routine.

Building and installation of the engines conceived by Quantum Fields would happen on orbit. Quantum hired the design engineers and then oversaw the entire propulsion project. The engines were just too massive to launch from earth plus it would take almost five years to build them and that put the entire project at risk. Any more time spend on earth than necessary amounted to a threatening delay. A side benefit, the added effect of near zero gravity would help the fabrication of the ZPV drive. *Independence* would also be home until new space quarters were ready.

After seven years of evasion, Maria longed for an end to the hiding, surveillance, and suspicion. Once *Independence* reached orbit, the entire world would know but, by then, all eight of the scientists and most of the initial crew would safely orbit off planet and out of reach of any government. Let the governments fight out the jurisdiction battles. She covered as much of that as she reasonably could, setting up the necessary legal challenge as part of her advanced planning. If these efforts paid off, Mexico would have the final say and Maria and her people would be out of reach, off world and in space confronting a completely different set of problems.

With long, easy strides, Erik's footsteps echoed around the cavernous hangar. Maria joined him in the signal-deadened conference room, certain no outsider could hear their conversation. Every electronic or sonic wave that entered or left the room did modified beyond usefulness.

"Well boss," Erik's favorite name for Maria, a title she had never sought and discouraged at every opportunity, "We estimate almost two hundred lifts to get what we've received so far on orbit." Erik's small talk surfaced at times, especially if he could inject a little humor. Often accused of being a closet comedian, Erik denied the label, saying overt leaned more toward his true nature. Often, humor put people at ease and probably made his job easier. Particularly, in Mexico, where despite becoming a citizen, he remained a *gringo* to the locals.

"A lot of work for two lift ships," Maria muttered pensively.

Erik nodded. "But we've got a bigger problem."

Maria eyed her friend, and poured two coffee cups. She kept one gave the spy the other, wondering how she would feel when the other shoe dropped.

"It seems someone ID'd me about a month ago. Mexico City and it wasn't one of Verson's people." His face remained a mask of calm.

Maria's gut churned as she waited. They'd come so far and were so close to achieving her plan to leave earth. Dealing with this jolted her even though they'd all lived with the thought, maybe fear, for a long time. "How do you know?" She wasn't sure she wanted to hear the answer.

"Since we pulled our disappearing act, I've had Martin monitor NSA. Yesterday he learned NSA had issued a BOLO on all of us about a month ago. Apparently, right after the Mexico City sighting. It would appear someone no longer believes we're dead. Yesterday, General Wallace Verson, NSA boss, contacted me."

Maria gave the spy a look that belonged in a scabbard. "NSA? Why them and what's a BOLO?"

Erik fielded the anxiety-tinged question. "I know CIA procedure and Martin knows NSA's. With both my and Martin's disappearance," Erik's lips pursed, his way of acknowledging someone's concern, yet nodded and continued, "Both agencies do a computer search anytime a former employee or more important an agent dies regardless of how. All the files would end up on the director's desks if anything were flagged. I wanted Martin to see if the search spiked any further looks and if they had taken any action because of whatever they found. I had him take a peek off and on over the years. He got lucky and hit them right after all this took place."

Maria shook her head clearly worried that this had gone beyond an acceptable risk. "Won't NSA detect the hacking?"

Erik stared at the bare wall, "Maybe. But, Martin knows more than any other human about their software and system. They might pick up on it, probably will, but Grabel will know it immediately. He's seen no sign that they have. I think we have a little time." He paused then added, "Sorry I didn't let you know. Just routine action. You knew we were in almost every computer system the government has. You name it, Treasury, Social Security, FBI, CIA. I just assumed you knew how extensive our poking around had been. We didn't see it as that big a deal."

Maria waved him off not wanting Erik to know her own anxiety.

Erik continued, "A BOLO is *Be On the Look Out.*" He paused, apparently searched for words that wouldn't unduly alarm Maria. He finally said, "When Verson, issues a BOLO, it's understood that if someone dies as a result, no questions are asked. He said he'd cancel it. But sometimes it takes days for that information to filter down to the boots on the ground.

"So, I met with Verson. He knows our whole story. I didn't leave much out. He meets with the President today. I think the guy is on our side but his number two wants us locked up.

Maria's lips press together and her eyes flared for an instant. "I think we'd better convene the group."

CHAPTER SEVEN
The Plan Falters

An hour later, still in the silent room, Maria, took a deep breath and sat to hide her weariness. It had been a long and anxious day. She asked Erik to bring the group up to speed. While the matter wasn't routine, Erik didn't add his concerns about the *no questions asked* dictum associated with the BOLO. No one spoke for a few moments.

Gramina Fiora broke the silence with news that stunned most of the group. "Bhani and Martin will require some help." At first, it seemed she would ignore the problem just laid before them.

As if on a swivel, all eyes turned toward the two, now seated on the small side sofa.

Bhani, dressed in a blue satin sari, hands folded in her lap, spoke. "I'm pregnant." She cast a glance at Martin.

He sat stoic, except for the red turning purple cast his face reflected, his eyes locked straight ahead. Despite best intentions, sometimes nature deals with matters in its own way.

Gasps broke the silence that for a few seconds filled the room.

Ann, the first to collect her wits, jumped up, stepped across the room, and hugged the Indian. All eyes switched to Grabel. He hadn't moved. The mathematician's face, rigid, had completed the change from a deep red to purple. Martin had most likely never been to bed with a woman before Bhani but now would be the first of the group to father a child since the explosion.

Maria smiled at the couple, all the while realizing her plans to get everyone except Erik and Ann off the planet in the next day or two had just gone to hell. "Congratulations. I don't want to sound clinical, but you need to keep the most detail records possible. This will be the first chance to see how the effect of our condition works out on offspring—genetically." This was our opportunity to learn how a pregnancy progresses. The affects on a child had its plus side. All the biological questions surfaced. Would the long life characteristic be inherited? Is the gestation period affected? What about maturing, does it happen at a different rate? These questions needed answers. But it did present herculean problems and raised hell with her launch plan.

Bhani cleared her throat. "There's something no one has mentioned."

Everyone waited for her to continue.

"Martin has the Rhesus protein. He's Rh positive." A gasp went up, mostly from the women.

A stunned silence permeated the air. Grim expressions were on all faces except Maria's, as she rose to the occasion. Martin sat unmoved, but then he'd never made high marks for his humanitarian side. Just when they didn't need it, and when they all thought they had two major problems, a third had surfaced and one that had far reaching repercussions. Changing the baby's blood presented no serious problems except they would have to make sure the

44

replaced blood was destroyed. Delaying the launch could condemn their escape.

Macon shook his head as he cast a tender look at Bhani.

David said, "Roberto, looks like you get to put your medical degree to work. You'll have to monitor this pregnancy." They had no idea how long the gene, or however the mechanism worked, remained active after transfusion. The major concern remained Bhani and her unborn child. How they would deal with it if either needed blood.

Macon broke the lingering quiet. "We can handle Bhani's treatment clinically. But the baby may be a different story. It may require a complete transfusion. Won't know until I can run some tests." Macon seemed to realize this wasn't the time or place to discuss routine clinical matters and with raised eyebrows returned to his seat.

Nothing Maria had done prepared her for these revelations. She pursed her lips, "Well, with this new information and no time to digest it, what are your feelings?" This had to be particularly unnerving. For the last seven years, each day had been lived as if those words would greet them. Now here they were and no better prepared than when this all began.

Excluding Erik, all had lived pastoral lives and these disclosures could only cause trepidation and fear. Most of Maria's life has been more like a monk's or nun, but that wasn't the case for the others. Born to parents who were both scientists, and over fifty, and an only child, she'd never experienced many of the casual growing up episodes of most children. David's life had been almost the direct opposite. Maybe that's why she relied so heavily on his judgment. She always seemed to have her head and heart going the same way and sometimes, that just didn't work. Learning to lead in life and death situations had gradually changed Maria and she knew it.

She tried to pay attention to the conversation but her mind stayed busy re-planning a schedule she'd spent seven years putting together. Her original plan had been for all but Anne and Svern to be on the first shuttle. They were to be the last to leave Earth. But now—Bhani couldn't launch until her baby arrived and then only when the living quarters habitat in the space station had artificial gravity. And of course that meant Macon would have to stay with her.

But that brought up the question of whether to relocate. Once the 747 and *Independence* lifted off from Bahia de Los Angeles, news people, and agents from every government anxious to find out who we were would overrun the place even though all contacts would be directed to the *Los Quatro Socios*. It would be OJT for them but so be it.

Macon said it would be a mistake to leave Mexico. He remained confident they could continue hiding until time to launch. Mexican authorities had assured Svern they could handle any attempts a foreign country might make to enforce extradition. He added, "Besides, if I understand what's happened and what could happen, the laws we've violated, faking our deaths, are ones that restitution can resolve. We've hurt no one with our actions. Maybe cost the government a little money searching for the airplane wreckage and our bodies. Most countries are reluctant to send you back if there's no victim."

45

They relied on Svern's knowledge of how the Mexican government would handle this. Maria for one had no doubts. She'd placed her trust in this man due in a large part to his tough-mindedness and ability to see any matter through to its end. His thoroughness, what any scientist would apply to day-to-day activities, short-circuited would-be problems before they became real. Most bureaucrats would defer to him, never fully understanding what the man had done either for or to them. Nevertheless, Svern had made it a point to never lie or mislead anyone in the Mexican government. After a few years of dealing with him, their trust came close to matching hers.

"I really don't want to live in another country." Macon, being Spanish, had little difficulty in adjusting to Mexico. Picking up the speech nuances and colloquialisms had taken little time. His Castilian birth placed him in the upper class of Mexican society.

Maria said nothing, preferring to let the conversation flow where it might. For the next hour, every option received its due. Some of the more bizarre ones brought chuckles and a few outright laughs.

Bhani, Martin, Gramina, and Macon would remain in Mexico, as would Erik and Ann. It had been their sanctuary for seven years, maybe it would hold until they could safely take the baby into space.

They'd just need to get lucky—as they had so many times before.

Over two hundred people had received blood donated by various members of the original eight. Seventeen had died by accident or from disease. The living, all to a person, had changed and were no longer aging as they should.

All survivors had volunteered as part of the crew. Ten had high technical skills. David had assigned them to handle the engine fabrication and of course, they'd signed on for the voyage. Of the six shuttle pilots, only the two flying Independence would be available for reassignment. For the rest of the airmen, Ann's recruitment had delivered Maria's full flight crews.

The Mexican government had agreed to shelter anyone who had to remain on Earth until final launch and keep at bay the growing throng wanting to be included. They'd received over four thousand requests to be included, some by various governments and those were only the ones reported.

The forty newcomers who had passed the blood screening tests, and the last contaminated, were completing orientation and scheduled to help load, prep the shuttles for turnaround for at least three months would remain here on earth. And that all depended on how successful the food and habitat modules proved out as they came on line. Another eighty-seven had arrived over the last two months and complete Orion's crew. As needed, they would transfer up to Orion, a one-way trip.

Maria waited until the conversation had run its course then instructed Roberto to set up a registry for everyone who will board Orion. Those people who had received blood donations would be first. Research over the past few years still hadn't revealed precisely which the gene transferred as the result of a blood transfusion even though it seemed to occur one hundred percent of the time. Remaining unknown was how the recipients longevity compare to the original donor. "Martin can help you with the programming."

Martin wearily nodded. Maria knew it would be almost demeaning work but Bhani had assured her, her husband took seriously his new role as soon to be father with pride and for him, that meant total commitment.

"Gramina," Maria turned to Roberto's wife, "Work with Erik and set up the necessary security for all of these people who will be coming and going. You know the rules, no strays, no visitors, no stowaway's—in a word, no one goes on a shuttle or gets onboard Orion who doesn't belong there. You and Erik will say who belongs and who doesn't. Be ruthless if you have to."

She paused for a moment, the athletic, robust woman seeming to lean forward anticipating Maria's next thoughts. "I would like for you to work with these newcomers, do a job skill aptitude test, you know the whole regimen of tests. Try to get everyone, or at least as many as possible, into jobs for which seems best for his or her aptitudes. And for those who don't fit, your job will be to convince them of their usefulness."

Roberto's wife seemed pleased with the attention and responsibility she'd been given. Maria sensed the large woman's concern that she may not have a useful role. But that all seemed to disappear if the grin on Gramina's face could be believed.

Maria stood, reached for the carafe, and poured each a cup of coffee. She rolled her sidearm chair across linoleum-tiled floor to the front of the desk. Juggling the brew, she brushed the longish hair from her grey eyes then sat. She placed her right arm on the wooden tabletop and offered a mild steady gaze, her demeanor taut yet receptive. There was nothing pretentious about her actions. She had made her mark in the sand and it would stand. She had always let his little band know how the odds stacked up. And now they were a lot greater against a successful launch than they had been a few days earlier.

Erik added, "I've been in touch with NSA boss General Verson. He wants to meet again. I think I should."

For an instant, Maria thought it would take all of her strength just to remain upright. "This puts everything on the line doesn't it? If they've penetrated this far, they have to know a lot more about what's going on."

"I agree," Erik said.

Maria turned toward the group. "Any comments?" Getting no response, she shook her head and not in a mocking way, "You people sure are a trusting bunch?"

CHAPTER EIGHT
The First Flight

Two men from Avionica Del Sur stood on the tarmac at Bahia Los Angeles. Unbeknownst to them, two others stood on the West shore of the Sea of Cortez, less than a mile away.

Rogue CIA agent Harold Bassett along with his Mexican counterpart assembled his team. Six men would accompany him—forty would wait for his signal to move against the hangers. The remaining hundred would hold the beachhead they'd established an hour earlier and be available if needed at the hangers. The thousand Mexican soldiers on the east shore of the Sea of Cortez were far enough away that Bassett wasn't worried about them. They just wouldn't be a factor. He'd be gone by the time they could interfere.

* * * *

The tall man jumped when his hand-held transceiver coughed to life. Long awaited, yet on time, the Boeing 747 requested landing instructions.

Along with all but Bhani and Martin, Maria watched the giant plane start its final approach on their only runway—designated one seven. Even though licensed to fly jets, David marveled at how something that large could fly—not to mention how graceful it appeared.

A collective sigh went up from the audience as the plane touched down and rolled onto the tarmac toward the hangar.

That night the aircraft maintenance crew, which accompanied the plane, set about preparing for the next flight.

Eight hours later, the self-propelled mate/de-mate crane, modeled after NASA's, lifted the shuttle *Independence* onto the plane's back at the near end of the runway.

By morning, the loaded spacecraft sat atop the jumbo jet, secured by six explosive bolts ready for the two-member plane crew and twelve *Independence* passengers. Less than twenty hours remained until take-off.

David's engineering skills would be fully tested now. Every effort, years of work, pointed to this moment.

He glanced at his wristwatch as he moved toward the giant aircraft.

Three A.M. Fifteen hours until take-off.

He walked around the coupled pair, touched the RATO rockets as if giving them a good luck pat. On those rockets, along with the new jet engines, rested the only chance for the heavily loaded plane to make it safely off the shortened runway.

Against the gathering dark, white high thin clouds peppered the sky. Mexico's federal weather office assured David weather would not hinder the launch. *Independence*, firmly anchored to struts protruding from the 747's top, stood ready to receive its passengers.

Shaped like a high-backed tortoise shell that reached from the planes cockpit and tapered to the empennage, the physical size of the joined pair awed him. The two three-foot diameter, twenty-five feet long solid booster rockets that would take them to their first orbital altitude, completed the picture. The mate/de-mate crane had cleared the runway and stood parked on the apron in front of the main hangar. Eight technicians and the two pilots took the elevator up the loading gantry to the orbiters entry hatch.

As they waited their turn to board, Maria gave each of her colleagues a hug and made no pretense about how she felt, flinging her arms into the air, something quite unusual for her.

David shook hands with everyone. Through clamped teeth and pursed lips, he tried to contain his excitement. Dressed in their space suits, crewmembers would need only minutes to prepare for takeoff.

Despite her accelerated heartbeat and adrenalin rush, Maria tried to remain calm. She didn't succeed.

She broke out in a huge grin. Helmet in the crotch of her arm, she said, "No speech. We've all prepared for this day for over seventeen years."

She, like the original eight and the hundred or so specialized personnel added to the roster, were very aware that few of the systems, although proven in other applications, lacked testing as a completed functional unit. Most of the scientists and engineers had been around prototypes all their working careers and knew how great the risk of failure.

While Scaled Components completed the structural design and fabrication, Quantum Fields developed and produced the ZPV Casimir space drive engines or at least those parts producible on Earth. Some segments of the engines, due to their size or manufacturing preciseness needed, would require near zero gravity for fabrication and that could only happen on orbit. David had handled the preparations for turning *Orion* into a self-contained world, one that would have to sustain the group for more than two hundred years. Everything had to be reproducible or regenerative.

Apprehension abounds where loved ones remained behind. But, to a person, all agreed any delay could doom their efforts. Once on orbit, they were a factor known to the world and no government could deal with them as a renegades. Mexico's resolve remained untested and therein rested their fate.

Maria faced the group remaining behind. "Erik is the CEO and responsible for everyone's welfare and—"

"Someone's coming," Ann interrupted. A gasp almost to a person pierced the quiet. Erik seemed to take the intrusion in stride.

David and Erik stepped away a few paces for a better view as the headlights approached.

"It looks like our van," David said.

A touch of a smile crossed Erik's lips, which he quickly wiped away.

Instead of using the blacktop road, the vehicle cut across the dirt infield leaving a billowing trail of dust and onto the runway as if to block any movement of the 747 and orbiter. It swung in front of the big plane, stopped ten feet short of the nose, headlights reflecting off the huge aluminum belly.

Two men dressed in army fatigues stepped out and approached. The taller one was armed with a holstered sidearm, the other had already drawn an automatic pistol. They stopped a few feet away and the taller man said, "I'm Harold Bassett, special envoy from the United States Embassy, Mexico City. This airplane is impounded and you are all under arrest." Even in the darkness, a smile of obvious satisfaction creased his face.

David's heart raced. Instinctively, he started forward.

He felt Erik touch his arm, a signal to wait as the CEO stepped between them, denying their accoster a clear view.

Erik called to a mechanic standing near the right landing gear wheel well for a flashlight. He shined it into Bassett's face and heard a weapon cock in response.

"Well, well. You're the guy who ID'd me in Mexico City. You must be very good and certainly very CIA and now with an added title of special envoy. You cover a lot of territory. Does the Mexican government know of your new job and authority?"

He flashed the light on the soldier behind Bassett and revealed a sneer, from his appearance most likely a Mexican but probably not army. To Erik, it could make a huge difference.

For a moment, Bassett's grin was replaced with surprise that seemed to cloud his face—probably because of Erik's casual attitude.

The intruder signaled the van and three men in drab army-colored body armor stepped out brandishing automatic weapons. They formed a semi-circle off to one side, giving each shooter a clear field of fire. Bassett reached for his sidearm. "Please do not resist. As you can plainly see, we are well-armed and will do what's necessary to enforce our orders."

David recalled what Erik had said about General Verson's BOLO's; even though Verson came out of NSA, rules have a way of being elastic. These people had license to kill, no questions asked.

As the three took their positions, Erik breathed a hidden sigh. The added men appeared to be Anglos. Had the Mexican government been involved, they would never have allowed anyone but Mexican soldiers to intervene.

He turned toward his group, "Please, everyone return to the hangar. You too," he whispered to David and Maria who had just joined them. "It might get a little dicey around here." His voice stayed low and calm but unmistakably not to be ignored.

Maria could only wonder what that meant. Five heavily armed soldiers and an unarmed Erik.

Bassett, his voice pounded through the night like a sledgehammer, said to his entourage, "If anyone tries to leave, shoot them," and in Spanish repeated himself. In unison, steel slammed against steel, the sound of cocked weapons dominated the night as the four guards responded to the order.

Maria forced back her rising fear. Adrenalin quickly turned her reaction to anger, surprising but satisfying even her. Looks of alarm and astonishment on those behind her steeled her resolve—not that she needed any encouragement. For the first time in her life, she wished she had a gun.

Erik's hard-laced voice smashed back at Bassett. "You son of a bitch." He raised his left arm and small red dots appeared on the chests or heads of the four gunmen and their leader. "Fire one shot and you're all fucking dead."

The finality in his voice stopped everyone including those who had moved toward the hangar.

What had been abject fear for people who could view a boiling test tube as something alarming, now justifiably reflected terror. Maria sensed death hung on Erik's every word.

Near panic appeared on the faces of Bassett's men as they searched the darkness in vain. One man noticeably lowered the barrel of his weapon. Bassett grimaced and sucked in air, his self-assurance a thing of the past.

Erik gave a wry grin. "In case you're curious, those little red dots focused on you are from CheyTAC LRM100 sniper rifles with armor piercing ammo. Go through four inches of steel at one thousand yards. At this range, your bulletproof vests are useless,"

Erik stopped and shook his head confident their imaginations would do more to get his message across than anything would. But he couldn't resist the temptation. "Your heads will explode like melons. Oh yes, I almost forgot," his casual attitude in itself, was more chilling than his words. "Those weapons carry silencers. Shit. You'll die, get dumped in the Sea of Cortez, no one will ever know. Oxalic acid will clean any blood from the runway. If it's diluted a little, it works great on concrete. Doesn't eat away the cement and just leave gravel pits like some acids." He let his needling comment hang for a moment. Darkness added to the armed men's misery intensifying Svern's admonishment that they were marked for death. "Put your weapons down now."

Despite the seriousness of the moment, Maria gritted her teeth to smother the smile struggling to form. Bassett seemed nonplused at Erik's cavalier attitude.

No one moved. "Your call Bassett. Live or die. Make up your mind." Erik nodded his head to one side. "Everyone into the hangar. Now."

Maria understood the ominous tone in Erik's voice but felt certain bloodshed here could doom their flight. "If these men surrender, they live." This entire scene was for her beyond belief. Somewhere, in the dark, people responded to Erik. The man had prepared.

"Get inside," Erik ordered again.

"No," said Maria her voice steady. "Not until I have your word."

"I promise you we won't start the shooting," said Erik even though he didn't like giving up that edge.

His calmness and matter of fact demeanor in the face of threat or violence swayed Maria—just one of the assets she'd notice and admired in Erik over the last seven years.

She knew that his answer had limits—it was what she would get and probably all that anyone could expect. This invisible army of was something new and unexpected, an army she didn't know she had. She was grateful for Erik's foresight and planning. She'd mentally prepared himself for someone or something to interrupt the take-off. Things had just gone too smoothly for some shit not to happen. She hated to be a pessimist but had learned from Erik that a little of that thrown into planning usually proved productive. It was equally obvious Erik had advanced information about Bassett and acted on it.

Maria motioned all but Erik and the intruders toward the hangar. She heard Erik slide the safety off his pistol and wondered where that weapon had come from. When all this started, Bassett and his guns had the upper hand. All that had changed in an instant.

In the dim light, Erik scanned the three soldiers who had exited the van just moments before.

Their faces contorted with what he judged as doubt mixed with fear. Not knowing what nationalities he faced, Svern slowly issued his warning in Spanish, "*Cedan las armas y viven. Esta es la unica advertencia que reciberan.*" And repeated it in English. "Lay down your weapons and you live. This is the only warning you get."

He watched and waited for what seemed an eternity.

One man, who appeared Anglo, had pissed in his pants. Experience had told Erik that the guys who lost control were the most unpredictable. He never took his eyes from him but kept his weapon pointed away—no sense in pushing or testing the man any further.

One by one, the men gently put their weapons on the tarmac,

Harlow Bassett, yielding to the obvious, followed suit. The red dots disappeared. A sigh of relief came from the man who had soiled himself.

"There are more of us," Bassett said. "It's only a matter of time before the remainder of my group arrives. I'm telling you this to avoid bloodshed."

"Shut-up you dumb son of a bitch. I ought to kill you where you stand." Erik spoke into his com unit.

"Move."

Gunfire echoed across the runway but quickly became sporadic and died completely.

Erik's mobile spat, "Objective taken."

With a few steps, Erik closed the gap separating the two men. "Ten seconds ago, you were willing to shoot unarmed civilians. And four of them women." He didn't mention Bhani's pregnancy. "You miserable bastard. You're not worth the shit it'd take to smother you." He glared at the CIA agent but found no regret in the man's face.

He walked away then stopped and turned. "We moved the Mexican Army into place last night. Your men didn't stand a chance. And the van... we left it there for you, dumb ass."

"Now, get back inside *our* van," Erik ordered.

As he spoke ten people, the owners of the little red dots emerged. Some, dressed in full desert camouflage, appeared from the Baja sand. Others, in black came from like backgrounds around the launch equipment. They surrounded the group then picked up their weapons. One approached Erik and the two quietly exchanged words.

First Contact

Maria, too far away to hear what passed between them, waited and worried. From the hangar door, her eyes locked on the men as the near disaster ended. Thoughts of what could happen sent a shiver through her. She had to admit to mixed emotions. Grateful this small army had been able to make the difference and yet the use of raw power grated. Physical threat was something she'd never had to use, in fact never experienced before today. Words and thought had always been her tools. At an age somewhere between physically close to thirty, yet experienced and emotionally seventy, she had entered a completely new world.

She started out the door toward the group. Erik waved her back but Maria's determination to make sure her orders were followed drove her.

"No Erik. I have to know what you're going to do with these men."

"Boss, you're being a pain in the ass. Just when I get a chance to act the big shot, you have to buck me."

Maria relaxed. Years of working with this man came into play. Satisfied the captives' lives were not in danger as long as they behaved she asked, "How are you going to handle this? What happens now?"

Erik stood next to David, who had never left his side, as his troops put plasticuffs on the five men, his pistol still pointed toward Bassett. "I'll turn the Mexicans over to one of our companies and they'll pass them on to the Federales. Any gringos along with this one, he yanked on Bassett's arm, I've got other plans."

"Why not all of them?" Maria asked. "Let the Mexican authorities handle the matter."

"Naw. It wouldn't be a nice way to treat Harlow. A gringo muscling in on their territory? Probably without Mexican approval." He shook his head, "Doesn't sit well. I'm afraid Mister Bassett wouldn't be treated very nicely." He toed the concrete tarmac. "Wouldn't live very long."

"So? What happens?"

"We let him go," his manner matter of fact.

Maria's lips screwed around in a sour way knowing more had to come.

"Look, he's been in touch with his people all the way on this, probably directly with Washington. Everything he knows, they know. So, why not give him back. His career's over. Let him go home to mama and the kids—if he can make it out of Mexico and back to the good ole US of A alive."

Almost in the same breath he said, "So, Mr. and Mrs. Rohm, you need to get the plane into the air. There're most likely people out there waiting to hear from Mr. Bassett, people who will try to stop you...again."

Erik's eyes turned hard as he looked at the prisoner, popped his fist against the agents shoulder, and asked, "Care to comment Harlow? Do we have other uninvited guests lurking out there somewhere just waiting for your beckon?" Svern laughed at his own foisted humor but those hard cold eyes held no amusement.

Maria took Svern's admonishment seriously and motioned for David to join her on the lift.

Bassett spoke, "Well, I'll be damned. You're Doctor Maria Presk aren't you? Washington was right. You and your people didn't die in that plane crash years ago!" His challenge ended with a wheeze.

Maria's heart skipped a beat. Bassett had told her more with that one revelation than she'd ever hoped.

CHAPTER NINE
Bahia de Los Angles

Grady Moffitt's clandestine army had failed to stop Maria and her determined group, at least this time. For whatever reasons the former NSA deputy director harbored, his efforts had been too little too late.

As quickly as Erik's amazing army had appeared, it disappeared into the darkness, along with the prisoners. Heeding Erik's warning to get into the air, Maria and David entered the crane elevator to the shuttle.

As the hoist neared their embarkation point, the outskirt lights of Bahia de Los Angeles sparkled in the distance. Maria stopped the lift, took David's hand, and said, "This is the last time we'll see a city, any earth city—at least up close. From now on, they'll just like satellite images we've all seen for years, only specks of light." She gave his hand a squeeze and even in the darkness, saw him smile.

Prior to boarding the lift, they had donned plastic shoe covers, as had the ten crewmembers before them. Meant to keep any foreign material from scratching *Independence's* outer surface, at the entry, they removed the coverings and stepped onto steeply slanted carbon fiber hull. Lack of handholds made traversing the ten feet to the entry hatch awkward but with practiced caution, both made it safely.

She saw Erik tap his earpiece and stopped mid-step. Maria put on her helmet, retrieved the phone jack hanging from its cable, and plugged it into a receptacle at the entry. "What's up?" Her gut told her Svern wasn't calling to wish them Godspeed.

In a quiet tone Erik said, "The UN is demanding the Mexican government stop the flight until jurisdiction can be determined; a peacekeeping force is on the way. They won't be the problem Bassett had been but even that we don't need. I've talked with our people in the Mexican capitol and asked them to send a couple of squads to protect our corporate offices. They've agreed." He didn't mention Bahia. "Should be there within the hour."

"What about Bahia?" Maria said.

Erik cleared his throat. There are already over one thousand Mexican troops surrounding us."

Maria shook her head a little angry Erik had not told her of the troops but thankful for his due diligence. "We'll move as fast as we safely can." The deadly calm in her voice did not betray her true nervousness.

Mexico's government faced its first real test of commitment. They'd come through so far, but to her knowledge, this was the first time the government itself had been challenged. A lot remained at stake on both sides.

She remained convinced their decision to leave and start a new life on another planet, had been their only real hope. There was no turning back.

Maria smiled, nodding as she and David stepped through the hatch into the reinforced carbon fiber tortoise-shaped craft that would take them into space. A few steps more and they were in the cylinder. Once pressurized, it would be their home until they had erected the ingress/egress chamber and habitat shells stowed around them.

The stowage area also held the hydrogen fuel cells that would be their only power source until the next flight up from earth.

The ten men already onboard had completed the required preflight checks and had only to strap themselves into their contoured seats. They helped Maria and David prepare for takeoff, cutting the time from the usual thirty minutes to less than five. Yet, they meticulously went over each item on the checklist.

Preparation of their space suits for orbital insertion would come after take-off. This may have been different from what they had practiced dozens of times in the simulator but they didn't have a choice. *Independence* had to launch. Maria had every reason to believe enormous pressure had been being applied to the Mexican government to stop their leaving. The UN didn't have the habit of acting independently.

As if the events over the last half hour coupled with the seven years of preparation weren't more than enough to raise her blood pressure dramatically, this last bit of news from Mexico City put the finishing touches in place. The adrenalin surging through her veins actually added to her stability.

For all twelve sealed in a pressure tight compartment inside the space module, the next few minutes went by in a whirlwind of activity. At the moment, the initiative remained theirs but that could change in a heartbeat.

The crew hardly had time to get nervous. Hardly time, but still enough. They'd applied the buddy system, each checking the others life support connections. Any mistake after release from the mother ship could be fatal. *Independence* had no way to return safely to earth.

Slowly, one by one, the four jumbo jet GE90-115B engines roared to life. Maria could only wonder how Erik had pulled that one off. He'd managed to get the world's most powerful jet aircraft engines retrofitted to their 747 while major aircraft manufacturers waited for delivery. *Another marvel to add to the list.*

Independence swayed as the turbines strained against the brakes.

Sitting almost sixty feet above the runway, every little move made by the behemoth below translated into a very large motion in the clamshell.

Even with David's long flying experience, the winnowing only added to the threatened vertigo. Tied together on the intercom, the other ten passengers soon let Maria know of their displeasure, voicing various degrees of anxiety and a few choice comments that were better kept within the group.

The kibitzing stopped when the co-pilot quizzed each crewmember— requiring them to give the okay that they were ready for take-off.

David, sitting at the control panel and the last interrogated, closed his visor, switched the intercom to the pilot's frequency and tied everyone into the 747 flight crew communications. Shuttle *Independence* pilots, Zhu Ling and Abba Dubaku, sitting to Maria's left, would actually be the pilots of record. A call from *Agencia Nacional de Espacio* (the Mexican space agency she'd helped bring to its current status) granted take-off and space launch permissions with a quiet

Via con Dios.

Maria breathed a sigh of relief along with short spurt of pent up breath. The Mexican government had not caved.

She glanced at David and managed a smile that went unanswered. Her eyes closed and gloves clearly clinched in a white-knuckle grip on the body-molded seat probably said it all. The next few minutes would tell their fate.

The 747 taxied onto the runway. The stripped down aircraft hull transmitted every noise, every nuance, every vibration the powerful engines introduced into the airframe and shook everyone and everything as the throttles commanded each engine to its one hundred fifteen thousand pound thrust.

Both the pilot and co-pilot strained against the brake pedals as the engines wailed.

Secured inside *Independence*, the crew sat and waited. Through their helmets, the jet noise sounded like the demons of hell screaming, wanting loose. Though gripped in shock absorbent carriers, instruments and computer screens jumped and were virtually illegible.

David listened as the co-pilot announced nose wheel centered and set for crosswind.

At one hundred percent RPM, the pilot signaled to release the brakes and the big, heavily loaded, 747 headed down the runway.

Instantly, the noise and shaking eased.

Less than five hundred feet into the take-off roll, eight of sixteen RATO rockets fired giving the plane and everyone in *Independence* a major jolt, ramming them back into their seats.

Another five hundred feet and the remaining rockets fired, delayed long enough to ensure the pilots had ground control since the airplane's speed wasn't high enough for the flight surfaces to have any measurable effect.

Although the initial G-forces had jammed everyone far back into their form fitting seats, the second salvo pushed them even deeper into what, once on orbit, would become their beds.

For a few seconds, the added thrust held them immobile.

Shuttle pilot Zhu Ling scanned the computer-generated flight instruments: the same as the cockpit crews. All too soon, everyone heard the co-pilot call *V-one in ten seconds*. The pilot had that much or that little time in which to decide whether to continue the take-off or abort, the point of no return. The runway, a little over seven thousand feet long, never seemed long enough. A fully loaded standard 747 needed a minimum of seven thousand five hundred feet for a normal takeoff. The rockets should reduce that at least one thousand feet. Not normal, suicidal may have better described what they were doing. There was no room for error. Their success remained totally dependent on the powerful engines' and auxiliary rockets' ability to provide the necessary added speed to generate the lift to make them fly.

They were cheating the take-off distance by nearly one thousand feet of white flat concrete.

A small TV camera looking over the pilot's shoulder gave Maria and David a clear forward view.

The runway end approached all too quickly.

Even with more than one thousand hours logged as first pilot, David caught himself pushing his feet against the bulkhead immediately in front and pulling on an imaginary yoke knowing his encouragement faced a test of nerves and that didn't help a bit.

The co-pilot's calm professional voice call 'VR (rotation speed) in six seconds, a command normally given for the ten-second mark but he could see the runway end. And V-one had passed, it seemed, a scant few seconds ago.

A quick glance at the airspeed indicator—at one hundred seventy knots or VR, the nose should have started to lift. The giant airplane tried to fly, struggling against gravity and drag to get into the air. The co-pilot's voice sounded strained as he announced *V-two now*. They passed one-hundred eighty knots… finally the aircraft's nose wheel broke ground. The familiar thump from the main landing gear signaled the 747 and *Independence* were flying.

A sign of relief heard through the mike went up even as the engine RPM indicator—reached one hundred ten percent. It had taken every bit of power the plane possessed to get airborne.

"How much?" David meant how much runway remained when they broke ground.

"Two hundred feet," the pilot answered. What went unsaid was in five tenths of a second and they would have run out of concrete runway.

David pressed the mike switch. "Gentlemen, some of the best piloting I've ever seen. Congratulations."

A general round of compliments and thanks passed back and forth and included the eight specialists and two pilots. The noise and vibration that had shaken them to the bone had become a low-pitched steady drone.

Once over the water, the co-pilot jettisoned the spent RATO rockets, eliminating their now dead weight. Far below in the Sea of Cortez, men in dinghy's stood by to retrieve the ejected bottles.

The pilot busied himself for what lay ahead—the point of no return.

The co-pilot commented on how little yaw they were experiencing as they continued to climb, something the engineers had been concerned about. The tortoise shape wasn't all that conducive to good aerodynamics. Particularly since Independence carried two solid-state rockets attached to the underneath side. In fact, the engineers had installed additional vertical stabilizers on not only the 747 but *Independence* as well. Still, the big plane handled the five hundred thousand pound payload almost as the computer models had predicted.

The space vehicle held no windows or forward cockpit windshield. Once free of the 747, they would fly blind, relying totally on computers and instruments to guide them into the proper orbit.

Zhu Ling could override the system, but that would only happen if some failure or malfunction, mechanical, electronic or software placed them in jeopardy—loss of nerve didn't count.

The craft maintained a nose up attitude. Coupled with the constant engine drone, that meant the flight parameters were as predicted.

Maria patted David's gloved hand. She turned and through their helmet visors, she saw doubt in his face—their ride with serendipity wasn't over.

Twenty minutes later, still circling over Mexican air space, the intercom crackled as the big plane leveled off. "Ms. Presk," a slight pause followed, "Captain Presk, we are at launch altitude."

Maria had played those words through her mind hundreds of times, yet she flinched when they came through her earphones. For the first time, she' been addressed as captain. But now, by law, not unlike maritime law that governed in space, she had total control. Any dispute or act against her authority constituted a mutiny.

David set the radio frequency and flipped the switch. "Bahia flight control, this is *Independence*. Come in please." His voice had projected the calm and self-assurance he wished his stomach and nerves felt. Soon this radio beacon would be their only connection with Earth. Maria hoped the entire world would hear this, their first communication. From now on, all communications would be available to anyone who wanted to tune in.

It only took a few minutes to confirm that the pre-launch numbers were good.

Zhu Ling and Abba Dubaku completed the pre-ignition check-off. The two solid-state rockets checked satisfactorily or in engineering terms, *all systems nominal*. She couldn't say that for herself, her breathing was too rapid and shallow. She told herself to settle down, and willed herself calm.

Maria gave the 747 pilot the command to start the speed run-up to their launch point.

At her signal and without any hesitation, David raised the switch safeguard and armed the two rockets that would take them into space.

All lights on his instrument panel showed green, except for the explosive bolts tying *Independence* to the braces. The umbilical cord, a friction joint, would separate from both craft when the vehicles pulled apart.

A studied look into the overhead mirror at the men seated behind him and brought a thumb's up from each one. A sideways glance at Maria brought the same. Apparently, they had all agreed to give him the identical signal and he acknowledged with an approving nod. He flipped the switch giving standby control to the computers. And waited.

Maria felt her heart pound as it never had before.

During her career as a scientist, she had experienced moments of exhilaration, moments that literally changed the world. But those had come after long tedious, deliberative experiments. This time it was different. No more questions about whether she or anyone else had the right to ask people to take such a risk, to give up their entire lives and leave family behind. But someone still had to make the decision to go ahead. And that fell to Maria alone.

Eyes glued to instruments, David saw the jet engine RPM increase to one hundred percent. The airspeed indicator slowly climbed above two hundred fifty knots. All their empirical performance data and computer modeling had shown at that altitude, at three hundred knots they had reached their expected limit. Once the airspeed stabilized for five seconds, the computer would send an electrical impulse and explode the bolts. The panel showed all green.

Again, without hesitation, he moved the switch one more notch and the computer had command.

Maria heard the hold-down bolts explode, and simultaneously the jolts, then a nudge from the springs inside the braces shove *Independence* up and away from the 747. The nose thrusters fired, aligning the ship the orbital insertion attitude.

She saw the effect also when the cockpit picture disappeared. Her earphones crackled. The airplane's pilot acknowledged he'd put the 747 into a speed dive and should have safe separation distance in five seconds allowing rocket ignition. David withdrew his hand from the override switch.

It seemed a giant fist slammed into Maria's chest as the rocket engines ignited. It made the RATO blasts seem like ladyfinger firecrackers compared to a dynamite-loaded truck. Maria's backbone and chest met, squeezing out all the air her lungs craved.

For seven minutes, the rocket thrust moved them toward seventeen thousand miles per hour and kept everyone pinned to their seats and struggling for breath.

She tried the techniques practiced in the simulator and they helped. Still, the fire in her lungs kept forcing gasps. She tried to talk to the other crewmembers but no recognizable sound crossed her lips.

Everyone knew all hell would break loose on Earth as soon as word spread that Mexico had launched something into space. Compared to the pain at that moment, she could have cared less about what people on earth were thinking or saying about her group, Mexico or anyone else.

While David anticipated the cut-off, it caught Maria still struggling for breath.

Pushing as she had against her shoulder harness and seat belt to help breath, she smashed forward against the restraints certain at the least she'd cut off all blood circulation below her waist.

The rockets had shut down.

David scanned the instruments and computer screen. They were on orbit, one hundred-eighty-six miles above earth.

Seven years of trials, tribulations and successes were behind Maria Presk and her intrepid followers. She pressed the computer entry key starting Orion's clock. It was anybody's guess how life would be from now on.

**PART
TWO**

Prologue ll

Ship's Log
First entry
Orion date: 00/00/00 Time: 00:00
Earth date: August 14, 2013 0000 GMT (Zulu Midnight)

What will become *Orion* achieved first orbit today with boosted shuttle from our Boeing 747. The flight was memorable if for no other reason than it was our first and final flight from Earth. All went according to plan, or *nominal.* Some apprehension remained for those accompanying me. I was there by choice. Had I given the others the same option or had they been coerced? David along with the two shuttle pilots, Zhu Ling, Abba Dubaku and ten permanent crewmembers were the first to agree to leave Earth for another world.

Orion's clock started. Twenty-four hour circadian cycle—Year start date to coincide with Earth year August 14, 2013. Computer programmed to maintain a running Zulu correlation.

Presk, Maria, Captain

* * * *

Maria leafed through her diary. Soon the ion engines would be started and Orion would slowly make its way out of system. She had done what she could to prepare her little band for what lay ahead. They would be vital in helping the others who had joined them and those yet to come.

The task that lay ahead would not be easy nor had their road to get into space. Something she considered important was to set a measured pace, one that made the most of real work and minimized idle time.

The entire crew would not be on board until the habitat ring construction got far enough along to induce at least point six gravity. Once the crew of one hundred twenty seven settled in, leaving the solar system would be only a matter of time.

Bhani Patel Grabel gave birth to 7-pound boy (looks like mother—a few comments expressing gratitude for that). Gestation: full term, christened: Chaman Martin Grabel.

Certainly, Bhani and Martin's baby would be among the last to join Orion on orbit. Dr. Macon had already set in motion his plan to monitor the Orion inhabitants who had received the blood transfusion giving them some sort of extended life. How much, no one knew. The child's development would answer some of the biology unknowns and inherent traits. Macon's meticulous records on baby Grabel were the orders of the day. Understanding the effects of the aging process would prove critical to the entire crew's future.

As they were to find out, young Grabel shared his father's penchant for mathematics but as his first name suggested, a great love for botany following a desire of his mother. Chaman in Hindu means great gardener. His contributions to growing and maintaining the food supply were to become a matter no one would deny. Successes in cross-pollination made the trip more tolerable along with other derivatives he developed. On Earth, this work would have brought a Nobel; on Orion, just part of the day's work, just expected.

It had taken seven years to complete the main structure from which the habitat ring sprouted and neared completion. Crews had completed enough of the bridge, engine room, storage areas, and docking bays that work on the habitat ring stayed well ahead of schedule. Serious planning for leaving Earth orbit and heading into deep space occupied much of their time.

Furnishings or anything to flesh out living and working spaces were slim to nonexistent. But with time, that would change. The creativeness of people to improve their lot within the limits imposed by their resources graced any living or workspace.

Three years into the construction, Orion experienced its first casualty. One crewmember failed to follow safety protocols, first failing to attach a safety cord, and second, disregarded the buddy system going EVA alone.

The incident spurred David to start a high priority program of robotic development. His determination that robots do a large share of the EVA work and the dangerous jobs seemed almost an obsession. He had asked Martin Grabel to assist, primarily to do the computer programming. After some codling from Bhani and assurances he could work alone, the volatile mathematician agreed. The program exceeded all expectations. Robots became an essential part of the daily life aboard Orion.

* * * *

Ship's Log
Orion date: 02/11/03 Time: 22.43
Lt. Mary Sizemore, OD

Main engine room, warehouse, and bridge assembly enclosed. Installation of plumbing and equipment started.

Last of permanent complement came aboard including Bhani, Martin and their son, Chaman.

Permanent Crew now numbers one hundred twenty seven souls.

Presk, Maria, Captain

Maria turned away from the consol. "Mr. Svern, you have the con. I'll be in sickbay if you want me."

"Aye, ma'am. You are relieved. I have the con."

It had been an easy decision to adopt the civilian cruise ship command structure. Every person on board had a title that matched their job assignment. The only thing missing were passengers. Erik had pushed for a military style command and his orders and responses often reflected the authoritarian strictness. Maria didn't see the need for that regimen and kept control on a much more informal basis.

She didn't want anything to delay the ion engine start and told David so as he joined her walking down the deserted, as were most, passageway. "Why don't you come with me to sickbay? Roberto has something on his mind."

He nodded. "What do you think about Earth's edict restricting communications with Orion to limit our contacts?" he asked.

"Probably the right thing to do although on a personal level I'm not fond of the idea."

"Sound like a contradiction."

"It won't be long until we'll be out of useful range. I don't want people standing around waiting on messages. We can't afford that."

A few minutes later, they entered the empty sickbay waiting room and spotted the Doctor in a nearby treatment cubicle just as he came from behind a white curtain. Macon had done wonders building a first class medical center. Every devise known available for trauma and day-to-day care was in place and functioning. Any doctor would have been delighted to have such a facility.

"Maria, David, over here." He motioned toward the office. The short bald man dressed in a white smock closed the door. By now, the emergency medical quarters looked like the sickbay on any naval ship—clean, austere, antiseptic, and impersonal.

Having no idea why she'd been summoned, Maria asked, "What's on your mind, Doctor?"

"The Casimir engines. I'm concerned about the radiation from them. They may generate some kind of radiation or radiation levels we've not considered."

The crew had planned in detail for over five years to deal with the consequences of the Casimir engines on crew and equipment. The potential effect of starting them too close to a star system was well understood. Safeguards had been put in place to measure in system variances to make sure no such mistake occurred. Navigation had worked diligently to maneuver Orion to get out-system at the earliest possible time. But that was just normal and expected. That was their job. Macon had more than ample time to complain and maybe save the crew a lot of dangerous and unnecessary work.

Troubled by the remark David said, "Well Doctor, I don't want to appear condescending but it seems to me that is an area of science that we'd better master. After all, everything we encounter from now on certainly has that potential."

It bothered Maria that Roberto, as the lead medical officer with authority to overrule any non-combat decision that may put the crew's health in jeopardy, wasn't making the obvious choice, which was clearly within his say-so.

After a studied delay, Roberto said, "I could order you not to start the engines."

"No, not this time Doctor," Maria, said holding her voice steady. "This is an operational decision and the engineers have assured me the risk is minimal and well within acceptable limits."

Macon fidgeted with a stack of empty Petri dishes sitting on the waist high counter but otherwise didn't respond.

But Maria had known this medical genius far to long and recognize something else troubled him. In all the years they'd worked together, she'd never seen the man quite so anxious. "That's not what's bothering you. Care to tell me the problem?"

Macon, not a forceful man, had made it known acts of heroism didn't fit his makeup. Rather he'd try to find compromises—even where they didn't exist. Where a medical decision was required, though, he stayed resolute. His manner suggested he wasn't the one you'd want watching your back in a fight. But then you never knew for sure. Combat tested people in unpredictable ways and brought out the best and the worst.

The Doctor rubbed his hands and paced before the far bulkhead; small droplets of sweat appeared and glistened on his forehead.

Maria waited—in no hurry and occasionally casually glancing at the man. Experience had told her not to push too hard. Macon's temperament stayed at best fragile when overly excited and that's where they found him right now. She could only wait to learn what news or information had so upset the man.

Finally, Maria laid aside her command voice, opting for a softer tone. "Roberto, what is it? We've been through too much far too long for you to be reticent. Tell me what's on your mind and obviously bothering you."

Almost in a panic that acerbated his Spanish brogue, he finally blurted out in an unending stream, "No! No! You cannot start the engines. I forbid it. And you know I'm within my rights. I have the authority; all the authority—that I need and I intend to use it. I'll put this before the crew. You can't stop me. Either they should be involved in the decision-making or someone else should be in charge and..." his hands fisted, the tremble in his voice more pronounced as it trailed off.

Maria had casually walked up to the desk. She rested one leg across the corner, and while startled, outwardly remained calm. "Doctor, you need to think this through very carefully. What you're about to attempt will set you apart from our most talented minds. They will not follow your lead. There is nothing to be gained by this absurd action."

David waved his hand, "Roberto, what do you depend on me for? Medical opinion? I think not. In the same way that I respect but do not seek medical opinions when making an engineering decision. I tell you again, every question you have placed before me I've answered with precision beyond anything I can recall. You have no reason to be concerned. If the Captain tells me to proceed with the start, I will do so."

Macon continued to wring his hands; his eyes darted around the room seeming to focus on nothing. "You cannot. You don't understand the consequences of such action."

David's eyes took a strained look. "Are you telling me something will happen, something that puts the ship and people in jeopardy? What do you know that you're not telling me?"

Maria said, "Roberto, this is a command order. If you are withholding information that could be injurious to this ship and crew, you must tell me now."

Doctor Macon hesitated then added offhandedly, "The lab completed your tests today."

"What?" Maria shook her head in disbelief. "Roberto, you are making no sense. What in the hell is wrong with you?"

Maria knew the results without Macon's diagnosis. Pregnant. Seventy-four standards years old, maybe forty-two long life years and expecting a child, her first, and David's first. Where did he plan to take this?

They had been busy, each at their assigned chore for too long; months in fact and hadn't talked all that much.

But this irrational action by was of a greater concern. The Doctor's words rambled and the Captain kept quiet and waited.

The words came bumbling out almost in a panicked stutter, "You're pregnant."

David's eyebrows shot up and mouth hung open and then turned to a wide grin. "I'm going to be a father." He turned to Maria, "Why didn't you tell me?" Pure delight and joy covered his face.

No smile crossed the Doctor's face. "She's entering her second trimester."

David, stunned turned to Maria, "How—how were you able to keep it from me? I had no idea."

Without giving Maria a chance to answer, David embraced her. Roberto hurriedly walked to the door, opened it and made a quick tour of the sickbay, returned and quietly closed it. The Captain stood in the same spot, a broad grin in place, holding David's hand.

Maria was satisfied Macon's pronouncement was nothing more than a diversion and as happy as she was, particularly for David, she'd have no part of it.

She extracted her hand from David's. She'd seen enough. Macon's irrational behavior warranted immediate action. Of course, she'd have to present her reasoning before the review committee, Orion's answer to a board of directors. "Doctor Macon, you are relieved of your duties effective immediately."

He shook his head. "You're making a dreadful mistake. You must listen to me."

A semblance of sanity returned to David, replacing the euphoria that had engulfed him. He shook his head as if still unbelieving, took a few deep breaths, paused in between each, working his professional will over the headiness he now felt. He had to push aside the moment and focus on the problem not the giddiness that made him want to shout. His pulse slowed and deliberate thought took over.

"I will not submit to your command." Roberto said. "I will not relinquish my command authority."

Maria stared, hard, unyielding, fixed on Roberto. "Mutiny is a very serious charge, Doctor. Conviction under maritime law and the UCMJ carry the death penalty." She kept a cool demeanor, which fit her nature, a normal response for her. Roberto seemed highly agitated. A lifetime of working virtually alone in a laboratory wasn't an asset right now. Old habits were hard to break. Especially if you're comfortable and don't recognize them as a problem.

Roberto faced Maria, with a plaintive, almost apologetic look. "I can only tell you if you start the Casimir engines, we will be in danger."

Maria's eyebrows shot up. "Are you telling me someone has sabotaged the engines?"

Roberto bolted from the sickbay leaving Maria and David angry and confused. She had to keep her cool.

She commed Erik and filled him in on the events of the last few minutes. "Name someone to take over as chief medical officer." She left sickbay and headed toward maintenance looking for Gramina Macon, David at her side.

It wouldn't be easy telling her friend she'd just relieved her husband of his post. Most of all, how would she explain his erratic behavior when she didn't understand it.

Gramina wasn't in her office and no one had seen her lately.

Maria had scheduled the general crew meeting to precede the Casimir engine start and hoped she would get to Gramina before anyone else did. Among other matters, it would be the one hundred or so temporary crewmembers last chance to return to Earth. Soon, Orion would turn toward deep space and 55 Cancri in the Constellation Cancer.

Maria started the crew meeting a few months earlier in response to concerns expressed about involving more people in decision-making. She expressly wanted to give everyone a chance to be heard. Attendance was open and voluntary.

Gramina wasn't in her office and no one had seen her lately. Maria left maintenance and headed for her day cabin immediately behind the bridge, David walked toward the engine room but not before reminding her of the need for caution.

Mixed feelings raged from having never been happier and apprehension about Macon for spoiling maybe the happiest moment in her life.

Maria, never married had always wanted a child, as had David. His first wife had died a few years ago with that marriage childless. For him to get the news along with Macon's inappropriate action angered her.

Her cabin wasn't overly large but could comfortably accommodate eight people. An elongated carbon fiber table covered with a plastic laminate formed the centerpiece; swivel chairs fixed to the floor surrounded it. A recessed area held a pull down cot next to a toilet and shower giving her a place to rest when long hours on the bridge were required. A small kitchenette occupied a spot to the left. Wherever possible, carbon fiber laminate found it's way into furnishings and served as an emergency storehouse. If the need ever arose, a large part of the ships interior would double to make repairs on critical structural systems. Framed pictures of earth-sights selected by the crew filled most of the remaining open wall spaces. Originally, it had been home to her and David, until more space became available. As did every crewmember, they had to *build* their own two-room efficiency and furnishings in the habitat ring. All materials came from ship's stores but they had to put it together and then decorate to suit their tastes. The result was some imaginative work in a number of cabins.

She keyed the intercom when it signaled.

It was Erik. She asked him to come to her cabin.

In less than a minute, Svern stepped through the hatch and took the offered chair.

Maria, still standing next to the screen controls, keyed up the dossier on Macon. "I am at a complete loss as to why Roberto acted as he did. Have you any thoughts on it?"

"No, not really. But I'll be ready for whatever."

"Oh? Are you always ready? The boy scout?" Sarcasm was evident in her voice.

"No boy scout here. Just a cynical bastard."

He smiled and she relaxed.

Erik, slowly stood, his head turned, mouth pursed to no more than a thin angry line as she explained what had happened. The same look he had when he confronted Harold Bassett on the tarmac at Bahia de Los Angeles. Someone could easily die.

Never questioning his leader, he simply asked, "What do you want me to do?"

Something still bothered her about Roberto's actions in sickbay but she couldn't nail it down. His unpredictable actions of themselves were enough to throw her of stride. Her uneasiness went beyond that. She finally wrote it off as a personal reaction.

"I wish I knew. Roberto acted so strangely. He continually warned me not to start the engines." David had assigned a crew to look for sabotage but even he admitted there are a thousand and one places the most inept person could foul the start up.

She added before her number one could respond, "I'm pregnant. I'm going to be a mother."

Svern, already on his feet, embraced her. "Maria, I couldn't be happier for you and David." He stepped back and eyed his friend and commanding officer. "You may be the oldest woman to have a child, certainly on this ship. Let's see," he paused, "You're eighty-five. Right?"

With a feigned look of distain and pain, the answer came back, "Not for another ten days. I'm only eighty-four."

He laughed, his eyes still fixed on Maria until the Captain held up a hand and asked, "What do we do? I believe Roberto sincerely wanted to tell us something but couldn't."

CHAPTER TEN
The Mutiny

"Any ideas how to handle a mutiny?"

The XO bit off his words. "Yes, Captain, but we can't use them." His hand made the familiar image of a pistol, his thumb the hammer hitting, with emphasis. "Shoot the bastards."

"But we don't know there's a mutiny in the planning. Usually, there's some erratic behavior or behavioral change and we've seen nothing like that." Maria's voice carried a razor edge that wholly illustrated her focus.

Erik knew the Captain's sentiments even though he personally believed Captain Presk would use violence if and when the need arose. Violence begets violence—maybe there was something to that. His sworn first concern had to be the safety of the ship and then the Captain.

"I'll have something ready for you. And we *will* take care of it, decisively." He paused then asked, "Doesn't mutiny get the death sentence?"

"Death's the only named penalty although the court can mete out lesser punishment if it chooses."

Years ago, Eric had said the best defense was an offense and that meant going all out, no quarter. Apparently, in all these years nothing had changed his mind.

Maria recalled a maritime legal paper she'd read on such matters. Mutiny remained the most serious offense that could be committed aboard a ship. Unlike murder, which usually involved one person against another, insurrection festered on resentments, suspicion, real or imagined. People took sides and not always with full facts. Positions hardened and that made it all the more difficult. Seldom did one group hold the high moral ground and the other totally wrong. Time had never proven to be a healer where rebellion against authority was concerned.

"How are you going to handle it?"

A concerned look crossed Maria's face. Orion had adopted maritime law as the governing protocol. A rendition of the United States Constitution and Bill of Rights had become their guideline. However, those documents would be guidelines only as long as they were in space with the real authority encompassed in the United States Uniform Code of Military Justice (UCMJ) and the Captain with absolute authority. The Mexican government had approved the plan and thereby conveyed autonomy to Orion. Even though everyone accepted the fact that Orion had been responsible from day one for their own actions, this just let the world know. Orion had the same status as any free and independent state, thereby keeping in place international law.

"You know the rules." Maria's comment wasn't a judgment, more of a statement of mutual awareness.

How they handled a mutiny, if it in fact was and if the mutineers actually tried to pull it off would set a number of precedents. The irony was under

Orion's own rules, any sedition had to actually take place in order to be an offense. Talking about an uprising or change of command is not, in and of itself, a punishable offense. The old hack, no body, no crime.

The Marines had been the only police force since getting underway and had never had a capital complaint filed against them. Petty stuff, yes, but nothing major. So far, years of living in close proximity had not fostered any major crime; for the most part, people were far too busy building the ship that would ensure their survival. A number of fights, and some stealing of personal belongings had happened. These had usually been handled without legal action.

Those instances where a Captain's mast applied had helped establish the authority of the Captain to conduct such hearings. She doubted it would be any different if this matter went to a court martial. And the possibility existed it would not. But, construction of the habitat ring kept adding requirements and the marines were worked to near exhaustion. If something happened, things could get out of hand.

This ship and crew had a lot of togetherness ahead of them—just short of one hundred forty-five years from earth orbit to 55 Cancri—their destination. If the current birth rate held, and allowing for some deaths, population would approach nine hundred souls by the time they arrived.

Erik left the Captain's day cabin and headed for his office only a few meters down the passageway, his resolve, and anger building with each step. He stopped before entering. The feeling he'd had a number of times during his CIA days had resurfaced, the sensation when you hunt another man. The predator. There were few other feelings like it.

The XO called up a security protocol that until now had lain dormant in the computer memory. A series of keystrokes, and hidden cameras, in addition to those in normal use and known to everyone, came to life. Every inch of the ship would be surveiled and recorded except for bedrooms and toilets.

With that done, he headed out for a tour.

Over the past few months, he'd taken to strolling around Orion, never repeating his pattern or times. His appearance in maintenance drew no overt attention. After all, the Captain had the job to run the ship and the XO's was to make sure that everything stayed in working order—including the personnel.

In a ship this size, almost one million metric tons, with the small crew and most space taken by stores, it wasn't common to find himself alone. Since there would be no forward view available, engineers had put the control center amidships; forward, and to port, the hangar deck and main materiel storage area, starboard hydroponics, aft the engines and maintenance. None of this had moved to the habitat ring except crew quarters and anything else that added comfort or distraction. Crew quarters now sported mini streets and aptly named Comfort City.

He spent some time studying a rig under construction that would capture and dissect any comet they might encounter. Three maintenance men casually acknowledged his presence and continued their work.

Erik leaned over slightly, matching the smaller man's height before conversing with him.

Nothing seemed out of place with this crew.

He patted the worker's shoulder and headed for the exit stopping en route to inspect the assignment board. In truth, he'd laid the first line of action if anyone tried to take control of Orion by force.

The other man he wanted to talk with worked in the engine room.

An hour later, having made that contact and firmly ensconced in his office, he sat with the head of the Marine security.

Erik poured each a cup of coffee. Both ignored the cream and sugar. The Marine had a habit of swirling his drinks while studying any surface pattern that formed—a throwback art practiced in the swamps.

Colonel Jimmy (James) John Jabari, born in the bayous of Mississippi, had seen the worst racism had to offer. Despite that, he'd worked his way through the ranks, the youngest mustang in the Corps history. And in spite of treatment he'd received, the man didn't have a biased bone in his body. It almost seemed incongruous, this public temperament Jabari displayed, and what Erik knew of his battlefield exploits. In addition, over the seven years he'd been aboard, the man had handled hundreds of minor scrapes between people and usually got them resolved on the spot. His smile could disarm, while at the same time, his eyes could rivet a troublemaker to the floor seemingly plumbing his soul.

Without a doubt, he was the kind of man Erik wanted at his side in a fight.

Jabari's quiet drawl seemed lazy but Erik knew it to be anything but. Unmistakably, the hungry look of an unfed lobo came to his eye as he considered the possibility of a mutiny. Like Erik, Jabari was a predator.

"Anyhow, without being obvious, I want you to make sure Doctor Macon's wife, Gramina Fiora, stays out of harm's way. He was so unpredictable, well, we don't think he'd harm her but you never know. We'd better not take that chance."

"We don't know if, when, or where something might happen. I can't very well assign a guard to the Captain without alerting the enemy."

"What's wrong with that? In fact, it just may be enough show to put a stop to any trouble. Head it off at the pass."

"Might work. But Roberto was emphatic about not starting the Casimir engines and that isn't an option. With that to work with, we're only looking at today. It has to happen in that time frame. It could be anytime and any place."

"Today, Captain Presk will conduct the all-crew meeting as usual. Place your people so they're inconspicuous but have the entire bay covered. If you can accomplish that and still have what men you can spare mingling with the crowd, it might be useful."

The lights dimmed through signaling nightfall in Greenwich, England and Orion. The twelve hours of bright lights and twelve dimmed had worked well. Erik didn't like the fact that he had only ten Marines and two undercover men. But that's all there were—they would have to be enough.

* * * *

Deep inside one of the storage areas and minutes before the crew's general

71

meeting with the Captain, Basil Cooper bided his time. He waited as the unsuspecting David Rohm made his way to what had been reported as an engineering emergency.

Cooper had made sure only he and his group knew the elaborate hoax he'd concocted. He checked his watch—almost thirty minutes until the Captain's meeting with the crew.

In his hidey-hole, well back in the shadows, Cooper tensed as the footfalls neared. Once he identified Rohm, it would all be over in a few seconds.

As David passed, Basil Cooper swung the small sack of lead washers, striking David at the base of his skull.

He dropped like a dead man.

Cooper pulled out a syringe and injected his victim with Rohypnol. He didn't like using the date rape stuff but it that's all he could steal from Macon's sickbay. He had no idea what the side affects were of an overdose and he'd given David more than three times too much—almost a third of the bottle. Still, it was his insurance in case the knock to the engineer's head didn't keep the man down.

Cooper quickly sealed David into a black bag identical to every other cargo bag used throughout the ship.

With little effort, he had the bag secured to a two-wheel dolly and headed for the forward storage area—the one part of Orion seldom visited and even more rarely used.

Cooper stopped the dolly in an obscure alcove where his human cargo wasn't visible from the aisle and returned to his quarters confident his actions went unnoticed.

He'd intentionally used passageways seldom traveled and Orion had a lot of them. The ship seemed a labyrinth that a person could get lost in very quickly. Most of the forward area provided a warren of storage spaces, cubicles, and aisles leading in and out and some to dead ends. The maze made the Pentagon look like a cakewalk.

He had no idea how long the drug he'd shot into David would keep the engineer out but he bet it would be more than the four hours he needed to pull off the coup and take control of the ship. The knock he'd administered to the Captain's husband's head might have been a little strong but so be it.

He recognized a number of the crew would have to cross over and join him to make his takeover work.

Knowing how people could be led, particularly rebellious people, he fully expected half a dozen to join him. Maybe even a dozen. More than enough. He also knew the majority would do nothing. That had been the history of mankind. Most were followers. If all went well, he'd revive Rohm. If the takeover didn't go as planned, his captive would become his insurance.

Checking his appearance in the wall mirror, he left for the meeting.

* * * *

Maria, dressed in her casual uniform, stood to one side of the slightly raised dais. An area big enough to accommodate about two hundred people had been outfitted as a theater, stage and all. A kaleidoscope of color covered the walls with a light blue ceiling, all part of the effort to break the routine black carbon fiber structure.

Dozens of muted conversations were going on laced with occasional laughter. On stage, Orion's information director finished the latest news updates from Earth and then turned the mike over to the Captain.

Dressed in casual khakis and hatless, Maria prepared to address the crew. Behind her, a number of charts stood on easels providing illustrations and talking points she planned to cover.

Svern had the bridge watch.

Jimmy John Jabari had taken up a position off to the right and about halfway toward the back of the room. From there, he had complete visual command of everyone and everything in the bay.

Maria eyes swept over the gathering—she acknowledged some, smiled at others, and started to speak.

Basil Cooper, in hurried strides, reached the platform and in something approaching, a yell said, "Stop. It's time for us." His arms waved to encompass everyone, "for all of us have a legitimate say in who runs this ship and how it's run. Captain Presk has used this as her private fiefdom and ruled without our consent. It's time for others to step forward, to take control."

Maria leaned toward the microphone, switched it on, and said in a mild voice, "Perhaps the crew could hear you better if you used this."

The mutiny had started and Basil Cooper headed it.

Her apparent lack of concern didn't seem to cause any conflict in Cooper even though she knew his confidence to be only skin deep. She stepped back giving the mutineer free access to the slightly raised platform.

The maintenance officer, in blue slacks, and tan blazer, didn't hesitate. In almost a run, he grabbed the mike. His eyes, wide and voice excited, he yelled, "I am now in command." As he spoke, two collaborators, Piet de Groot and Dan Dakarai emerged on the balcony circling the hangar bay, each carrying automatic stun rifles.

Cooper pulled a small handheld from his coat pocket and spoke into it. In the quiet that had settled over the gathering, the open mike picked up the answer for all to hear, "Bridge secured."

Cooper continued, "It's over. Captain Presk, you are no longer in command of Orion."

A collective gasp escaped the assembled but no one moved.

Cooper ordered, "Marines, lay down your weapons." With his right hand, he pulled a pistol hidden in his belt—it wasn't a stun gun but a Glock 19, which he pointed at Maria. "Someone, one of you," with his left hand pointed to the assembly, "take the Marines' guns."

No one moved. Cooper barked his command again.

Nothing.

He motioned toward the gunmen above, and one fired his stun rifle at a far bulkhead, intentionally close to the assembled.

The electrical discharge danced over the wall startling many who had never seen one of these weapons in action.

Still, no one moved to help the mutineer.

For an instant, he seemed dismayed, his forehead peppered with perspiration.

In that moment of confusion, Maria stepped toward the microphone.

Cooper swung the back of his hand and struck the side of the Captain Bresk's head, knocking her to the deck.

Colonel Jabari had moved to less than ten feet of the mutineer. The instant Cooper struck, Jabari yelled a command. In the time it took for the words to reach the balcony, his Marines had subdued the two rebel guards.

Cooper dove toward the prostrate Maria. He shoved the pistol against the Captain's head. "Stop or she's dead," he ordered.

Almost as one, the assembled people surged toward the Captain and Maintenance Officer, but Jabari's command voice stopped them cold.

He held up his hand, yet those hungry eyes locked on the mutineer.

For the first time since he'd started planning this takeover, Basil Cooper clearly showed the fear that now engulfed him. Cooper again pulled out his two-way and spoke into it.

Alyana Zlata still controlled the bridge.

Using the Captain as a shield, Cooper stood, pulled the still dazed Maria to her feet. "Make a hole," the rebel ordered and pointed toward the exit.

Jabari motioned for the people to move, clearing a path to the access leading to the passageway.

As they neared the door, Maria dropped to the floor and in that instant, Jabari, no more than a blur, crossed the remaining few feet, grabbed Cooper's weapon and slammed his right fist against the man's head.

The blow devastated Cooper, the mutineer dropping to the floor like a drunk who'd lost all control.

The Marine knelt beside the skipper, "You okay, Captain?"

She answered with a large grin.

Maria extended her hand and said, "Thank you, Marine. I counted on just that reaction."

Jimmy John pried the Captain to her feet and saluted.

"You ready to rescue our XO?" Maria asked.

Jabari answered, "Sir, with no disrespect for my superior officer," (suggesting that Svern would need help in a one on one to retake the bridge) "I would be delighted to assist you."

Jabari ordered his men to place Basil Cooper and the other two in chains and confine them to the brig.

"After you sir." Looking at the Captain, he gestured toward the bridge.

A few feet from the entry hatch, Jabari pulled the sound power headset and mike from its bulkhead niche. He spoke briefly and then turned toward the Captain. "No contest, Mr. Svern is in control of the bridge."

Maria smiled, nodded, took the headset, and called around for Gramina and

First Contact

David.

CHAPTER ELEVEN
David Rohm

Maria opened the hatch and stepped onto the bridge. The fourth mutineer, Alyona Zlata, was alert but her defiance evaporated as a crewman snapped handcuffs to the Captain's chair base.

Erik, now standing, saluted and said, "Well done." His remark directed more at the Marine. "Watched it all on the monitor."

"Have you seen David?" Maria's eyes searched the array of monitors all displaying some portion of Orion.

"No, sir," answered Erik. He pressed an icon on the master control board and the monitored pictures changed every two seconds switching in a preplanned sweep of the over four hundred cameras strategically located around the ship.

With David's image, the computer driven search went full bore. Svern leaned over the keyboard, entered a few strokes and the screens showed images from the mess hall, corridors any place where people were likely to be.

Soon, only two monitors displayed a picture following the program code only if they detected a human presence.

Maria punched the consol and the lab answered.

"Is David in the laboratory?"

Shortly the answer came, "No, sir. Haven't seen him for a couple of hours."

Maria thanked the voice and ended the contact. As her mind searched for where he might be, a solemn aggravated call came from the brig.

"Captain, you'd better get down here."

Maria, despite being pregnant, didn't ask why but broke into a run to do just that. A few minutes later, she entered the small room revamped as a cell, the Colonel less than a step behind.

Dressed in fatigues sporting an outfit of crisp creases, the guard stood at attention and saluted. "As you were Marine," Jimmy John ordered.

The two stood waiting, eyes fixed on the guard.

In a comment crisp with intense dislike the guard said, "Captain, the prisoner has something to say to you."

Maria had no way of knowing what Cooper could offer the angry look on the guards face gave her no illusion this was going to be anything pleasant. She nodded and motioned for the turnkey to lead the way.

Maria approached the cell.

Sitting on the bunk, hands resting on the mattress, Basil Cooper looked up, his lip curled in hatred, but he didn't stand. Maria didn't address him but instead waited.

Without any hesitation, his voice with a honed edge, Cooper defiantly stared at Captain Presk. "If you ever want to see your husband alive again, you'll drop all charges, release the four us and let us return to Earth."

Maria, stunned, fought the rage about to erupt. David had chided her about her sometimes-stoic demeanor but now it served her well, masking her fury.

Before she could answer, Colonel Jabari punched the transmit button on his shoulder mike and ordered the ship searched in an immediate and detailed sweep.

A smirk crossed Cooper's bony face as he stood and then replaced by a look of contempt. Casually, he said, "He'll be dead before you get a good start. Turn us loose and I'll tell you where he is."

Jabari who had turned to leave the brig and join the hunt stopped in his tracks. He recognized the impossibility of searching the almost four million square feet that made up Orion not to mention the vertical as well. That amounted to forty million cubic feet.

He still carried Cooper's pistol and pulled it from his belt, handed it to the guard. With his eyes locked on the prisoner he said, "I don't trust myself with this," then left the brig.

Erik, still on the bridge, had patched in Jabari's call. He quickly started a search of the camera data storage banks. There were over four hundred separate storage sites but an algorithm Ann Bartlett had written would make the scan at least one hundred times faster than any prior computer system could manage. Even at that, precious time would be lost.

Ten minutes into the search one image froze across the screen. A man with a two-wheeled dolly filled the monitor, Cooper.

Erik hit the normal speed button. Whatever or whomever he had on the cart the man wasted no time. He checked the location—the forward warehouse area, more specifically, just behind the hangar bay where construction materials were stored. Not only did the area seldom get visited, whenever workers went in or out with a load, it usually required a cart. Dollies were a common sight. In fact, the rarer scene had to be someone with out some heavy load carrier. The kidnapper had picked his spot well.

Erik punched a few icons and increased the scan speed; Cooper stopped at a cubicle and entered; the XO returned the feed to normal.

He keyed in the location, and switched on the heat and night vision cameras. The maintenance officer turned toward the camera and for the first time, Erik could clearly see the cargo. Involuntarily, his breath sucked. Tied to the dolly a baglike container normally used for long carbon fiber fragments. Cooper could have wheeled his cargo in front of the bridge crew and not raised any suspicions.

Deliberate but unhurried, he stood the dolly upright, untied the container, and laid it none to gently on the deck. A plastic cord that held one end closed yielded to his efforts and the bag opened. In one quick motion, he yanked the lanyard. David's head lolled to one side, his eyes closed. A shiver raced through Svern's body. Angrily, he pushed aside his fears and could only hope his friend's unconsciousness was temporary.

Erik keyed the mike and delivered the coordinates to Captain Jabari without waiting for an acknowledgement. He turned to the Officer-Of-The-Deck, "You have the helm," and ran from the bridge.

As he raced down the passageway, on his two-way, he called sickbay, ordered a team to the site and told Dr. Macon to have every facility they had available ready to treat David.

"I've been relieved," Macon responded.

"Fuck that. Get your ass to sickbay," Svern ordered. "Now!"

* * * *

Maria sat in the sickbay. The wait seemed interminable. It had been over two hours since Dr. Macon and his medical staff started working on David. As soon as each could relinquish their duties, Erik, Ann Bartlett, Martin Grabel, Bhani Patel, and Gramina Fiora joined the wait.

Slowly, the door opened and Macon stepped out of the room, stripped off the surgical gloves, and discarded them. Obviously anxious, he rubbed his forehead. His eyes avoided the group and he turned directly toward Maria.

The Doctor seemed nervous and to be searching for the right words. "Maria." No one moved and as if on signal studious avoided looking at their Captain. "It's too soon to tell for sure but so far, he's non-responsive."

The Captain visibly paled, pain etched her face, and then the noted stoic façade took over.

What seemed an interminable time, Macon added, "The drug and blow to the head have had a severe effect on him. I have no idea how long it may be before a more definitive diagnosis is possible." He paused.

Still no one made a noise.

"I won't be able to give any better evaluation until he regains consciousness but the prognosis is not good. I'll start running genetic tests, if there are any more problems maybe we can spot them and who knows, even head them off."

Maria swallowed hard but forced her voice steady. "Can I see him?"

"Of course."

She stood at the bedside, her eyes longingly caressing David.

That night, in her cabin, Maria tried to cry but tears wouldn't come.

Numb beyond grief, watching the only man she had ever loved taken from her just months before she would bear his son. Something they had both talked about for endless hours.

* * * *

He moaned. Maria reached out from her chair next to David's bed and touched his hand, which felt cold. She gently rubbed his palm remembering how he liked that—but it brought no response.

Dr. Macon stepped into the cubicle, brushing the curtain aside. "You been here all night? Decent rest will help all of us. We—the entire ship needs you at your best." He paused, "And so does the baby."

Maria merely nodded as the Doctor picked up the chart. Overnight, the nurses had noted David's vital signs but could do little else. There had been no change.

Macon checked the instruments displaying David's running condition, and then retraced them back through the last few hours looking for any encouragement.

As much for Maria's benefit as for the microcorder he wore, he said, "No substantive change. Breathing's normal. That's encouraging."

Maria stood. Her shoulders slumped as she took a few steps toward the exit. She tried to put a little more life than she felt into her voice. "Let me know if there's any change. I'm going to freshen up. I'll be in my bridge cabin if anyone wants me."

Having disposed of the amenities, she keyed the intercom, "Erik, can you come to my cabin?"

Maria poured two cups of coffee. She read the notice from radar—navigation had detected a comet that would be within range of Orion in about a month. Knowing it would have to wait, she laid it down and picked up the day's printout from earth's transmission lying on the desk. This could have been a thousand pages, but only useful information now made the cut and therefore it boiled down to only six. She quickly scanned the words and put it aside at Erik's knock.

On entering, he gathered his cup, took a seat across the table, and asked, "You get any sleep?"

"Enough," she lied. In truth, she'd not slept at all.

The XO gouged at his ear, a habit he'd had for years. "If you say so."

Maria could go a couple of days without sleep—she'd done it many times when research was at a critical stage and an interruption could destroy or at the least, alter a result. But this was different. What had become her reason to live was at stake.

Erik knew he had to say something. "Macon is the best. If there's anyway or anything available to help David, he'll find it."

"Yes, I know that." She paused, let out a deep sigh approaching a sob, "I didn't realize until now just how much I depended on David."

The tone and quiet of her response was a distraction in itself. After a long wait to reclaim some composure she said, "You know, David is the only person who can start the Casimir engines. He's it. Without him, we don't go anywhere." She had encouraged everyone to cross-train and train backups and for the most part that had happened. But in this case, being a backup meant understanding the Casimir effect and the quantum mechanics involved as well as the physical engine mechanics. No one on the ship came close to David. He was simply just that much smarter than the understudies were.

"When's our next transmission to earth?" She knew as well as anyone that Thursdays at noon the transmission went out. "We need to contact Quantum Fields and have them start training someone. Question is, who?"

"From where I sit, only two people, other than David, have the brains to learn, let alone understand those engines."

"And."

"You and Martin."

"Martin, Yes. But I don't know about me. I'm just a chemist."

"Yeah. Me too. But there's as much difference between your chemistry and mine to create a completely new field of science. But then, of course, that's what you did."

"And that's what got us where we are; over six billion miles from earth and no one to crank the engine." The only experience anyone had, including David, was with the auxiliary Casimirs. Other than providing the ships internal power, they were necessary to start the large Casimir engines, something that had never been done on earth or in space. These were the first and only working size designs of this technology. Maria mulled this over. She would have to delay the Casimir startup.

"Okay." She punched the intercom, "Martin." She waited knowing the mathematician would be in no hurry to respond.

"Yes." The high-pitched voice answered. "What do you want? I'm very busy."

Maria made sure her voice was calm before answering. "Something important has come up. Can you come to my cabin for a short meeting?"

That short session turned into over an hour. To Maria and Erik's surprise and elation, Martin was excited to learn everything he could about the Casimir process. Several times, he had even considered asking David if he could coattail his work just for the chance to learn but hadn't ever gotten up the nerve. He admitted David's knowledge intimidated him, something not easily done or for the mathematician to admit.

With Martin's departure, Maria and Erik settled down to the question of Basil Cooper's indictment and trial.

"Well, one thing's for certain. I'll have to recuse myself and Mathew Hammond will be trial judge. He's got experience in civil and criminal cases but not under the UCMJ."

"What about defense lawyers? We're kinda thin there."

"Yeah. Let me talk to Mathew. He may have some thoughts that can help."

"Basil Cooper's reason for attempting the takeover of Orion showed a lack of clear thinking. Like most demagogues, reason did not run deep. As for his commitment to Grady Moffitt, as far as I can tell it was tenuous. Each had his own reasons for doing what they did. Cooper, saw money when he took Orion back to Earth. Strictly greed.

Grady Moffitt, something clicked in this guy's head. The general consensus is that he went off his nut. Became irrational when confronted with the idea there were beings who could and would come back to haunt Earth."

With that the meeting broke. Maria asked Hammond to meet her in sickbay. Roberto stood by as the two discussed the legal aspects of what might be possible and how to proceed. The judge left, telling Maria he'd study the UCMJ and put together a brief defining how the court would conduct itself.

Maria turned toward David's room and immediately knew something was wrong. "What is it? David?"

"He's awake."

Maria started past the Doctor but the almost distraught Roberto grabbed her arm. "Let's talk first."

The Captain strained against the pull but Macon's grip remained firm. "He's not well. The drug or the concussion, most likely both, seem to have affected his mind. It's still too early to tell how severe or permanent it is—but frankly, I'm not hopeful."

Maria went lax and no longer tugged against his pull. "Go on."

Macon seemed to regain his self-control. "There's damage to the frontal lobe, the Limbic system. There's a great deal we don't know about how all this functions but simply put, the cognitive recall of faces, names and personal associations are stored and processed there." He paused seeming to search for the right words. "It's the part of the brain that makes us humans more than robot. His motor functions appear to work satisfactorily. Another way to describe his condition is it's beyond the most severe case of autism I've ever seen."

Maria snapped. "What are you saying—that he's anti-social?" She immediately regretted the outburst.

Macon flinched. "I'm afraid it's much worse than that. Who he is, who I am, why he's in a bed, any of that is of no concern to him. He simply doesn't respond to that kind of stimuli."

Roberto's grasp relaxed and Maria walked into her husband's room. The sheet covering him clearly outlined the body David had so rigorously kept in shape. A look into his hollow unknowing eyes sent a chill through her. She approached the bed and smiled but got only an uncaring, grim-faced stare.

Her heart sank.

She touched his arm. The skin felt warm, soft. She held out both hands to take his but David offered no reaction. It was if he looked through her and never responded. The lines of strain that crossed her face brought no reaction.

Maria retreated and closed the door. She tried to hide the despair that wanted to overwhelm her.

Doctor Macon laid out a routine of mental exercises that he thought might help David although there were no assurances.

Maria left, went to her day cabin and again did not sleep. She had no desire to return to the place she and David had shared—their home in the habitat ring.

The next few weeks brought no change in his mental condition. Surprisingly, he soon returned to work. In fact, that was all he seemed capable of or wanted to do. Technically, he was as good as ever. Maybe better because nothing distracted him.

David Rohm was at peace in his technical world. Nothing else existed and he seemed blessed with tranquility. Concerns over starting the Casimir engines evaporated as he poured his many talents into the effort. As Martin excelled in the non-social atmosphere, the two were able to work effectively, the mathematician making sure he stayed out of David's way and followed his lead.

Bhani was elated that Martin's attitude had improved now that he had something totally new and physical to do. The idea of someone other than David learning the science and engineering involved in the quantum engines had found a home to everyone's satisfaction.

Maria didn't adjust as quickly. She suspected everyone on the ship sympathized with and for her, but that wasn't the issue. It wasn't their sympathy or understanding she wanted, for her or David, just the acceptance of things as they were. She wasn't being calloused or uncaring, she just had to deal with losing him in her own way and of course, in the hostile environment of space, safeguard the lives that were Orion.

Maria stayed busy during the days and nights leading up to the trial. She watched the proceedings without incident from the bridge or her day cabin.

Cooper's defense was the same as his reasons for attempting the mutiny. His three accomplices could only offer excuses of personal vendetta's that they would carry out against picayune wrongs committed on them by other members of the crew had the coup been successful.

"That verdict was a foregone conclusion. Two trials, four convictions and there'll be four executions unless you commute," Erik said walking into Maria's bridge cabin. He took a seat and kept an eye peeled toward the seated Captain. "Any thought on what you're going to do?"

"I haven't decided," she answered, her back to the XO.

"Well, if you commute, we have to keep them locked up for an awfully long time. I suppose we could build a prison workshop and get some good out of them. But, I must tell you, the sentiment among the population for commutation is non-existent. Most people don't trust them and don't want them around. In fact, the general sentiment is brutal. Just space them. Send them out an airlock. Don't even give them something to knock them our before the heave ho."

"Erik, don't be cavalier." Maria had always been against the death penalty but now she wasn't so sure. She surprised herself because it wasn't what happened to David but because of the danger, Cooper represented to the very survival of Orion.

"I'm not. Maria, what I'm telling you is exactly what the people are telling me. I have found no one who wants to keep them on board, never mind alive."

"What about the men's wives. All were married."

Erik's face showed his own disgust, lips pursed he said, "Sorry, I didn't ask them."

"I did."

Erik, his own self-depredation quickly put aside, mouth open, with a blank stare on his face seemed to want to say something but somehow couldn't.

"Care to hear what their thoughts were?"

That brought no more than a nod.

"The wives, all of them, want divorces and they want them before final sentencing. They want no stigma attached to them or their families once this is over. Can't say as I blame them."

"I'm not surprised either. Beside, that does make matters simpler to deal with."

Ship's Log
Orion date: 09/19/05 Time: 10.11
Bartlett, Ann, Con & OD

Closure of habitat ring achieved. Ion engines at full power. Engineering reports nominal. Leaving earth orbit will be a long slow process. Small Casimir engines nearing final construction and testing. Preparation of nuclear device to start the mini Casimir engine progressing on schedule. Main Casimir engines years from completion. By the time ready, Orion should be far enough out of system, away from Sol's gravity well, to permit Casimir engine start.

Presk, Maria, Captain

CHAPTER TWELVE
Lives changed
Self-Rule

The Captain started toward the hatch but when Erik didn't move, she asked, "Something else on your mind?"

A momentary grin crossed Erik's face. "Damn, you read me like a book. I couldn't get away with lying to you if I tried. Have you talked with Judge Hammond?"

Maria had made it a point to avoid all contact with any of the trial members. Outside of checking on David and standing her bridge watch, she'd kept to her cabin including taking meals there. She did find time to go to the gym and exercise. With the baby due in three months, she'd decided to do everything she could to stay fit. It was only after the trial had concluded and the verdict known that she contacted the ex-wives of the convicted men.

"No, in fact, I shouldn't talk to him until I've made my decision on whether to commute the sentences." The appearance and intent as well as obeying the letter of the law was important and something she'd held to steadfastly throughout the trial.

"The judge and I had some significant discussions. I wish circumstances had been different so you could have been there."

Maria had a distant look about her as if distracted. "What was so notable about this talk? You've had dozens, probably more, without me and we've managed quite well."

Erik pawed at an imaginary spot on the deck and seemed ill at ease. It was the first time Maria had seen him act this way.

She waited.

The Exec ran his tongue over his front teeth and pursed his lips. "Maria, this trial was about an attempted mutiny. Of course, we took pretrial depositions and tried to make sure that the crew felt they were involved the process."

He stopped, took a deep breath, slowly let it out, then leaned forward in his chair, elbows on his knees, hands open, and extended. "While the attempted mutiny generated no following or sympathy, we did uncover a very large consensus that people who would like to form some kind of government and have a voice in it." The rest of the pent up air rushed out as if he'd exploded.

Maria didn't reply. She kept her eyes pinned on Erik looking for a reaction. The fact of the matter was the Captain had anticipated this very thing. It seemed to her that the importance wasn't in whether they wanted to participate but how they, as a group, presented their feelings. Everyone on Orion knew how they got there and the oath each had sworn. But it wouldn't be all that long until second-generation voices would join the chorus, voices not locked in to the pledges of their fathers. However, if raised in a political and social environment agreed to by their forbearers, prospects for maintaining order were much better.

"Your thoughts?"

The XO rubbed his chin and took his time answering. "I guess it was inevitable this would happen. Most of these people came from democratic societies," he hesitated, "In the same respect most were also raised where a military co-existed with civilian governments. It's just that the civilians had the final authority but I don't see how you can allow that here." He seemed to hesitate not sure what the Captain's reaction would be.

In all the years he'd known, worked with and for the woman, he was at a loss to predict her reaction. Everything they were or were not was because of Maria Presk. Without her foresight and action, every one of them could be in some hospital used as a guinea pig at best. For many of them, they'd simply be locked away somewhere so that a select few would get the blood transfusion that would greatly extend life.

Maria walked to a wall safe, opened it, and pulled out a manila envelope. "Here, read this."

Erik opened the folder, drew out the first page, and scanned it. "Well I'll be damned. I should have known you'd already have thought this through." The preamble lay open as if daring someone to comment. The XO looked up but kept quiet.

"Think the people will buy it? My not giving up final authority on matters determining the well-being and fate of Orion might not satisfy the itch for self rule."

The XO answered with his own question. "Mind if I show this to Judge Hammond?"

The Captain nodded. "Go ahead, but it goes no further until I've made my decision on Cooper and his group. Then you, Hammond, and I will talk this matter through."

"Understood." Erik arose, put the envelope into his coat pocket, saluted, and left the cabin certain the Captain had just told him the fate of the mutineers.

* * * *

Doctor Macon put away his stethoscope, closed the bag, and signed the papers stating method and time of death. He left the room that had been set up as the temporary execution chamber without saying a word.

Captain Presk and Colonel Jabari waited in the passageway. Both gazes were on Roberto as he approached.

The Doctor avoided eye contact.

Maria struggled with her next comments. "Roberto, I think you still owe all of us an explanation for your actions. Your concerns about any of us not realizing the consequences of our actions were empty at best. Had you been more forthright with us, perhaps all of this could have been avoided."

Macon nodded and walked away. What Maria said seemed to have little positive impact on the Doctor. Something was eating at him and Maria had a pretty good idea what it was. She suspected Gramina had never overheard the mutineers, that Roberto's first report had been a lie.

Jabari understood why Maria's comments were so labored. He signed the order and handed the skipper the clipboard. The Marine saluted and said, "Cremation and spacing of the ashes will be done within the hour."

This was a first in many respects. The first time Orion had had to deal with a capital offense and the first time Maria had ever been involved in the death of other human beings. Under different circumstances, she would have commuted the death sentences, but that hadn't been possible.

It was her turn to say nothing. She nodded, returned to her cabin, changed out of her full dress blue uniform into khaki's, and took the few steps to the bridge.

Erik had command. Assuming Maria would take control, he stood but Captain Presk turned to the OD and said, "Lieutenant, You have the bridge. XO, assemble the staff in my cabin."

"Aye sir," both responded.

After the formal transfer of control, Erik followed the Captain off the bridge. "Well, I misjudged you."

"How's that?"

"I thought you'd commute on the three and only allow the sentence on Cooper to proceed."

Maria didn't answer.

Erik a puzzled look settled on his face as he stepped into the cabin. Seated, the Captain still had not addressed the Exec's statement and left no indication that she intended to do so.

The XO took his usual position immediately to Maria's right, eyes fixed on the Captain. Bhani, Martin, and Roberto had entered by the time he sat, leaving only Ann and Gramina. Shortly afterwards, the two arrived. To everyone's surprise, Colonel Jabari entered with a sidearm strapped to his waist.

Except for the Marine, Maria motioned each of them into chairs No one spoke. The looks on their faces clearly showed the apprehension that seemed to suffocate everyone.

Maria's eyes finally eyes locked on Erik. "Mister Svern, would you repeat your last comment?"

A puzzled look crossed the Exec's face—it had been at least ten minutes since he'd last addressed the Captain and it took a few seconds for him to fathom what she wanted.

He slightly shook his head as if to clear unwanted cobwebs and then said, "I think it was," he hesitated, "Um, I thought you'd commute the three and only execute Cooper."

As abruptly as anyone had ever heard her, the Captain curtly said, "Close enough."

Maria pointed toward Grabel. "Martin, tell them what you know."

A nervous sound came from the mathematician clearing his throat but in his squeaky voice managed, "During the interrogation of the three mutineers, one, Piet de Groot, told us they'd been paid by Grady Moffitt."

"Moffitt," exclaimed Erik interrupting.

Maria's eyes swept the group as she held up her hand to stop Svern and in the same move motioned Martin to continue.

"They'd been paid by Moffitt to sabotage Orion and make sure the ship never left orbit." Martin backed away, a clear indication he'd had enough.

Maria picked it up. "That's what the fertilizer missing from the farm was for —an explosive. The purpose was to force a return to earth. Moffitt's reasons you'll learn later."

Martin nodded toward Maria, whose look had never changed.

In a strong steady voice, the Captain said, "Moffitt retired from NSA when he disagreed with the President's decision to allow us to leave Earth. He wanted us rounded up and made wards of the state. I must admit something about this mutiny effort seemed not to fit. I'm sorry to tell you I was suspicious and de Groot's admission only confirmed my fears. I ordered Martin to do a computer search. He found that Moffitt communicated with Orion a number of times and not with the same person. It seems he had contact with five different people."

Maria stood. She touched one hand to the tabletop, resting the other on her very large stomach. Her face became a mask of despair, her eyes hollow. She focused on each person but the look never changed.

Everyone understood unless there had been a total breach of security, no one outside this room had access to the main computer.

A stunned silence permeated the crowded cabin. It was as if someone had sucked out all the air. No one moved and only gasps could be heard. The close-knit group, which had been through so much together, was stunned to silence. The trust that had tied them together in that instant shattered.

Maria waited, hoping Roberto would, on his own, step forward. In actuality, she was hoping someone other than the Doctor would be the fifth mutineer although she doubted it. The wait was interminable.

As if one, they all turned at the sob.

Gramina cried out in anguish as Roberto dropped to the floor, his hands rose as if asking forgiveness. "They threatened to kill my family if I didn't go along. They said my presence would sway many other people to join."

His wife fell to her knees and embraced the sobbing Doctor.

Maria remained stoical, and then knelt next to both. A gentle smile touched her lips. It was obvious she was straining to keep her own emotions under control.

"What has happened to us no one can change. It may well have turned out no different even if you had made us aware of the mutiny earlier. I hold no malice."

The Captain believed what she said and realized the ship and crew needed the Doctor now more than ever. Certainly David did.

Maria stood and said, "Grady Moffitt's distinguished career ended in disgrace with his arrest for conspiracy, treason and other high crimes. He will stand trial for his acts."

She paused for a moment searching her thoughts. "In light of what we now know of the circumstances surrounding this mutiny, I doubt that Roberto could be judged a willing participant. However, if we are to be ruled by law and not by men, that is for a court to decide. Colonel Jabari, please place Doctor Macon under arrest and take him before Judge Mathews. He's to be charged with aiding and abetting the mutiny."

A hushed cry rose from the assembly. Maria had no idea how the people of Orion would react.

* * * *

A cheer went up from the bridge crew. Judge Hammond had declined to accept the indictment. In his writ he said, "In light of the information made available to me, Roberto Macon acted as I think most of us would have. I see no reason to pursue this matter." And then he attached a most injudicious comment, "Besides, since I would offer to serve as his legal council, who would preside as judge? On top of that, I doubt you could find six people willing to sit as a jury."

Maria folded the decision, placed it in her pocket, smiled, and took the Captains' chair and almost as if the mutiny had never occurred said, "Mr. Svern, how goes the business with the comet?"

The comet discovered a few months earlier was now in range for capture. About as long as a football field and almost the same in girth it would add to the supply of water and other minerals aboard Orion.

The mutiny and Roberto's involvement a matter that now belonged in the past. The ache she felt for David went far beyond the mini-revolt.

Without any doubt, the worst result from the short insurrection was David Rohm's injury. Cooper had intended for Rohm to be his out in case things went wrong. And they had, but in a way, Cooper had never considered. David Rohm was a savant.

He maintained his extraordinary engineering talents but the man's personal skills were definitely gone. It was tough for the crewmembers who had worked closely with him to watch him stand alone, foul himself and see nurses rush to minimize the problems. Those problems were many and often.

David required around the clock attention. He never resisted their effort, indeed never acknowledged them. He always stood patiently as the nurses attended to whatever they deemed necessary. He acknowledged no one. The ability to recognize technical problems and solve them without input from others seemed the man's only capacity. He became Orion's roving engineer. Martin Grabel effectively became the resident engineer. Hardly up to David's engineering skill level, Martin often took suggestions or criticism personally. Still, he proved invaluable.

Even though no words or other forms of communication occurred between the two, they would work together on problems and projects. Whatever happened, whatever the cause, it was to the benefit of Orion.

<u>**Medical Log**</u>
Orion date: 05/11/05 Time: 11.11

Maria Presk Rohm gave normal birth to a 7 pound 6 ounce boy. Mother and baby doing fine. Christened: Michael David Presk-Rohm

Macon, Roberto, ships physician

<u>**Ship's Log**</u>
Orion date: 08/08/06   13.00 Zulu

Gave command to start one small Casimir engine. If all goes well, second auxiliary comes online within the next day or two. Casimirs will provide more than enough energy for all the ships functions. Broadcast start order to the entire ship something they had all been waiting to hear.

The initial process required a small thermonuclear explosion. Of course, the shipping of the fissionable material into space had caused havoc on Earth. But that was long forgotten, at least on Orion. Now, they had only to detonate the device without destroying themselves and in the process start a Casimir engine.

Presk, Maria, Captain

<u>**Ship's Log**</u>
Orion date: 11/7/10 16.00 Zulu
Erik Svern XO, OD

Monopole captured today; expectations run high that artificial gravity will become a reality in near future.

Presk, Maria, Captain

<u>**Ship's Log**</u>
Orion date: 3/7/15 11.00 Zulu
Lt. Mary Sizemore, OD

The problem of man-made gravity solved. Engineering successfully established artificial gravity in the small portion of Orion. Habitat ring still has centrifugal gravity. Ordered engineering to design a reconfigured Orion. Habitat ring to be disassembled and incorporated into the main fuselage center structure making a more traditional design. Materials removed will be added to main hull dramatically reducing overall profile and hazard exposure. Having the habitat area separate from the ships flight and engineering sections had its advantage but overall, logistics should improve with the new design.

With some of humanity's finest minds onboard, major science is being done. The development of artificial gravity became a most important milestone adding a normalcy to life that buoyed spirits. Communications transmitted this discovery along with the required physical and engineering specifications back to Earth.

Conducted graduation exercises for seventeen high school students. All will go for advanced studies, some for trades, others on to graduate studies.

David has shown no improvement. Still does not recognize other people including his son, works entirely alone. When outside mechanical assistance is needed or help in moving a large or heavy object, David accepts it as part of an ongoing process. When he needs assistance, he simply stops until someone figures out the needed process and presto, everything is as it should be. He never acknowledges help and fails to recognize even the presence of others let alone communicate with them. But he remains the best engineer on Orion. Martin Grabel is fascinated and seems to take the attitude that David is a kindred spirit. Obviously, this is a one-way expression on Martin's part.

Grabel developed probably the most comprehensive mathematical definition of the Casimirs. David is an avid watcher when Martin is teaching a math class. If he recognizes problem or solution, David goes to the chalkboard and adds insight that might otherwise be lost.

By the time the mini Casimirs started, Orion was over one light year from Sol, more than enough to minimize any in-system solar gravitation problems when starting the main engines. Martin took over the responsibility for the Casimir power plants.

Maria noted Orion was now over six billion miles from Earth. Engineering, under Martin's direction had informed her it was safe to start the four main engines. The only experience anyone, including David, had was with the auxiliary Casimirs. Other than providing the ships internal power, they were necessary to start the large Casimir engines, something that had never been done before on Earth or in space. These were the first and only working size designs of this technology.

Martin has shown a keen interest and learned everything he could about the Casimir process. When he could, he had coat tailed David just for the chance to learn. He admitted David's knowledge intimidated him, something not easily done or for the mathematician to admit.

Presk, Maria, Captain

Orion's design allowed for no forward viewing areas so everywhere needed video screens festooning the bridge and other areas throughout the ship. Over one hundred cameras provided external views and internally two hundred cameras strategically located through out the ship tied in to the bridge.

Night was distinguished from day by diminished light throughout the ship remained the bellwether for controlling sidereal clock. The navigation consol stayed bathed in red light. The crew had long since acclimated to Orion's day-night standard.

Turning her chair toward Svern as the XO cleared the bridge hatch the Captain asked, "What do you think? Is capturing the comet worth the risk?"

"Frankly, if we take our time, I don't see much of a problem." In a whisper, he added, "And I'm a believer that you never pass up a chance to take a piss or a drink." In a normal voice he added, "We can use the methane and ammonia that the lab analysis detected."

"Agreed," Maria, looked chagrinned in response to Erik's off color remark. She keyed the consol, "Engineering, are you monitoring the comet?" _

"Yes, looks good from here. We can use it."

Svern issued orders for the runabout to close on the icy hulk and get final test samples. If these carried no bad bugs, the maintenance crew would cut the icy hulk into chunks and secured them to external pylons. This drifter could be their water supply for some time, adding precious stores.

CHAPTER THIRTEEN
Main Engine Start

Engineering idled back the two small Casimirs for preparation to start the main engines. They had performed well for over a year but not flawlessly. Lessons learned were applied to the four large engines, perhaps saving Orion from a fatal catastrophe. With new technology, no one was complacent about possible problems. The small engines had provided the needed opportunity to gain some operating experience with the new technology. It wasn't only the engines that were of concern but the maintenance crew that had a trial ahead. Many, in fact most, of the engineering gang had brought cots into the area not daring or wanting to be away for any lengthy period during the complicated startup.

Martin Grabel stood watch at the engineering computer consol confident the software he'd written would perform flawlessly. No one saw fit to argue with him. Computers controlled most of what happened over the next four days. Even though it would be a stepped or phased progression, everyone expected a myriad of glitches, mechanical and electronic to plague them. Watchful eyes would monitor every step and each power increase.

Maria tried to relax but wasn't sure how successful a show she put on. She watched the bridge crew and how they took all this. Usually, whether they were up tight or taking things in stride was a good barometer of whoever had the con. Her crew seemed relaxed, and if they were stretched, it was well hidden.

The boson's whistle sounded and Maria, standing at her consol, keyed the ship wide intercom. "May I have your attention please? Today is a momentous occasion for Orion." She paused, "Engineering, start the main Casimir engines." Applause went up from the bridge crew and Maria joined them.

Well into the second day, with one main engine on line at its lowest power setting, the second Casimir progressing well, three and four ready for start, the maintenance crew idled down one small Casimir and moved it to the space ship's nose. Eventually, both of the small engines would run there, their exhausts pointed in the direction of travel to deflect any space debris Orion might encounter. During the main start up, the small engines would compensate as vectoring engines for any side thrust generated by the mains.

Ship's Log
Year: 06/22/15 Time: 04.10
Lt. Abba Dubaku, OD

All four main Casimir engines operational. Engineering reports nominal performance.

Presk, Maria, Captain

* * * *

Over the next twenty-four hours, the main engines reached one-third power plus enough to offset the two small Casimirs' forward thrust. Only a slight noise and minor vibration gave any indication something had changed. Adjusted dampeners compensated, virtually eliminating any noise. The thrust increases were small and spaced two seconds apart making it impossible to tell something as unique and special as the first space ship designed to leave the solar system accelerated away from Earth.

Orion's destiny was in the hands of the astrogator, its nose pointed toward their hope for a habitable planet.

Ship's Log
Year: 07/12/15 Time: 04.10
Gramina Fiora, OD

Port side upper Casimir engine shut down. Severe vibration. Initially, cause unknown. Thrust of opposing engine throttled back and two forward engines adjusted to maintain vector heading. Problem in Casimir determined to be a malfunction of a vibration dampener. Repaired; small Casimir removed from nose position to restart engine. Underway at 11.20

Presk, Maria, Captain

Maria spent as much time with Michael as possible, many times bringing him to the bridge while doing her duty stint. During his first year, his world remained either the bridge or her day cabin. On occasion, she'd take the baby to see David but finally acknowledged it was a waste of time. By age ten, Michael was as much a fixture throughout the ship as any crewmember—his assigned task, school. He had shown the same intellect as Maria and David. To Maria's dismay, Michael showed a proclivity for military history and spent most of his free time at Colonel Jabari's office asking the Marine questions. He spent hours reading from the immense library Orion carried. By the time he turned twelve, the boy could recite in detail the major battle plans or 'order of Battle' history had recorded.

Jabari conceded the Mike had all the makings of a superb strategist. Even at that age, Jabari could see the boy's father in his mannerisms and mothers sweeping intellect. By the time he'd reached age fifteen, he'd completed all of his postgraduate studies and received Orion's first Ph.D. Bhani and Martin's child remained close behind him, much to Martin's consternation. Bhani seemed unconcerned.

Orion and her inhabitants again faced a major milestone. "We've reached three-tenths c, Captain," announced the Officer of the Deck.

"Reduce power to maintain current speed," Maria ordered knowing they would soon reach the point of no return. Engines failure from now on would leave the ship and its inhabitants no way home. Their destination, 55 Cancri in the Cancer system, was forty-one light years distant, one hundred twenty three earth standard years away. But they were already one hundred sixteen billion miles from earth. An engine failure at that distance would mean they had little chance of shedding their forward delta-v with the small Casimirs and ion engines working at maximum thrust. Simply put, without the main engines Orion could not make it to 55 Cancri or back to Earth.

Ship's log
Orion Date: 11/16/20 Time 22.10
Bartlett, Ann, OD

Aging process appears to favor the four-hundred age estimate. Blood samples taken from the original eight every six months. All offspring of original eight carry the gene as does those having received blood transfusions from the eight.

Genes causing aging identified but this information not sent to Earth.

Presk, Maria, Captain

Ship's log
Orion year: 10/02/25 Time: 01.00
Bhani Patel, OD

As other children were born to the long lifers, the early development showed no extraordinary effects from the parental life span. By the time the first-born reached puberty, subtle changes were noted. Around twenty-five years of age, it became evident they too possessed at least some portion of the parental long life gene. How much, only time would tell. Those crewmembers who gained their place in history by receiving blood from one of the original eight and subsequently had children, exhibited similar results.

Macon computerized every aspect of these children's mental and physical development. Perhaps more data were collected and records maintained on this group than any in the history of mankind. If Macon's data were respected, inbreeding would be impossible.

Some good news. The question of what caused the long life reaction has been answered. Research continues to define the matter in detail. This information was also restricted to Orion.

Orion's hydroponics farm showed near-miraculous results. Productivity had increased over seven hundred fold. This information, they transmitted to Earth, immediately as it became known.

Presk, Maria, Captain

Ship's Log
Orion year: 7/15/42 Earth year 2055 CE, Time: 19.00 Zulu
Bhani Patel OD

Orion now under Constellation Cancer's gravitational influence. Approximately ninety Earth years remain until encounter with 55 Cancri.

Experienced a severe meteoroid shower yesterday. Little structural damage thanks to the sweep of forward facing mini Casimir engines. Some damage to antennae and remote cameras. Repairs under way.

Presk, Maria, Captain

Ship's Log
Orion year: 7/15/59 Time: 19.30
Zhu Ling, Lieutenant, OD

Orion has become a closely-knit city-state. Population approaching six hundred. Ability to feed inhabitants satisfactory. Shortages of structural materials have required some original thinking.

Comets and asteroids mined at every opportunity. Over one thousand have contributed to Orion's welfare.

Committed additional areas to both Botany Bay (Hydroponics) and Machine shop. Most time and resources committed to food and repairs.

David Rohm remains a social non-person. His engineering skills seem to improve with the isolation and are unmatched by any member of the crew. Doctor Macon believes he is all he will ever be although research directed at improving his condition continues. Nurse with him twenty-four/seven as he neglects personal care and hygiene.

Presk, Maria, Captain

Maria reflected over the past one hundred seven years. She'd guided a crew of one hundred twenty seven plus one baby, now an adult, through the construction, habitation of the first deep space ship peopled with humans to leave planet Earth and then their perilous journey to 55 Cancri D. Many unanswered questions faced the inhabitants of what would one day be a new world but to a person they remained committed to seeing their mission through.

The remaining twenty-five years, she would devote to preparing them for the rest of their perilous journey to their new home 55 Cancri 'D'.

Ship's Log
Orion year: 8/23/62; Earth year 2075 CE, Time: 13.00 Zulu
Erik Svern XO, OD

55 Cancri twenty light years away—we are halfway there.

Artificial gravity installed in habitat areas. Estimate additional year before installation complete through out Orion. Need to capture a few more small asteroids for raw materials.

Ordered design and construction of four shuttles and two fighters. With anti-gravity installed, all will have orbital and terrestrial capabilities.

Presk, Maria, Captain

Ship's Log
Orion date: 8/31/88 19.00 Zulu
Gramina Fiora, OD

Under influence of Constellation Cancer. 55 Cancri's gravitational pull detected. Estimate seven earth years to destination.

Ship's Log
Orion year: 8/31/0120 Time: 08.30 Zulu
Gramina Fiora, OD

Arrived 55 Cancri, still five million kilometers distant. Reversed Orion's attitude: Engines now pointed at 55 Cancri. Deceleration commenced at 07:20.

Maybe a significant moment; David seemed to respond to our son's one hundred two earth years birthday. Doesn't look a day over the eighteen years equivalent. Doctor Macon says he's mystified by David's improvement. Work continues to help him.

Captain's personal entry: Little good news. David's response to his son led to nothing. Absolutely nothing gained.

The relationship between David Rohm and Martin Grabel has lost ground. Resentment seems evident at times. Will continue observation.

Presk, Maria, Captain

"Captain, radar's got a live one. A really good sized ice cube," the boson's voice boomed over the com.

Maria smiled, rubbed her forehead, and punched the stud, "Okay. Do you want to bring it aboard?"

"Nope, Captain. Too big. Anyhow, they think it's got some volatiles."

Good news and bad news Maria realized. Orion was always looking for esters but bringing them on board had to be controlled. Over the years, established routines were in place to handle most situations.

With nothing on her schedule, Maria strode to the bridge and opened the recently redesigned forward and side view panels, watching the maintenance tug approach the icy berg. For over an hour, she watched the choreographed activity. The explosion spewed water, ice, and the tug tumbled into the void of space. She jabbed at the emergency alarm button. The Klaxon blared its warning and sent emergency crews scrambling. She grabbed the nearby mike and, interrupting the squawking claxon, issued instructions.

Her main concern—the crew on both the berg and the tug.

"We're on it Captain." It was Erik. She watched the display as the Pinnance launched.

Erik guided the launch toward the tug. "Any contact yet," he asked.

"No XO, no response."

"Power?"

"Aye, Sir. The Tug has power. Just no one on the radio or the flight controls."

That could mean anything. Crew injured, equipment malfunction or worse, dead crew.

"Anyone know what happened?"

"Not yet. Explosion of some kind. Knocked the Tug off the ice cube."

Erik keyed the comet crew, "Give me a headcount."

"Thirteen," came back the answer. "What's your condition?"

"Three injured, one severe, looks like a broken leg. Got him in a can. Other than that, we can handle it." In the can meant, the casualty was in a portable hyperbaric chamber just in case of a space suit leak. Typical for any excursion.

That left one person aboard the Tug.

Erik cut the throttle and extended the grappling hook. Some clever maneuvering stopped the tug's erratic tumbling and he initiated the clamping sequence. Boarding the tug, he found the worst. He keyed his mike, "Crewman dead."

He assigned a pilot to fly the tug back to the comet and headed the pinnance in the same direction, now some fifty klicks off Orion's starboard bow. Without the tug, the comet had started to tumble. Erik pushed the throttle.

A few minutes later, the pinnance nudged the ice cube, bringing the tumbling under control.

Three people exited the pinnance to help the injured. Positioning the tug and pinnance, with thrusters at idle, the comet moved toward Orion. Erik made the decision not to bring it aboard but secure it to the hull. Ten hours went by before the detail secured.

PART

THREE

Prologue III

Their log encompassed many entries—the chronology of a race of humans seeking a new life, learning how to work and live together as few if any had before. New science occurred almost daily, mining asteroids and comets, constantly expanding and improving Orion. The establishment of a civilian government, subject in fact to the Captain in matters of safety, purpose, and destination set Orion on a course of democratic civilian rule not unlike a constitutional monarchy. They'd constantly strived to improve their lot while raising families and become very innovative at relieving and avoiding boredom. This group, remained bound together by a reason mankind had never before experienced.

Orion continued to transmit and receive data from Earth although at this distance, no semblance of meaningful communication was possible. Over the last fifty years, things have not gotten better on Earth. Two major wars ended with major political realignments. The Third World War, WW 3, between Muslims and Christians many called the second crusades. Except this time, the death and destruction horrified even the most cynical. WW 4 pitted the Russians against the Chinese. Fortunately, the United States and a very fractured European Union were able to broker an end using their favorite tool, capitalism.

Following the last Great War, United States, Federated Russia, and Republic of China tried to form a troika to keep a lid on things. Their economic and political interest required, at the least, the absence of war, but at the last word Orion had, things were not going well.

To a majority of Orionians however, Earth conjured up nothing more than a name and pictures. They'd been born in space and had no direct knowledge of Earth.

CHAPTER FOURTEEN
55 Cancri

The entire bridge crew stood transfixed—hardly a soul breathed. Some people shook, others cried. All over the ship, every eye found available screens and stared.

Maria steadied her voice and said, "Once we're close enough, we launch both shuttles to begin a systematic search of the planets." 55 Cancri 'D' appeared no more than a bright dot. Only a hint of light, but there it was. She intentionally kept her choice of words almost indifferent. Speculation among the crew had run ramped about the probability of one planet becoming home. A series of fly-bys, radar scans and spectral analysis of the four planets orbiting 55 Cancri, 'D' seemed to meet most of the criteria needed to sustain life. "Cancri 'D' it is." Getting there had taken one hundred twenty three years.

"Time to orbit?" Maria struggled to keep the quiver from her voice and only partially succeeded—a sentiment not lost on the bridge crew.

"Seventy-two standard hours," Mory Brix, Astrogator answered as she jabbed at the icons, "Present heading, orbital insertion altitude, one million kilometers."

Maria returned to the command control consol and hit a key, "Engineering, You may deploy all assets arrayed for first scientific investigation of all four planets in 55 Cancri."

The cheer going up from the bridge crew got rid of the awful tension that had built over the last few hours.

"Mr. Svern, assign the OD."

"Aye, Captain, I have the bridge." Svern had never varied from their goal, Maria's leadership, and his loyalty, both total.

Captain Presk said to the XO, "I'll be in my day cabin. Please ask President Hammond and my staff to join me. We will address the ship's company in one hour."

"Aye, Sir." He noticed Maria had never wavered from addressing the *ship's company*. Hammond on the other hand, always used *the People of Orion*. On occasion, he said the *Citizens of Orion*.

Maria took the few steps to her cabin. The faint background hum noise had become so much a part of every day life that she had no trouble picking up the soft footfall. She stopped dead in her tracks. David stood looking at her. Her heart raced. For a rare moment, recognition seemed to replace the vacant look that had so long been a part of their lives. Her pulse leapt as a wellspring of hope overtook her even as she tried to shove it aside. To a crewmember, all agreed they would have not made it this far with out David, even as a savant.

"David." She reached for him but he didn't move, causing Maria to pull back. Confused, she took a small step toward him. The entire bridge crew now focused on the two.

Maria paused, wanting in the worst way to touch him, nevertheless forced herself to wait. She'd lived with warnings that any improvement could be sporadic and unstable.

Slowly, his eyes shifted from looking past her to her face. She hung back not knowing what else to do. Macon, in a hard run, appeared in the passageway, stopping just behind David. That brought no reaction from her husband.

Reaching past her, the Doctor opened the cabin door. Maria, taking the cue stuck out her left arm toward the opening. "Won't you join us?"

David slowly turned and stepped inside, never acknowledging the gesture.

As Maria and Roberto entered, Mathew Hammond followed. No one spoke for a few moments. Maria motioned the two men to seats and slowly placed one for David. She then stood at the table's far end as the man she'd never stopped loving took the seat. Slowly, the rest of the staff filled the room. No one seemed concerned that David had joined them. Even though it was the first such time.

"Thank you all for coming. We've identified one of the planets orbiting 55 Cancri, designated 'D', as our target. Sensors indicate it is rich in minerals and has plenty of water and a breathable atmosphere. For the moment, we will call it New Earth." Much of what Maria had to say was available to anyone who wanted to take the time to study the results of the orbital investigative reports. How she would approach, first contact, if there were any sentient beings on the planet remained what everyone wanted to hear.

"Tomorrow, our journey may be over." She waited for the light applause and polite *yeas* to end and gazed into faces beaming with pride and anticipation. "Pilots, Zhu Ling and Abba Dubaku, will fly the first shuttles to enter the planets atmosphere. Some of you, a few anyhow, may recall these two piloted the first shuttle from earth that started us on our way." Maria turned the meeting over to Harper Crowfoot, one of four Native American Indians onboard and squadron commander.

Crowfoot laid out how they would implement the plan approved for first exploration. He noted nothing resembling cities or encampments of any kind showed up in the orbital surveys. In fact, the instruments showed nothing suggesting sentient life. The flyovers had shown the planet ideally suited for habitation. Mountain ranges, localized storms, generous cloud formations, a few arid areas although most of the planet had plenty of foliage, radiation level well within tolerance, and breathable atmosphere.

The next few days Maria concentrated on the expedition, going over every detail. Colonel Jimmy John Jabari would have overall command and Gramina Fiora would handle any botanical, biological and geology surveys.

Macon strongly objected to her going. As he'd noted before, he was a confirmed coward. But Gramina insisted. She'd studied hard for years learning these sciences and this was her chance to contribute as never before. Roberto couldn't talk her out of going or stop her for that matter.

Maria stayed completely out of what she considered no more than a family argument. Besides, as far as she was concerned, Gramina had earned her place on that expedition.

Over the next five days, data from the survey group flooded Orion's computers. They had detected no hostile life forms. So far, only small vertebrates and a few invertebrates appeared in and on both land and water. These early missions omitted marginal life forms. Right now, they needed to find a site for New Earth's first permanent structures.

On the sixth day, the shuttle returned the weary but excited explorers except for Jabari and his small well-armed squad. The second expedition left less than an hour later with orders to remain on the surface and establish a base camp. Ann Workman had scheduled a shuttle to leave as one returned until one hundred twenty people, along with their supplies, were transitioned along with supplies to sustain them. Four shuttle trips would get the people down but it would take another twenty flights to handle the supplies and equipment.

These would be the first colonists. Four people, selected by lottery, became a part of the historic first settlers to New Earth.

CHAPTER FIFTEEN
New Earth
55 Cancri 'D'

"Two hours," said Maria contemplatively. "Any word from the expedition? They missed their one hour report-in."

Already nervous regarding recent reported noises from unseen whatever, she had become extra cautious about taking unnecessary risks.

Colonel Jabari had signaled his readiness to send out a recon team. Maria decided to wait.

Two weeks on New Earth and so far, nothing lethal in fauna or flora had cropped up. Classifying the habitat kept the botanists and biologist busy and excitement ran high. A tree is a tree is a tree was no longer true. Soil samples were not all that different from Earth's. Both some animal and plant species were very close to known botany and biology; most others would require detail study and new classifications. Grass and vines seemed peculiarly different, inedible. The biggest challenge would remain the microbial life that helped sustain the flora. Lagoon water carried little bugs that would tear up any human if not boiled or chemically treated.

Svern shook his head. "No," he too had expressed concern about the group. "But that isn't unusual. We still haven't solved the atmospheric interference problem. At best, line of sight transmission is all we have. And you know about Amon Isaacs's rebellious streak."

Gramina Fiora walked up. "Hey you two, take a look." She held out a picture. "Just came in. From Isaacs. Over the new tight beam we just got set up. Isaacs says everything's going well. And everyone's okay. "

"Doesn't look that way. I need to talk with him," Maria sensed something wasn't right. The animal certainly looked dead. They were all under strict orders to kill nothing unless threatened. A dead anything didn't suggest things were going well.

"Ugly looking bastard isn't it," said Erik. "Look at the size of those claws and teeth. What do you suppose it weighs?"

Maria didn't answer; she had already headed toward the command center.

A few minutes later, she had Isaacs on the com and didn't like what she heard. Things hadn't gone well and the explorers ended with having to kill the animal. The beast had attacked the survey group but luckily, none reported injuries.

The expedition found refuge in a cave about one hundred feet above the valley floor. That added height provided the altitude needed to communicate with the base. Isaacs promised that, if matters didn't improve, they'd activate their anti-gravity units and return to the compound. Engineering calculated New Earth's gravitational field within one-tenth Orion's, just point one five less than old Earth's. It didn't escape Maria they could easily have used an anti-grav unit to bump up the antennae and kept in touch. For that matter, Orion had put a communications satellite in stationary orbit to ensure that contact with the group remain unbroken. Over Amon's protest, she ordered the entire group back to camp.

"Well, I've got to get back to Orion." Ann had the next forty-eight watch. She kissed Erik and headed for a shuttle parked a thousand meters further out on the peninsula. Two other members and the flight crew joined her and shortly, shuttle Enterprise headed for orbit. Maria decided David would come down on the next shuttle. No one had any idea how he would react to the new environment.

Jabari picked the most defensible site, an elevated peninsula, for the permanent settlement. While it gave them access to water, and space for shuttles to land and take-off, making forays into the rest of the planet on foot could be problematic if any kind of threat occurred. The narrow access leading into New Earth remained a defensive problem for the Marine.

In the six weeks since the first encampment, a rudimentary form of cement proved out and concrete slab walls were going up all over the clearing. Mild temperatures and occasional rain coupled with few insects had construction moving at a faster pace than anyone had anticipated. Anti-grav cranes made the slab wall erection little more than child's play. Completing the mess hall, warehouses and barracks made securing life essentials a lot easier. Of the 986 souls who'd been aboard Orion when it arrived in system, one hundred thirty had transferred to New Earth. As accommodations on the ground could handle them, additional people would move from Orion. Just being able to provide food and protection were major hurdles, and solutions, while slow at first were showing promise. Some Orionians were looking forward to seeing real dirt, plants, and just being off a satellite world. Of the original 127 that boarded Orion, one hundred twenty were still alive and were the only people who'd ever experienced living on a real planet. Others were apprehensive about saying goodbye to their world—the only life they had ever known. Maria had decided not to push anyone into leaving the orbiting ship.

That evening, she assembled the remaining settlement team, except for the posted guards. Orion engineers had developed a most impressive bug-repelling device, making the outdoor meeting a festive gathering for most. Specific wavelength lighting rendered humans virtually invisible to the bugs identified so far. David had not reacted any differently once on the ground than he had aboard Orion. He sat amongst the others—alone in his own world.

Seated Maria said, "I've asked Colonel Jabari to increase the security."

That brought more than the usual groans along with a few shouted questions as to why—some very angry.

"This location is very defensible," someone brusquely interrupted. Most of the people facing him became silent, maybe even curious as to what threat was so eminent, particularly since Isaacs had easily killed the only large animal they'd seen, with no one injured.

"We have no idea if anything will happen as a result of the attack. I'm not willing to take unnecessary chances. In due time, we'll know enough about this place to make more informed risk assessments." Where a threat existed, and Maria considered killing the animal a risk, she meant to be as thorough as possible. She'd never been a confrontational person, but changing her behavior meant avoiding losing people, she'd change. All her life she'd relied on her intellect along with gut instinct and her gut directed her now.

Consultation with Erik Svern and Colonel Jabari on security matters seemed to meet the most people's approval.

"From what? Someone yelled.

Maria turned to the Marine. "Jim. Care to tell them?"

Colonel Jabari, all six foot four inches and two hundred fifty pounds, cast an imposing sight as he walked to the front of the group. No one had ever had the temerity to question his courage or commitment and finding takers for sparing sessions bordered on the impossible.

He spoke in a matter-of-fact no-nonsense manner. "We've detected a number of anomalies over the past week. Since the killing, the noise level under human audible range, has increased significantly. We think that beast Isaacs shot wanted to herd a group of smaller animals into a blind canyon and isolate them. Based on the increase nightly activity around the compound, we believe that an attack may be coming. From now on, everyone will be armed at all times."

Stunned silence greeted the pronouncement.

"That's pure speculation. Pure BS," said another voice. You talk as if these were sentient beings planning an assault. These are nothing but big dumb animals. I'll admit they're different from what were used to but still dumb animals. Our weapons and brains are more than a match for them. So why panic?"

"No not beings," said Maria, "at least as we understand beings. And sentient, we don't know. Maybe, probably not as intelligent as we are but that doesn't mean they couldn't formulate an attack. I just don't want to take the chance. We've come too far for too long to get careless. I ask you to remember, some of us came from a world where carnivorous creatures were quite capable of organizing a coordinated attack on humans and other prey. You only know that world through videos and books. On these matters, I insist you follow our instructions. It is not a matter for debate."

Rapid-fire questions came at her.

With enduring patience, she handled most of them. A few questioners were not looking for answers but assurances. Others were simply scared. Isaacs had become so incensed and raised his rhetoric until he seemed on the verge of personally attacking Maria.

After the meeting, she asked Amon Isaacs to stay. "Amon, I've tolerated your insolence and disobedience longer than I should have. You're an excellent botanist, but I cannot afford to have you leading expeditions and unnecessarily placing people's lives at risk."

Isaacs stood and started toward the door. Maria responded, "I'm not through."

"The hell you aren't. You may be the great one to some people aboard

Orion. But we're not on Orion any longer. I can leave this compound any time I want and you can't stop me."

Isaacs joined the group as a third generation Orionian. His grandfather had received a blood transfusion qualifying him and died during an asteroid recovery, leaving Amon without major parental discipline. The grandfather had never been able to control the young man. Amon had been disciplined a number of times for often small acts of cruelty. Maria suspected the confrontation with the now dead beast could have been avoided.

Jabari's hand held squawked to life, "Colonel Jabari, we've got movement.

In an instant, his com unit barked orders as he headed for the perimeter wall.

Maria, on the dead run, yelled to the group, "Into the mess hall and that includes you, Amon." The concrete slab walls would withstand an attack from anything they'd seen so far. Maria couldn't imagine something getting past the main barriers at the neck of the peninsula. But if it did, her people would be ready. She issued weapons and formed a perimeter guard using gun slots cast into the walls. "Keep your weapons on safety until I tell you otherwise." Maybe he could at least keep these people from shooting each other.

"Colonel," Maria said into her com unit. The perimeter floodlights now illuminated about five hundred yards in front of the slab walls. Then the lights went off. "What's going on?"

Jabari replied, "Can't see anything with the floods so have shut them down. We'll go to night vision, heat signatures, and x-ray. Will keep you posted."

Almost twenty minutes passed before Jabari, his voice calm and deliberate said, "Got more movement. Stand by."

The wait seemed interminable. Maria's first reaction had been to head for the wall but she'd reluctantly decided she couldn't leave these armed civilians without leadership.

The hairs on the back of her neck stood out as Jabari's calm deliberate words slammed into her consciousness. "Captain, you need to get up here and see this."

Maria bolted from her watch position near the mess hall entrance. "Ann, you're in command. Keep in constant contact."

She would have preferred Erik in charge, but he had the watch on Orion. Her decision to put Ann in command during a high stress situation came easily though. Ann would shoot if she had too and wouldn't think long in making the decision—a tendency everyone understood.

Less than a minute later, with anti-grav assist, Maria reached the wall. "What's going on?" She deliberately kept her voice calm.

Jabari headed for her car but Maria stopped him. The Colonel growled, "I've got to go after David."

"What are you talking about? What does David have to do with this?"

Jabari turned back toward his portal, put his back to the wall slid down until he sat on the ground, his knees forming a rest point for his crossed arms. He stared in the dark for a long moment at the Captain. "I've failed you and David.

Everyone!"

"What do you mean?" Maria's voice struck an alarming note. "What are you saying?"

Jabari shook his head in dismay. "Maria... Captain. David's out in the field with what appears to be a herd of animals. I have no idea how he got past the guards and away from his nurses." His hand motion generally took in the men around them.

Maria sat stunned almost afraid to look. She accepted the night vision binoculars and gazed into the dark. Three hundred meters away, David faced a partially visible group that she estimated at ten creatures like nothing she'd ever seen before. A gasp escaped her lips but she managed, "They're not showing any signs of hostility. In fact, they seem to be greeting David."

Jabari wanted to mount a rescue team to bring the engineer back but Maria insisted they wait. He did order his men to keep their weapons trained on the aliens admonishing them not to shoot unless he gave the order and to make damned sure they didn't shoot David. Jabari, now with a scoped rifle, had what appeared to be the leader in his crosshairs. "If that son of a bitch so much as blinks the wrong way, I'll cut it down before it can reach David."

"Don't shoot," ordered Maria.

The creatures remained standing where they had stopped. "In fact," she said, "I think we're being wooed or enticed or lured in some fashion with an offering." She pointed toward the slit from which she'd been viewing.

Jabari cradled his rifle, stood, accepted the binoculars, and studied the scene. "All I see is a pile of what looks like fruit. Is that it?"

A grimace touched her face. "Colonel, I think you're right. Question is, is it a lure or effort to show us some kind of deference?"

"It had to be a peace offering of some type. Otherwise, David would have already been attacked."

"Keep an eye out for another beast." Maria said.

"We're on it."

"And what did the fruit donors look like?"

Jabari didn't answer immediately. Finally, he said, "Lemurs except their upper torso is a carapace. Looks like knights' chest armor. Head and lower body's lemur. Half bug, half lemur."

Maria leaned against the wall beside the Marine. "Lemurs?" She didn't doubt the Colonel. "Bug-Lemurs? They were bipedal, upright and not on all fours." She tried to remove the disbelief from her voice. Since lemurs did both, she expected Jabari would say 'both'.

"Upright. Used their arms and hands to carry the fruit. More importantly, they seemed to communicate among themselves."

Maria never looked at the Colonel and that seemed to upset the Marine. "I know it sounds crazy but I'd swear they were talking to each other."

"You think they're sentient?"

He shrugged. "They were jawing back and forth. May be no more than monkey talk. I'm sure of what I saw. I've only seen hand gestures made toward

David."

"Maybe their giving thanks for Isaac's killing that beast earlier today."

"That's as good a guess as any but may be wishful thinking."

Neither wanted to discuss the matter further until they had David safely back inside the walls.

Maria wondered if man's first contact with another sentient being had to begin with a conflict. Uncounted words of speculation, written by both scholars and fiction writers pointed to this moment or at least something like it. Elated as she was, she had nagging doubts about this being the first meeting between intelligent species. Maybe because the creatures standing with David were something less than the advanced beings she'd expected. Were humans, mankind the dominant creation? Somehow, she doubted that. Even with all she'd read pointing toward this moment, Maria Presk wasn't as prepared as she'd hoped. She sat down beside Jabari and looked straight ahead into the dark for a few moments.

Jabari questioned, "Do you think it wise to let this play out? I don't like leaving David out there."

"Nor do I. But right now, it seems we have little to say about it. We can't take them all out quick enough to keep at least one from attacking David. Beside, if we're these little guys saviors, maybe we should do something to demonstrate our own friendship without tackling another beast."

"I still don't like it."

Maria nodded her understanding. "Send the armored grav-car out."

Jabari turned to survey the area again through binoculars. "They're gone. David's standing out there alone." Jabari set a watch for the night and ordered three sentries to join up with him in the rover. A second quick check on David confirmed the bug-lemurs had left. David already headed for the enclosure, ambled leisurely across the open field, and seemed not to notice the car speeding toward him.

Maria stood, activated her personal anti-grav. As David had moved out of harms way, she headed for the mess hall in long bounds.

Shortly thereafter, David returned to the enclosure never giving any indication that something new and different had made its way into everyone's lives. As he entered the hall, a distressed nurse took him by the arm and led him to his quarters.

At sun up the next morning, with most of the settlement people at the wall watching, Jabari ordered out the armored patrol car with six fully armed marines to retrieve the fruit. The bug-lemurs nowhere in sight.

From a walk near the top of the wall, Maria watched intently as the car slowly approached to offering. "Colonel, I think you should hold your position for a few minutes. Let's see if you attract any attention."

Jabari acknowledged and the grav-car stopped. Twenty minutes went by. "Got some movement." The Colonel's voice didn't indicate anything out of the ordinary.

"Yes, I see them," said Maria quietly, no alarm indicated in her words.

"Bug-Lemurs. They're walking toward you from the east. About a dozen. I see no weapons or anything that would pass for a weapon. One is carrying something."

Ten meters from the grav-car, the bug-lemurs stopped. Each took whatever they carried and spread them on the ground. "They're mats. They're putting them on the ground and sitting," someone exclaimed. Beyond any doubt, these beings had some level of sentience.

Over the next few days, first contact had become ordinary. Communication with the bug–lemurs, still no more than gestures, their language more guttural noise than real speech remained a long shot work in progress. David and his group mastered some of the sounds but the bug-lemurs seemed to respond only to gestures. Every sound and gesture recorded was sent up to Orion for analysis. Symbolism meant little or nothing. Clearly, the *natives* couldn't match human intellect, yet their ability to care for one another perhaps equaled man's.

Maria made the decision to allow the bug-lemurs into the compound, and, to everyone's amazement, they accepted the gesture.

At the end of the day, the creatures withdrew. Only the one beast had been reported and no other reports even hinted at another sighting. So far, the one Isaacs had killed was it.

The bug-lemurs appeared completely at ease coming and going from the compound. If these beings had a village or encampment, they never extended Maria and her group an invitation to visit.

She directed Jabari to form up a squad to follow their guests. New Earth needed to know everything they could about their neighbors. She ordered Orion to survey the departing bug–lemurs just in case the Marines lost them. Not unexpectedly, the bug-Lemurs made their way to a cave—their home.

During the ensuing six weeks, contact between the two groups increased. If trust between different species is manifested by a seeming willingness to be together, then trust was building. However, interpreting or deciphering a language or getting the bug-lemurs to understand the English language all led to dead ends. As far as the earthlings could detect, the bug-lemurs issued only grunts. Jabari never let the aliens' apparent harmlessness get in the way of being prepared for any eventuality. Every bug-lemur inside the compound came under the sights of an unseen rifle. Maria had made no effort to suggest to their guests that the she wanted an invitation to the bug-lemur's encampment. She had no idea how to ask.

Svern's turn came to take the forty-eight hour watch on Orion and he left for the six-hour shuttle flight.

Routine ruled the next day and Maria went to bed early. About two a.m., she flicked on the overhead light and reached for her handheld.

"Captain Presk." Erik's voice carried the steel he hadn't used since the mutiny attempt or Harold Bassett's assault on the tarmac at Bahia Los Angeles one hundred forty seven years ago. "You'd better get up here."

Maria's heart jumped. She forced her voice calm. "What's going on Erik?"

"We've got company. Radar's showing something approaching. From its speed and vector, it is headed directly for us and it isn't a meteor or asteroid."

CHAPTER SIXTEEN
The Visitors

Maria stopped halfway out of her bed, her mouth dry. An involuntarily swallow only aggravated the parchedness. She choked back the emotion, unsure whether fear or something else—maybe pure excitement—had taken over. She regained her composure and asked, "How far away is it, and when will it be here?"

Erik answered, "Seven million klicks. At current speed, twenty-two standard hours. However, I have no idea how quickly it can shed delta v so the arrival may be triple or one third that."

Occasionally, Maria had imagined this moment but never seriously. Now, all that would change. She had always dismissed the idea of space-traveling aliens as just too far out. But, it was here and she had no suggestion of what to do.

So be it. She'd take what came and deal with it as best she could. She had highly competent people to draw advice from and she would use them.

Erik asked, "Do you want to assemble the council?"

Her voice cold, she said, "No. In fact, just the opposite. The last thing I want is for the all the leadership to be together. If whatever's coming our way is hostile, that would make it easy for them to knock us all out at one time. We have little with which to defend ourselves. Especially against superior technology."

She gave a slight grimace wishing there had been more moderation in her tone. The governing council, established shortly after they'd reach New Earth, and modeled much along the lines of the American constitution, had not handled anything like this situation before. They'd had their moments of crisis and gained some experience in dealing with domestic issues, but there'd been nothing as potentially devastating as this. She could only hope their usual calm deliberation would prevail.

Mathew Hammond had set up a constitutional court, and representatives elected to a congress. With the election of a president, New Earth would have its government—but that remained weeks away. That meant there wasn't anyone to foist the problem off on—not that Maria wanted to. Deep inside she realized she enjoying the feelings of discovery, danger and fear. Making first contact with an alien sentient species went beyond momentous—just being a part of it would make history. Of course, they could all soon be dead or worse, taken captive. She had no intention of losing the new life they'd endured so much and come so far for—at least not without a fight.

She ordered Erik to awaken everyone on New Earth and assemble them in the mess hall. Same went with Orion personnel—he had to roust them also. She would address them all from her shuttle.

Within minutes, the shuttle airborne, Maria headed toward Orion, which sat in a stationary orbit four hundred kilometers above New Earth.

She instructed council members to arm themselves and get to some type of shelter. Everyone had at least three methods of communicating with the other members and Orion. Standing orders "Do not fire unless fired upon. Only defensive action without expressed orders from Orion.

"Have the space fighters, fueled, fully armed, and standing by," she ordered. "They're not to leave Orion without my explicit order."

Fully armed meant a complete range of weapons: twenty mm armor piercing Gatling gun, rockets and lasers, all fully operational. Right then, she wished more than two fighters made up their airborne armament.

"Yes Ma'am."

Maria left Colonel Jabari in command dirtside with orders to organize a defense as best he could. Both knew he couldn't do much against a determined attacker, especially if the attack came from space.

She urged the shuttle pilot to push the craft to its max acceleration cutting transit time by nearly one third. The next hours would be critical for the residents of New Earth and Orion.

Maria maintained a composed attitude even though she felt less than that. Not knowing whom or what the nature of threat had everyone on edge and how she handled it could make all the difference. The sudden realization that another species with space venturing capability far superior to their own was headed for them could cause panic. She had to make sure her every action reflected calm and self-assurance, even though she didn't feel that way. The crew would follow her lead and even she had more than enough apprehension.

Maria and Erik, in contact with Jabari, worked out the best defense possible with what little they had. Orion, designed as a transport not a battleship, had no external defenses other than the two fighters and ten laser canons. The inhabitants never considered the need for more, maybe with the exception of collision avoidance for comets, asteroids, or space debris.

Dirtside, following Jabari's lead, the one hundred twenty or so inhabitant, organized into squads. His defensive prospects no better than Orion's. His only advantage—he could disperse his band making targeting more difficult.

Back on the ship, Maria stood on the bridge watching the radar blip come ever closer.

A signal chimed and she pressed the intercom button, "Yes, Ann." Her voice held calm.

"Maria, Martin, and I have been working on computer code for a universal translator. Actually, we were just finding some way to keep from being bored once we arrived at New Earth."

Ann wasn't one to mince words, so Maria never doubted her comments and wasn't startled with her uncomplicated straightforward attitude. She punched a few icons and had Martin Grabel in the hookup. Time had not allowed for any meaningful testing of the translator. In fact, the two had planned to try it on the bug-lemurs in the next few days. The test would take about the time they had until the unknown visitors arrived to get the all the loose end tied up. Usable? Total unknown. They could be going nowhere with this gadget. They had absolutely no idea if their effort would work. A translator may be no more than a colossal waste of time, universal or not. The biggest drawbacks were that all comparisons for sentence meaning, structure, and individual word interpretation came from Earth languages. That might not mean a thing when they receive their first alien signal.

Maria wanted the crew alert when the aliens arrived. Four on and eight off watches were ordered.

For four days, Maria watched the blip approach. What little she understood about an attack vector told her this ship's vector wasn't that of an aggressor. "Turn on all our external lights."

One million klicks out, the intruder stopped. At that range, Orion would not be able to see the same lights, but Maria had no way of knowing the alien's capabilities. Orion's had little maneuvering ability, so running wasn't an option. She'd err on the side of caution and diplomacy.

Radiation patterns emitted by the alien ship soon reached Orion. Sensors displayed erratic readings. Who or whatever loomed out there clearly wasn't looking for a fight. She keyed the chair mike, "Ann, Martin, are you receiving their transmission?"

"Yes," he answered, his voice unsteady as if excited by anticipation. "But it's just driving our instruments crazy. We can't tell what kind of signals they are let alone stand any chance of deciphering them."

Ann said, "We've got a hello signal worked up along with a picture of you and Orion ready to transmit. We can send it out on all frequencies."

Me? Maria thought for a minute. Actually, having the ship and her pictures made sense. "Go ahead. Transmit the message but on one frequency."

"Will do," responded Ann. "I think we might want to send a signal for hydrogen. Send it on a low frequency band and keep transmitting it."

Physics are physics. They don't change out here. "Makes sense." Maria gave the go ahead.

An hour later, the alien cut its broadcast to one wavelength.

For the next eight or so hours the two ships held their positions unchanged. Electronic signals passed between them—but with no understanding.

"They're moving," said astrogator Mory Brix, "toward us at about one thousand klicks per hour and accelerating."

Maria let a smile touch her lips, thankful for Brix's calming voice.

Silence settled over the bridge. Occasionally, a pent up gasp escaped from someone.

Quietly, Maria said, "Relax everyone. If these guys wanted a fight, it would have all gone down differently. I think they're as startled as we are. Let's not do anything that might upset or be misconstrued by our visitors."

Erik stopped beside her. "What you really mean is *don't screw up this first encounter.*"

Maria laughed and soon the entire bridge crew joined in. She tapped her number one's shoulder, "Thanks." The tension visibly eased among the crew.

"Bogey has stopped accelerating. Speed, one-hundred thousand klicks per hour. At that rate and considering how quickly it shed delta v earlier, it should be within visual in about thirty hours," Brix reported.

Maria quietly commanded, "Launch the fighters. Have them take up station in our radar shadow. Only under my direct orders are they to leave the ship's umbra."

Erik's head snapped around. A nod and smile accompanied the move. "Yes, Ma'am." The XO relayed the orders to Harper Crowfoot, squadron commander.

Maria addressed the crew and people dirtside. She had prepared them as well as she knew how. She had no history to go on. After all, the first encounter between what up to that time had been called extraterrestrial species marked a milestone in mankind's march through time. With no credible offensive capability, any response she made must come across as non-aggressive.

She remembered her father's admonition when the odds are against you. "If you can, run. There's no dishonor in not being killed. If you can't run, then talk. If you have to fight, then fight to win.

Well, Maria couldn't run. Orion just wasn't designed as anything but a transport. She had little to fight with so that left talk. Maria could only hope talking could see this first encounter to its end.

CHAPTER SEVENTEEN
The Aliens

As predicted, thirty hours later, the alien spaceship took up station one hundred thousand kilometers off Orion's starboard, out of visual range.

For the next seventy-two hours, Ann and Martin worked their magic.

"We've got it," Martin finally shouted. "We've nailed down the frequency and interpreted a message. Without confirmation, we can only believe our interpretation is correct. We're putting our hello and your picture on this frequency and sending."

Maria squelched her own excitement. "And what did their message say?"

Ann cleared her throat, "Yes Ma'am, sorry. The closest we can translate into English is that they call themselves the *First*. What they sent literally means *before the apes* in English although they would have a different word than ape. We don't yet know what that would be. So, we're calling them *Prosimians*. They may not appreciate the comparison."

Maria mused for a moment. "So they consider themselves the first sentient beings. Interesting since mankind most often took the position other beings had preceded them. Maybe we're both right." She thought for a moment. "I hope that doesn't translate into the chosen."

What seemed an interminable period slipped by.

"What's happening? Has there been any change in the data stream?" Maria asked. She was concerned Orion might take in the moment and overlooked something critical, like a sneak attack. A diversion. A decrease in the data stream could be a prelude.

Ann responded, "The aliens continue sending single stream data, we're recording and also trying to decipher it. We're also entering it into our language interpreter, starting a data base."

It could take a while to get enough of the alien's vocabulary and word-meaning base before any interpreting would happen. She assumed the alien had the same idea.

Once exchanged communications became constant, Ann sent a message in the limited language she and Martin felt comfortable with, suggesting both sides add more channels for faster data transmission.

Almost instantly, thirteen additional frequencies flowed simultaneous broadcasting from the alien spaceship each one preceded by a frequency identifier in English. "At this rate," Martin said, "we should have enough to open meaningful dialog in the next eight hours or so."

Maria cautioned. "Even though it seems these folks aren't looking for a fight, be on your toes, people. Remember we don't know what we're dealing with here."

Anne said, "We've got a picture." Quiet settled over Orion's bridge all eyes glued on the monitor. A full-face image appeared on the bridge forward screen. "Very look-a-like bug-lemur but definitely not a lemur." This one did carry a sidearm. Behind the figure, stood two more lemurs carrying what must pass for them as rifles.

"Don't look too friendly," a voice muttered.

Martin asked, "What happens if they start shooting?"

"They won't," responded Maria not at all confident she was right.

Martin persisted. "But what do we do if they decide to shoot?" Even he recognized Orion couldn't possible outrun the leviathan sitting off their starboard.

"Not much to do." Erik said, "Those are probably energy weapons of some type. Each Lemur's rifle seems attached to a pack on his back. Most likely the power source. If the ship has external weapons—like I said, not much we can do."

"Look at those helmets. What are they?" someone asked.

What are they seemed like a dumb question until one bug-lemur's visor snapped shut startling Orion's bridge crew. For the most part, they expected the next sound to be from one of the aliens' external weapons. Instead, the lemur framed in the picture, turned and spoke to the offender. He left the image. By then it had become apparent that the helmet design included protection for the lemur's large protruding eyes.

In the background, more bug-lemurs moved around, probably going about assigned tasks. Not particularly muscular, their movement resembled ballet dancers' graceful steps.

Judging by appearance, rifles, and pistols left a question and seemed a contradiction to the almost delicate body movements. Which were they, decent beings—or warriors?

Just as the com quieted, astrogator Brix announced, "They've launched a shuttle. It's headed dirtside."

Maria hit the com button, "Colonel Jabari, have you been monitoring?"

"Yes, Ma'am. Do you want us to intercept?"

"No, but have someone tail them in a grav-car. See if you can find out what's of so much interest that they'd risk a confrontation. They must know we have people dirtside."

The shuttle made no effort to avoid detection as it headed straight for a series of cliffs about one hundred klicks southeast from the New Earth colony, not far from where Isaacs killed the beast.

As much as possible, the Marines kept to a ravine trailing the shuttle by about one thousand meters. The shuttle gave no indication of the Marines' presence or that they cared if it had.

"Well, I'll be damned," the grav-car driver said, "Colonel, the shuttle landed and was roundly greeted by the bug-lemurs." The Marines stayed on station visually recording what they could of the encounter.

Colonel Jabari's ongoing dialog with Orion abruptly changed, becoming more intense. "We can see the shuttle passengers. Six of them. They're very much like the bug-lemurs except the carapace looks more like a clavicle. And they don't look peaceful. These guys have more weapons among themselves than we have on Orion." Mats were place in a circle on the ground and what appeared as a serious palaver started.

* * * *

"We just got word the shuttle has left dirtside. Headed back to the mother ship," Brix, the astrogator said.

"Be alert everyone," Maria repeated. She sat in her command chair and keyed the com. "Ann, Martin, are we able to communicate?"

"We can try." Came back Ann's answer. "It's a gamble."

"How so?" The Captain asked.

Martin answered. "Without some confirmation and no experience, we have no way of knowing if our decoding is correct. To quote a famous submariner, we may be sending our dirty laundry list." It was the first time Maria could remember Martin using any kind of humor.

"I think we've got to try. Put together a message and send it in English and their language simultaneously."

Maria wrote out a few words and read them. "Here's my thoughts. 'Greetings. We are explorers seeking a place to live. We mean no one harm.'"

There seemed to be general agreement that said what everyone felt. Shortly the message went out. They waited.

Several hours passed when the screen again came alive with an image but different from the first.

Ann announced, "We're receiving a message." After an interminable time, the translator crackled, "Unauthorized life form: agree to a meeting on Usgac (their name for New Earth) or be destroyed."

Brix broke the silence. "The ship's accelerating again. Straight for us. At about one thousand klicks per hour. Be here in ten hours."

"Pretty damned sure of themselves aren't they?" asked someone.

Absentmindedly, Maria said, "Talk or fight," recalling her father's earlier advice.

"Ma'am?" Brix asked.

"Tell them we'll talk." That brought a number of stares but no one raised an objection.

As Brix predicted, ten hours later the alien ship took up station about four thousand klicks off Orion's starboard. Orion's inhabitants thought their own ship large, but the alien dwarfed it by a factor of four. The ships forward third bristled with armament; the last two thirds apparently housed engines, storage and probably shuttles and fighters. This species obviously had some serious problems with someone to carry that much firepower. Apparently, space held more dangers than the earthlings had reckoned.

Shortly after achieving orbit, the *First's* ship simply seemed to shut down. "Why would a warship, armed as this one, apparently become dormant? No pickets out to protect it. No radar probing approaches. No visible means of defense?" Maria sat bewildered in her Captain's chair and pressed the com button, "Keep our fighters on station and set the watch," she ordered. Suppressing her urge to do something more, she went to bed.

For the next two days, the big ship remained powered down. Orion registered no activity, no lights, no emissions, and no transmissions. Only at departure time for the surface and the meeting did things seemed to get very busy. Puzzling behavior.

"We sleep for eight hours, these guys for two days," Eric said.

Maria, Ann as translator, and a yeoman to scribe and photograph the meeting, boarded the shuttle for New Earth and the get-together with the *First*. It would be the first meeting between sentient beings from different worlds, a historic moment. Then Maria remembered the armament of the alien ship and decided that perhaps other sentients had met. For the new inhabitants of New Earth it remained a first.

Jabari picked a location that he thought suitable. They would meet at the spot David and the bug-lemurs first met. No weapons would be allowed—and that included Jabari and his men. The Marine didn't like it but realized the Prosimians would be four hundred klicks from their own weapons, if as he said, they truly left their weapons behind. Justice Hammond declined an invitation. He may have to rule on New Earth's participation in any agreements and attending the meeting might compromise his judgment.

Maria sat behind the pilot as the shuttle approached New Earth. She keyed the mike, "Erik, with their armament, these beings could blow us all over space. And they want to talk. They can see we pose no military threat. But, I think they have a problem and are looking for answers. A very big problem."

CHAPTER EIGHTEEN
The Meeting

With more diplomacy than Maria had credited Jabari with, he'd put chairs for Orion personnel. For the guests, on an elevated piece of land, he'd placed mats like the native bug-lemurs used when they visited the New Earth compound.

A table sat between the two groups but a few feet from either.

The *First*, about a foot taller and heavier than the native bug-lemurs, but about six inches shorter than the humans, walked more upright and with more assurance, undoubtedly due to the greatly reduced carapace.

Large, black, round eyes locked on Maria, Ann and their scribe following every move. A shortened muzzle, shorter than those of the bug-lemurs, gave more of a chimpanzee look to the larger aliens' faces. Large by lemur standards, their head size approached that of a human. Their exposed body parts were covered in distinctive grey, white, black, and brown coloring with light well-groomed fur. They were magnificent to look at. Form-fit one-piece garments made up the clothing style. All wore the same color uniforms, with symbols probably for rank affixed to the shoulders. This group could pass for a meeting of royals. Maybe they were.

The *First* made a show of laying aside pads they'd brought and using those the Marines had provided. The first move of trust taken, they sat and waited.

Now, Maria should reciprocate.

Through the artificial interpreter, she asked if they would join her at the table.

A surprised look came over the *First* and several looked at each other. Prosimian facial anatomy apparently lacked the muscles of humans and therefore they had fewer expressions that told anything about what they were feeling. In fact, Maria could make no judgments from the few visible nuances. Like the smaller bug-lemurs, arm and hand gestures seemed to be an important part of their communication. Maria and her contingent had to find some way to put the conversation more on the electronic level. Hand gestures clearly were not transmittable. Without a doubt, what she needed was a more intimate knowledge of the language. To avoid a false step, a great deal of care would be required.

Clearly, there was some confusion.

Maria said, "We can move the table to accommodate your seating." She motioned to the Marines standing some twenty-five meters away.

First seemed pleased with the gesture. Sitting on the ledge placed them a few inches above the humans and that seemed to please them as well—they even sat a little taller.

Maria signaled her group to bring chairs and take their place at the table. Apparently, the Prosimians saw this as a move of deference, their look this time easily interpreted as a satisfied smug.

119

Once all were seated, Maria used the artificial language interpreter. "I am Maria Presk, Captain of the spaceship Orion and leader of this settlement. Who do I have the privilege of addressing? Who speaks for you?"

The *First* sitting in the center reached for the microphone. His three-fingered hand and opposable thumb deftly swept the instrument from the table. With guttural sounds, he spoke. Hearing the Prosimians then the artificial language seemed a contradiction. "I am *Cslic*, Prime of the long flyer, *Msminc*. We are the *Rshcococ* and the *First*. Our home world is *Gsnicic*, some fourteen light turns distant." That was the best the AI could do on names leaving doubt in Maria's mind that they were even close.

"These are my subordinates." He made a gesture toward the five sitting beside him.

After a lot of effort to fine-tune the translator, Maria said, "Prime and First, I fear we may not be able to speak your names. The human tongue is limited. May we give your names the human sound?"

Cslic gave what amounted to a nod and looked at his subordinates with what could only be another smug acknowledgement.

Maria said, "*Cslic*, you will be called Selic. Only time and practice would tell either side how well we're doing. Your ship *Msminc* will be Majestic, your race, *Rshcococ* and the *First*, Rococo and the First, and the home world, *Gsnicic*, Genesis." They had a long way to go.

Maria told of her groups origins, their one hundred forty three year journey and watched as the Rococo and the First eyes noticeably enlarged. They huddled for a few seconds and with what seemed greater interest turned to the matters at hand.

For the next hour or so, both sides worked to refine the translator results. It was frustrating at times but generally, it went remarkably well.

The beast Amon Isaacs killed some weeks ago figured prominently in an experiment the Prime had underway. Sensors in critical places told them something had happened, bringing the long flyer, Majestic, back to Usgac. In addition, the Rococo were involved in some kind of mining.

Maria apologized for the problem her people had created.

Selic nodded—not a gesture he'd picked up from the humans.

Jabari approached the group with refreshments, having learned the bug-lemurs preference for food and drink. Maybe Selic and his party had different palates. He, Maria assumed her counterpart male, sipped the drink, raised the plastic cup, and tossed down the entire contents.

Selic called for a short recess. Along with the subordinates, he huddled for what seemed a very intense discussion. All of the Rococo party joined the hushed but heated debate, which ended after a good five minutes. Selic returned to the table, along with his group and they resumed their elevated pad seats.

Maria invited Jabari to join Ann and the scribe.

Selic made a noise Maria took as clearing his throat. He pulled the mike close and said, "Perhaps you can help us. You have the knowledge of long life."

Somewhat wary, Maria said, "Of course. We'll help in any way we can."

Again, he cleared his throat. "We, the Rshcococ and the First, are a dying race."

Maria gasped and the scribe queried the interpreter. "Did you say dying?"

Selic nodded but said nothing. His eyes, as were his followers, remained riveted on Maria.

Striving to hold her emotions, she managed, "How? From what?" She wasn't about to insult them by saying how healthy they appeared. They were well enough to travel in space, work at ore extraction and establishing a genetics field test.

"We, Rococo and the First don't know. Our," they used a word she couldn't pronounce and the interpreter could only estimate meant scientist, "have worked for many turns (years) to find the solution and failed." He stood. "We started a reparative process—Usgac is one of twelve colonies involved in an attempt to regenerate our race. The life form you see here represents what we were thousands of years ago. We are trying to accelerate their growth into the Rococo we have become. It is our only hope."

He stopped. This must have been difficult for him although his face never showed signs of stress.

Selic spoke again. "Perhaps with this knowledge of long life, you can help the Rococo and the First." He sat down, still no emotion on his face or any of his subordinates.

Maria let out a small gasp. Apparently, the Rococo and the First have come to grips with their dilemma. Her mind raced. Two hundred ten years ago, she started Advanced Bio-Yield to do DNA research. And it had taken her and her band to this. She learned the Rococo hibernated every few weeks, explaining the dormant period they'd witness earlier. She shook her head, not in dismay but at the irony. Out of all the thoughts, she'd had about how this meeting would go nothing as bizarre as this had entered her mind.

CHAPTER NINETEEN
The Helping Hand

"We're starting from absolute zero." Maria eyes swept the conference room. All of the original Advanced Bio-Yield scientists were there except David. She didn't mention him. Her son Michael had become a key part of their strategy sessions.

"Well folks, that is about where we were a little over hundred seventy years ago. We should be able to handle this in a lot less time and with fewer dead ends. These beings DNA and gene structure will be different than ours, but our science should be able to unravel and understand both. They should fit nicely. "

She laid down strict medical protocols for the research to see if they could save the *Rococo and the First* dropped sometime before. If Orion's scientist could identify and isolate the gene-analogue responsible for the Rococo problem, coming up with a cure would be infinitely easier. Rococo insisted on their scientists being in on every detail, something Maria had tried to avoid. Without the training to understand what Orion's people were doing, the odds of them gaining any useful information were nil. She did learn the Rococo used the residents of Usgac as breeding stock—the beast was to challenge them mentally and physically. This had been going on for over seventy earth years but the offspring of this coupling was problematic, some progress but many more failures. Those few results from these unions hadn't advanced the species.

She shook her head in disbelief. "How in the hell could these beings have FTL travel, hulls made of material a thousand time stronger than anything we know about and have done nothing about investigating their own DNA? This is beyond my comprehension.

Ann had her own concerns. "I don't want to seem mercenary, but what do we get out of this. Any swapping of technology? That FTL is a pretty big deal."

Erik spoke, "I suspect the Rococo didn't develop the stuff they've got. Most likely got it through captured equipment or treaty. What we need is the FTL drive, metallurgy, and weapons information."

Maria said, "We're okay. I got agreements on all that in the first session. In fact, if case any of you haven't noticed, David hasn't been around Orion lately. According to Selic, David has already improved the efficiency of about everything we're expecting them to give us. You're right Erik. These guys haven't invented anything. Just from watching them, I suspect they're not that great in combat either. If we're unlucky, we'll find all that out in due time. Right now, we've got work to do. Everyone remember to keep on your toes. Don't be antagonistic, but alert."

That afternoon, Maria learned the Rococo had ordered a transport from Genesis due to arrive in about a week. Onboard were Rococoans ranging in age from very young to elderly as well as fetuses. They were to be her and Roberto's source for study.

After the second ship's arrival with the test group, the effort to unravel the mystery behind the Rococo infertility and high newborn death rate progressed amazingly well. As expected, the Rococo presence in the labs proved to be a hindrance but Maria couldn't throw them out even though temptation abounded.

Years earlier, Martin gladly accepted following David to learn all the engineering he could. That had gone on well for a few decades and Grabel became a brilliant engineer although it seemed he always lived in David's shadow. With the arrival of Rococo and the First, that all changed. The opportunities for someone with David's engineering talents soared with the new technology.

"Eric," Maria somberly noted. "Our old problem has resurfaced. David is again in his element and Martin Grabel is an unhappy man."

Despite David's infirmity, Selic, Prime of the Rococo, soon realized the valuable contribution the savant made almost daily. David went over every new technology with a fervor and dedication that was impossible to deny. Majestic's crewmembers became his greatest supporters, even though he never acknowledged their presence. The Rococo opened up all of Majestic, denying David nothing. David paid special attention to the gravonic engines, learning but never tinkering.

Martin quickly became second fiddle, something that didn't play well with the arrogant scientist. The mathematician did have the presence of mind to download all the engineering data, including design and calculations into Orion's computers. Orion's techs immediately began dissecting and digesting every detail. Maria had no idea how this would play out. It bore watching.

David remained an enigma. The Rococo treated him as special, as if he operated at a level most would call divine. To them, David could do no wrong, not that he would have reason to. Still to everyone's distress, if he needed something, he never asked but simply got it—no one stood in his way.

Six weeks after the first meeting, Erik walked into the lab and motioned Maria to the conference room. After pouring each a cup of homegrown coffee, he casually sat opposite her, elbows on the table. "Looks like the Rococo have a number of alliances and a few enemies as well. Kinda like we guessed, these guys are not very good warriors. Seems they get protection from a race called the *Pagmok* if we can believe the interpreter. A real tough bunch but not the originators of the technology. The *Pagmok* are the fighters in the area. It's a symbiotic relationship. The Rococo provides minerals and gets protection in return."

"And the technical?"

"Comes from a race that pretty much seems to stay behind the scenes. They design and make the goods, then trade, sell, buy protection, whatever the market offers to whoever has the cash. And cash in this case can mean minerals. Rococo are owners of the largest deposit of unique and highly sought minerals in this part of the universe. And let's not overlook, someone had to put this coalition together and they will not think highly of our muscling in."

"And the techies are?"

"*Kalazecis*. You realize these are approximations based on our computer interpreter."

"Yes, we may be insulting them just speaking their names. Do you know where these guys hang out? Is their part of the universe off limits to us?"

"Rococo seems to believe that if we solve their problem, these two races'll welcome us. Biologic technology hasn't had a lot of attention paid to it in these parts. We're the techies in that area and it would appear our services could be very much in demand."

"Any recommendations on where we go from here?" asked Maria pouring a second cup.

"We wait. Even with FTL, it takes a while to cover some of these distances. Both the Pagmok and Kalazecis know of our presence. We're waiting to hear back, communications being no faster than the fastest ship. And I have no idea what the Pagmok and Kalazecis look like. Seems the Rococo have no need for pictures of their allies."

Erik, ever vigilante said, "Captain with your permission, I'd like to place a few early warning satellites in orbit. Three of them. One at ten million klicks, another at one hundred million and one at five hundred million. Make them passive and transmitting to us on a tight beam."

"Agreed," said Maria. One ship had come in system without Orion knowing. Not that it made a lot of difference. Orion lacked the ability to take any meaningful action. "Would you have the OD prepare something for me to tell our people? Can't keep them in the dark." She stood her eyes stared beyond the lab.

"How's the research for the Rococo going," Erik asked.

"Really quite well. It's just a logical step-by-step process. No shortcuts. I'd estimate another three weeks and Roberto should have completely identified their DNA-analogue structure and we've already isolated some likely culprits. Could be very promising."

Maria studied Erik who at that moment seemed to be somewhere else. "Something still bothering you? Care to let me in on it?"

Erik took a swig then lowered his cup. "This is all too benign. It may be no more than the laid-back attitude of the Rococo but I haven't convinced myself of that. I find it hard to believe that as the new kids on the block, we'll be accepted with open arms. Too many self-interests here to let me think that."

"So, what should we do about it? Or maybe I should be asking what have you done about it?"

He pointed his finger at her. "You know me all too well. With David and Martin's help, Orion is arming—at least adding weapons. Ones that don't require the exotic metal. The hull is the same deal except a lot more material is required. We need processed metal from Genesis or at the least raw ore before we can build a structure that can withstand these kinds of weapons and FTL travel. Same goes for building FLT engines. Can't go that fast without all three being a lot stronger and able to withstand higher temperatures. A lot higher."

"And?" As Maria spoke, Ann and Martin joined those taking seats on either side of Erik.

"Still talking to them. Seems they don't have a problem with our having the material but they need Pagmok transport barges to move it. They, the Rococo, don't have a fleet for moving much of anything. Again, we're back to them relying almost entirely on the Pagmok. Seems the Pagmok do both the fighting and heavy lifting. Based on What Erik just told me about the Kalazecis, they may not take kindly to our processing any ore."

"Why don't the Pagmok just take over the Rococo planet? Eliminate the middle guy," asked Martin.

Maria answered, "As I see it, they have the best of both worlds as it now stands. The Rococo mine the material and everything goes to the Pagmok. Why would the Pagmok want to have to man, feed and guard subjected miners when they can get what they want without any hassle?"

Erik swirled the coffee in his cup. "I think we'd better prepare for the worst. The Pagmok are warriors. We've no way of knowing how they'll react to our presence."

Maria opined, "I agree, but how do we prepare? We've no weapons, no armament, no army and only two fighters that I suspect are completely inadequate, suicide for the pilots. What do you suggest?"

For a long time, his eyes locked on Maria, his face totally expressionless. He cleared his throat, "When we left Earth, I truly believed we had the opportunity to leave behind some of mankind's worst traits. Maybe I'm idealistic or worse, naive. Now, it seems we've walked in on someone else's galactic war. The Rococo ship armament isn't just to look good or mimic the Pagmok. It's because they have enemies. I suspect when the Pagmok get here, we'll see some serious space battle equipment…

Maria, cup in both hands, her lips tightly pressed said, "You're going to have to help me. I don't see where this is taking us."

"We still have the remaining nuclear material we brought on board in Mexico for starting the Casimir engines. It wouldn't take much to create a bomb. In fact, I could make a dozen or so very small but powerful bombs. One of those shoved up a spaceships tail and everyone would take immediate notice of us."

Not a soul moved. Only the far off everyday noises of Orion penetrated the quiet.

Maria quietly said, "Erik, you've never failed me. And I include this time in my assessment. But—"

"No buts," said Erik, his voice forceful. "We don't know what may be ahead of us. I suspect Pagmok warships will make the Rococo's look like a peashooter. Maria, we are up against races that with one shot can destroy us and not leave a trace—no one will ever know we were here. I've studied the weapons on Majestic. Any one of their photon energy weapons could take us out and they have twenty installed and operational. And that's as good as it gets. If I were the Pagmok, I damned sure wouldn't give the Rococo my best weapons."

Macon, standing in the doorway said, "You still have to deliver the weapon. Our little fighters wouldn't stand much of a chance of getting that close to a battleship."

"Not so," said Erik. That brought all eyes toward him and they were frightened questioning eyes maybe even hopeful looking for an answer. "Our fighters are reinforced carbon fiber. The Rococo's detection systems can't see us. We've tried it. They're blind as hell against radar absorbing surfaces. And we've got the best. Probably because they need metals for their faster-than-light ships, they never seem to have considered composites." That again suggested that the First's technology had not been one of discovery and development but had leapfrogged, never going through incremental stages. In other words, someone gave everything technical to them.

That didn't seem to ease the tension. Everyone knew if shooting broke out, that Orion could not possibly win.

Maria said, "There has to be a better way. We must find some way to take our place as a nation state." A general nodding of heads confirmed the majority agreed.

"Erik quietly spoke, "I totally agree. I do not intend to start a fight that we cannot win. That would be beyond stupid. It would be suicidal. All I'm saying is we must be prepared. At least with the bombs, if someone refused to negotiate and threatened us, we'd have a response. And bear in mind, their mindset should already be that we have some forms of superior technology. Otherwise, the Rococo wouldn't be asking for our help. We can use that. It may be no more than a threat in the end, but it may also give us the edge we need to survive a challenge."

Maria asked, "How long would it take to produce the bomb?" Just the way she asked the question put an even more ominous touch to the word.

Erik, without looking at anyone answered, "I have only to build a trigger and assemble the devices. About a week."

Maria pulled her com unit out, and asked Mathew Hammond, still head of their only court, to join them. She couldn't express her sense of irony that everything she'd done to save one race might just go into destroying another. Erik was so right. She had been naive.

Five minutes later and seated next to Maria, Judge Hammond listened intently.

His voice chocked with emotion he said, "I never thought I'd hear myself say this, but I agree with Erik. We must defend ourselves with whatever we have available. And God have mercy on our souls." The judge's ashen face streaked with tears, but his resolve remained firm.

* * * *

Everyone within earshot jumped when the bridge claxon sounded, alerting the crew that something had appeared on radar.

Ann Bartlett had the bridge. It wasn't necessary to summon anyone as Maria, Erik, and Bhani Patel were all at the plot screen almost as quickly as she was.

"What've you got," asked Maria.

Ann said, "Don't know for sure. But it is big and fast. Lots of power. It's shedding delta v at an incredible rate."

"Some kind of warship," Erik said. He quickly recognized the questioning looks and added, "Only makes sense. It takes as much power to stop as it does to go. And no one would put that kind of power on a transport or cruise ship."

That didn't ease any of the building apprehension. Maria pressed the com switch. "Who do we have on board the Rococo Majestic right now?"

A long pause then—"David."

Stoically, Erik said, "Permission to deploy the fighters."

Maria knew the fighters stood no real chance if they did engage and that any effort at a peaceful resolution could be wrecked with her next order. "Granted."

CHAPTER TWENTY
The Confrontation

"We're translating the Rococo transmission now. It's a Pagmok ship," the astrogator announced to a silenced bridge. "We're picking it up."

Maria punched the com key." Ann, Martin, how long before you can break down the Pagmok and translate?"

"Shouldn't be too long. With everything we've learned about the Rococo, maybe five minutes," Ann said.

A slight smile touched Maria's lips. She turned to Erik. "It seems to me, your statement about us being the techies as far as the Rococo are concerned could be used to our advantage with the Pagmok right now."

"My thoughts exactly," he responded. "In fact Captain, that may be our strongest weapon. I think we should become the strategists and let the tactical be implied. Their imagination might be our biggest asset. Let's play on it."

The com came alive. "We can transmit an opening message in Pagmok and Rococo. Got any idea what you want to say?"

Maria turned to the astrogator, "How far away are they?"

"Little over half a million klicks."

Maria realized Orion's ability to translate and broadcast in Pagmok in such a short time should give their new arrivals some pause for concern about who they're up against now. She jotted a message and read it to Ann.

She came back immediately. "You're tough boss lady. If you want the maximum effect, we can broadcast your voice and picture. Live."

"Give me about a minute." Maria stepped off the bridge to her day cabin and quickly slipped on her parade tunic, grabbed a visor cap, and returned to the bridge.

"Open the com to all hands, ship and dirtside." She adjusted her tunic, smoothed her hair, put on, and adjusted the visor. "Let's do it. Just the top half." She grinned to herself—her jeans anything but regulation or captain-like.

She pulled herself to full height, took a deep breath, and relaxed letting the air slowly escape.

"Vessel approaching Usgac." She had decided to use Rococo names realizing they would be less threatening and more understandable. "This is the ship Orion. We are here on a peaceful mission to assist the *Rococo and the First*. If your intentions are peaceful, cut your speed by half and orbit at your present altitude. The *Rococo and the First* and Orion look forward to your answer and meeting you."

Erik questioned with a wry grin, "Wonder what the Rococo are thinking about now?"

The new arrival response came almost instantly, but without picture. Orion's translation was virtually instantaneous. "This is the Pagmok cruiser Tusgan. You are in Pagmok space without permission. Stand down to be boarded."

Absolute silence settled over the bridge as the crew waited to see how their Captain would respond.

Nothing had prepared Maria for this kind of situation. During her lab career, she'd maneuvered to avoid confrontation, claiming her work always came first. That possibility no longer existed and she had no place to hide.

Maria thought for a long moment, and then took her place before the camera. "I had hoped this would be easier. Looks like the chess game has started."

She faced the camera and signaled them to record. "Pagmok ship Tusgan. I repeat. We do not want a fight. We are here to help the *Rococo and the First*. However, any effort to board us we will deal with in the harshest manner. Again, set your orbit at half a million kilometers. Do not come any closer." She ended the message. "Transmit."

Applause erupted behind her as the crew celebrated the stance.

Well, some of them did.

"Captain?" Macon questioned. "You've given them an ultimatum. What if they don't comply? We can't stand any kind of ordnance hitting Orion. They can and will destroy us with little more than pea shooters."

Maria didn't answer the Doctor directly. "Erik, signal the Rococo. Tell them to get off their butts. They know we're about to solve their dying out problem and if they want the answers, they'll stop the Pagmok where they are."

More than determination tinged her voice. The crew saw the toughness they had seen in other difficult situations—a few had seen it during the mutiny.

"Aye, Ma'am."

Erik carried out the instructions. Quiet settled over the bridge as, after a few exchanges with the Rococo ship, anger laced his voice. "If you want to stay alive, you'll delay your hibernation long enough to tell the Pagmok not to try to board us. That isn't going to happen. Tell them we are peaceful, but when provoked we have weapons they can't imagine. So, tell them and do it now."

Erik flipped the com switch. "Bastards, want to go to sleep for a few days." He shook his head in disgust then at the wide-eyed group gathered on the bridge. "Shit, if you're going to bluff, you can't go halfway. This is high stakes poker, folks. I'm good at it—damned good and so is your Captain."

Maria could only hope so and flashed back to Erik's demeanor when he faced Bassett on the tarmac at Bahia Los Angeles before they left Mexico. She had no doubt he would have shot the CIA agent and his men if provoked any farther. He wasn't bluffing then. Even with his nuclear arsenal, she couldn't tell if he bluffed now. Maria couldn't make much of a fight and couldn't run. What they had had been out to the test.

Silence reigned over the bridge where over a dozen people had gathered.

The astrogator said, "Majestic's transmitting."

Ann had the translator on line. "They're telling the Pagmok to hold their position. That Orion is a friend of the *Rococo and the First* and can be theirs."

"An appeal to the sense of cooperation. Something mankind never seemed to learn." Macon said.

Maria often disagreed with the Doctor but this wasn't the time or place. Besides, they'd had this dispute before. Roberto Macon was a pacifist and by his own admission, a coward. Gramina Fiora, his wife was the closest he'd ever come to having any guts.

They waited. For over a standard hour, not so much as static came from the com.

"They're slowing. Looks like they're establishing an orbit," said the astrogator.

An exhilarating cheer of relief resounded around the bridge. Maria breathed a quiet sigh herself.

Erik just cocked his head. "Told you we were good."

"Radar blip. Majestic has launched a shuttle. Looks like it's headed for the Pagmok ship."

"Let's hope they return with an olive branch," someone remarked.

"Yeah," came another response.

Maria knew these people would follow wherever she led. But they were scared, and rightfully so.

"Captain, this can't be right."

Ashen faced, the astrogator turned toward Maria, "I just received a tight beam message from Zhu Ling in one of the fighters. He says he's tucked in for the night. He's tailing the Rococo shuttle."

Maria eyebrows flinched up and she paused for a moment. "Flight Captain Ling has orders to tag along with the Rococo to the Pagmok ship. When he gets there, he'll hack their computer. We need to know as much as possible about them. Zhu will return the same way."

What went unsaid, as everyone knew, was the danger involved. If the Pagmok discovered Ling, they certainly would attack him and most likely Orion as well. Maria considered the odds against making it back to Orion so high, she wouldn't order anyone on the flight. Zhu Ling had volunteered.

"Majestic's shutting down. So's the shuttle. Looks like they're going to sleep for a couple of days," the astrogator reported.

"Makes sense," said Erik. "It'll take at last that long for the shuttle to get to the Pagmok ship so the Rococo can do their regeneration."

* * * *

Three days later, the Rococo shuttle docked at an external airlock amidships of the Tusgan. Zhu Ling would have much preferred a lock closer to the aft part of the ship away from the heavily crewed area. He had monitored every Rococo radio conversations with the Pagmok since leaving Majestic. When the Tusgan computer took control of the Rococo's landing, Zhu tied his computer in, using minimal power and trusting no one would notice the added signal strength his entry caused.

Actually, he counted on them letting down their guard since the Rococo had convinced the Pagmok they were in a superior position and that Orion wasn't a threat.

Fortunately, the Rococo never mentioned Orion had little armament. The two day nap didn't hurt a thing either. Actually worked in Orion's favor adding to the time the Pagmok and Orion had to get used to each other's presence.

* * * *

Zhu held the fighter directly above but less than a meter away from the shuttle. His timing had to be perfect. The fighter had less than a second in which to grab onto the shuttle or the docking would not mask the noise of his ship attaching. Using maneuvering jets, he positioned the fighter above the shuttle and lowered the craft to within a few centimeters. Only his mark one eyeball could handle this. When he saw the mooring clamps extend, he fired his maneuvering jets, forcing the fighter against the shuttles' hull. Held fast by his magnetic grapplers, he waited. If discovered, it would only be minutes before someone moved against him.

The Rococo shuttle's escape hatch closed, echoing through his ship.

Time was of the essence and immediately he hacked the Tusgan's computer —which were, fortunately, identical to the Rococo systems and like those systems, completely without advanced security systems. Everything Orion's engineers had seen of the alien technology was offensive and nothing very sophisticated for defense.

Slowly, carefully, he installed an algorithm Martin had developed to transfer data to his computer anytime the Pagmok computer moved data internally. If this mask didn't work, the Pagmok would know it in seconds and he'd be dead meat.

* * * *

Maria didn't expect to hear any time soon from Ling, thinking he'd leave as he entered, in the shuttle's wake. Instead, he'd piggybacked until at safe distance from the Pagmok released the magnetic hold on the shuttle and drifted, allowing the gap between vessels to increase for almost a standard day. Ling fired his thrusters pointing the fighter toward Orion.

How lucky can you get? Zhu Ling knew that sometimes a little luck can go a long way. And knew he'd just had his share and maybe then some.

A great collective sigh went up from the bridge as Ling settled his fighter into Orion's hanger bay. Maintenance crews removed the mainframe computer and took it to the mother ship's lab. The fighter pilot successfully downloaded virtually every program and file on board the Pagmok ship. Discovery would have meant instant death, certainly for the fighter and most likely for Orion. But in this case, information was power. Knowing something about the Pagmok, their society, the fighting capabilities of the Pagmok ship Tusgan, could give Maria what she needed to make sure they had a chance against the heavily armed Pagmok.

CHAPTER TWENTY-ONE
A new Strategy

"Damn, they're ugly," Ann said. Assembled in the engineering lab they'd accessed some of the Pagmok files Ling brought back.

"Is that the head guy?" another voice asked.

That brought no answer.

Maria asked, "What do you make of them Roberto?"

"Carbon based. Reptilian. Carnivorous, meat eaters," the Doctor responded.

"Meat eaters? I hope you mean like *we* are," said Maria.

"Doubtful," Macon who had expanded his skills to include a detailed knowledge of biology responded. "Those teeth are meant to tear and swallow, not chew."

Someone said, "Look at the size of that thumb—it's as big as a tablespoon. Three fingered also. The thing resembles a chameleon with teeth."

For some time, Maria and her staff studied the screen. Some moved to other stations and pulled up additional data. The Pagmok was about the same height as humans, head shaped much like the Rococo, mouth and resulting dietary habits certainly different. Even though it had shark-like teeth, its head and jaws were small enough to suggest wasn't the hunter-killer most were imagining. Its nose was no more than a pair of slits and eyes not as large as the Rococo's dominated its face. From the pictures, it appeared to walk upright with reasonable agility. Its skin was smooth—more like a frog than snake or alligator and a pale green in color. Maria could spot no noticeable vestiges of hair. They apparently need a humid atmosphere again suggesting an aqueous ancestry. Estimated weight—sixty to seventy kilos.

Maria said, "I assume we're looking at the male of the species. Anyone seen anything that might look different enough to be a female?" She added, "I wonder what the Pagmok consider food?"

Momentarily, that stopped all conversation. Thoughts of what the Pagmok dinner look like triggered imaginations and a few shudders around the bridge.

Erik studied the detailed plans of the Pagmok ship and said, "No match. They outweigh us by more than one million tons. And outgun us. Our peashooters against energy weapons, lasers, and ion canons. Over sixty weapons stations. One shot from their smallest weapon and we'd vaporize. This ship could handle some serious fighting."

Hours later, Erik, still working alone at a newly installed but vacant armaments station, came across the critical information. "Seems the Rococo's friends are kept in check by the Kalazecis. They're the suppliers of most of the foodstuffs as well as the technology. Kinda like an intellectual dog pile with Rococo on the bottom and Kalazecis on top. But then, a better way of putting it may be that the Rococo have the minerals, the Pagmok are the warriors who keep bad guys away, and the Kalazecis are the brains driving it all. In fact, there's a Kalazecis officer on this ship. He must have some say-so. According to this, every Pagmok vessel has a representative of the Kalazecis Emperor on board. And, every representative is a direct descendant of the Emperor."

Maria turned to Ann who was just entering the bridge. "Find Bhani. You two pull together as much info as you can on the Pagmok. Roberto and Fiora, dig into everything about their social structure of both groups. There may not be much in the database, but put together what you can. Erik, find Martin, and the two of you work on the armament and other technical aspects. Have Michael come to the bridge. We'll work on the Kalazecis. There may not be much in these files, but it would seem our getting along in this sector of space depends on what kind of relationship we can establish with them."

One hour later, Ann stuck her head through the bridge hatchway and said, "Got a picture of the Kalazecis."

She stepped to the plot table and hit a few icons.

"Well," Eric said. "That's better than the Pagmok. At least they have teeth similar to ours. Omnivores. We're faced with it all, vegetarians, carnivores and omnivores."

The Kalazecis' almost effeminate heads resembled a smaller version of UFO alien sketches that proliferated on earth in the mid twentieth century. A small, almost indiscernible nose, mouth no more than a slit, skin that appeared smooth and eyes resembling Earth Orientals. *Thai* Maria thought. But the likeness stopped there. A slender but wiry body that looked anything but frail. Four digits adorned their hands, one on each of two arms made useful with an opposable thumb. On their heads, she saw visible hair patterns similar to humans.

Later that day, Maria, Erik, and Ann walked down the corridor away from the bridge and entered the wardroom. Whether it was the long hours or concerns each of them had about how their world had changed in the previous few days, they looked bedraggled.

Michael Rohm poured each a cup of coffee and took a seat at a table.

Distantly, Ann said, "I'm afraid we've become involved in a world, I'm sure that's not the right word, but anyhow, we're not prepared for any of this."

Martin and Bhani joined them.

She continued, "We've got nothing to compare with anything we've seen."

Erik, a tease in his voice, said, "Dear wife, I really hate to disagree with you, especially in public." His attitude anything but apologetic and everyone knew he had drawn Ann into his little show for the benefit of all.

His act drew smiles including one from her.

The levity provided a welcome break in the near fatalistic attitude that seemed to be taking hold. "But, I think we have the best weapon. I just hope we get the chance to bring it to bear."

"Your nukes?" she asked.

"Well, those of course. But no, dear wife—I'm referring to our intellect. We know the Rococo and Pagmok are not Mensa material and if the Kalazecis couldn't fix the Rococo problem, maybe they're just not as smart as we've built them up to be. Smart, probably, yes, we'll give them that. Match us—maybe. I'm not ready to sell us down the river."

Maria said, "I'm betting they're as curious about us as we are about them. And they don't know what are capabilities are."

Erik said, "Possible. Looks like we're going to find out."

Maria's com unit strapped to her waist came to life.

"Maria…"

She recognized the alarm in Roberto's voice.

"You'd better get down here, to sickbay—and hurry."

Fearing the worst—that something terrible had happened to David—Maria launched herself toward the hatch. In less than two minutes, she pushed her way passed three techs into sickbay.

David stood in the middle of the room leaning on a gurney, shaking violently, his body soaked with sweat, his face a wondering mask of despair.

She managed a furtive stare at Roberto, who held a hypodermic syringe. The Doctor's mouth hung open, his gaze riveted on her estranged husband.

"What's going on?" The pain in her voice startled the crew standing around paralyzed by whatever they'd seen.

A trace of the crooked smile Maria had missed for so long touched David's face.

She grabbed at the doorjamb as David looked at her and acknowledged her presence, no recognition, just that he knew she was there.

David was fully conscious.

She choked back a sob. "David?" And could only repeat herself. "David? Is it you?"

Without realizing that she'd moved, she crossed the few feet separating them, reached out, and grasped her husband.

She got no sign of recognition but David's awareness of his surroundings and people around him surprised everyone.

Maria held his hand as if she'd never let go. She made no effort to hold back the tears. In fact, she welcomed them. Over one hundred forty years of pain and anguish flowed down her cheeks. After so many years, long-faded hope faded swelled renewed in her chest. She wanted desperately to believe but years of anguish cast a guard she couldn't turn loose.

Roberto and Maria eased David onto the gurney as Erik, Ann, Martin, Bhani, and Gramina stood nearby, almost afraid to believe what they were seeing. A crowd had gathered outside in the waiting room, each with the hope that this was for real and that a relapse wasn't the next surprise.

Roberto quickly sent them on their way.

David, confused and disoriented, searched from face to face. Maria clasped his hand to her breast. She turned to Roberto, "How? What happened?"

While checking David's life signs, Roberto related that when working the Rococo problem, it became apparent their cure would most likely be realized by regeneration. Essentially, the apoptosis and somatic cells had destroyed the germinal cells at an abnormal rate. That in itself focused the research. That's when it clicked. David's treatment would be similar.

Six weeks ago, he'd made up a concoction from David's brain tissue removed years ago and cryogenically preserved. Mixed with the regeneration solutions made for the Rococo, but modified to fit the human genome, he injected small, regular doses into David's brain. He'd kept his actions quiet in case it failed. After a few days, it became apparent something had happened. What, he couldn't say for sure. If it meant recuperation, how complete? However, it soon became evident David had regained some of the mental facility he'd lost years ago.

Today, they were looking at six weeks of remarkable brain regeneration. When Roberto noticed striking developments, he purposely kept David on the Rococo ship to give him time to acclimate, all the time sending him information on his past. Of course, his twenty-four/seven nurses had him under close guidance and protection.

"And if it had failed?" Erik asked.

Roberto answered, "I don't think anything would have changed as far as David is concerned."

Maria awoke the next morning in a ward bed, after having slept fitfully for only a few hours. For the next two days, she hardly left David's side. Michael, their ninety-year-old son, returned to his botany laboratory accepting that he remained just another strange face to his father.

* * * *

Erik sat at the bridge plot table reviewing translated Kalazecis data. Revelations about the Rococo, Pagmok, and Kalazecis piled up as the translator gained proficiency. The added transmissions filled many of the gaps that existed in their database but more importantly in their knowledge of the Kalazecis and Pagmok. On occasion, the translator would stop, obviously grinding away over a new word or use. He looked up as Maria stepped through the hatch.

Displaying a smile, Maria could only interpret as pleased, he asked, "Captain, how's David?"

"I really don't know, but I'm hopeful. I'm afraid to put too much into what's happened but my lord, Erik," she stopped to compose herself, "If this... if this works, if David has gotten better." She stopped again, "It needs some time and so do I."

"Understandable," he responded.

Maria took her seat in the captain's chair. "Anything new or exciting?"

"Everyone we can spare is translating and correlating all this information. Zhu Ling really cleaned out their computer. Can't tell how long it will take to complete the translation, but we should have a pretty good picture of what we're dealing with sometime today. The technical data is being fed directly to engineering so it's not involved in the correlation."

Maria stood, "Fine, let me know when you think we've got something to act on. I'll be in my day cabin trying to get some sleep."

"Aye Captain," Erik stood as she left the bridge. He still preferred the military protocol.

Seven hours later, Maria, awake in her bunk responded to the com.

"Captain, looks like another ship approaching. It's just outside our farthest satellite. I'm guessing, but based on in-bound signal strength, I'd say a million klicks beyond. From the information our boys downstairs are feeding us, it's a Kalazecis."

"ETA to in-system?" Bless Erik. His early warning system had already paid off.

"Don't know about their delta v but at current speed, about four days."

"Not very fast," said Maria. From a tactical position, that wasn't very smart.

"No, sir. Do you want me to signal any alerts?"

"No. Please ask my staff and Justice Hammond to meet me for breakfast in the wardroom, zero eight hundred."

An hour later, Maria walked into the meeting.

Erik looked up from scanning printouts. "Looks like the masters of this part of the galaxy are here to see us for themselves."

"So it seems," said Maria.

"Captain," Mathew Hammond said, "you seem rather casual about it. We'll soon have three alien ships standing off and us with little means to protect ourselves."

"My good Justice, I am very much aware that we have a very limited defense, no offense and I know of nothing that's going to change that."

Hammond quickly responded. "I didn't mean that as a criticism, Captain."

She quietly answered, "Yes you did, Mathew. And correctly so. You have every right to find out what I have in mind. What am I going to do about it?

"At the moment, nothing. I really don't want to cause panic in our own ranks." Maria remembered she'd earlier used staff instead of council and that she could have said population but ranks spurted out before she realized it. Military terms had become a more frequent part of her vocabulary. "I think raising an alarm this early would be a mistake. I prefer to announce to Orion and New Earth that the Kalazecis are about to pay us a visit."

Maria frowned at Erik. "Executive Officer, how many of those little bombs do we have available?"

"Ten." His eyes narrowed with the answer.

"Please send a fighter to the Rococo and the Pagmok, stealth of course, with four bombs. Plant one bomb on each ship. The fighter will remain with the Pagmok and when the Kalazecis' arrive, plant one on their hull."

"And the fourth?" asked Erik.

Without so much as a flick of a finger Maria said, "Have the fighter move off about five hundred thousand klicks, and place the bomb into a stationary orbit."

Erik stood exposing a broad grin. Before he could say anything, Martin jumped up. His voice was almost a scream. "You can't do that. Suppose they find out?"

Maria turned to the volatile mathematician and said, "You're right to be worried, Martin. However, if we are threatened, I plan to tell them about it. In fact, I plan to explode the orbiting bomb. Of course, after having done so, I'll also tell them there is a device like that attached to the hull of each one of their ships. And, just to be neighborly, I'll tell them specifically where they are located and that if any attempt is made to remove the bomb, it will detonate."

Ann looked at Erik then Maria and asked, "Haven't you ever wondered why the Kalazecis haven't been to Earth?"

Before either could answer, a crewman stuck his head through the door and handed Maria a folder.

It wasn't unusual for someone to pop into a meeting but this time, everyone waited to see or hear the contents. She opened the manila file, studied it for a few moments.

"Great timing. Seems the Kalazecis only recently got FTL. They've been busy conquering their own back yard. Also, 55 Cancri is on the far edge of their territory." She read further, "It appears the Kalazecis aren't aware of Earth's existence. They haven't looked in that direction. And they don't use anything aren't close to the frequencies used on Earth."

"Our being here will change all that," Erik said.

An ominous quiet settled over the group.

Eric stood, his face grim. "Yes sir. By your leave." Pagmok and Rococo bombs should be in place within the next eight hours and the orbital in another three or four. The Kalazecis, three or four hours after it achieves orbit."

CHAPTER TWENTY-TWO
The Third Alien

Martin again protested Maria's orders, calling them unilateral.

She held up her hand. Between that and a tug from Bhani, Grabel sat again, but clearly he was not ready to give up.

Maria leaned against the table. "Martin, you're rightfully concerned."

She moved her chair back from the table, stood and walked a little circle in front of the group. "Particularly if my maneuver doesn't work. But I think what we're faced with calls for extreme measures." She reached into a pile of papers Ann had left on the table and pulled out a manila folder. "Has Martin seen this?"

"No. He wasn't in the lab during the translation and compilation."

Maria, holding the folder said, "I'll not bother to read you the entire file. But it clearly shows the Kalazecis keep the Pagmok under control by controlling their food source. It seems the Kalazecis directly command worlds that offer a plethora of fertile land—and their home world is the best of the lot. In fact, the Kalazecis had designs on Cancri D. Only Pagmok intervention prevented the Rococo from becoming captives. One of the Kalazecis worlds has been used to raise a meat source, or at least what we call meat, exclusively for the Pagmok." She let that stand for a few seconds. "Meat that is made available to the Pagmok in abundant and never ending quantities. Some of the meat is what we would call animal and a natural food source." Again, she stopped, the delay clearly intended to drive home that she had more to say.

"In fact, the Kalazecis originally wanted to raise bug-lemurs as a food source. It would seem the Kalazecis had written this species off and are ready to make them the menu. That most likely explains why the Kalazecis hadn't made any effort to come up with a cure for the Rococo genetic failure."

His face pale, Martin reared back in his chair. "Do you know this to be fact?"

Maria slid the folder across the table.

Martin stared at but didn't touch it.

Her eyes intent, Maria looked about the wardroom studying each face. "It appears to be the Kalazecis position to let the Rococo die off—the sentient ones, anyway. Then they'll breed those on New Earth as an added food source for the Pagmok. Those same semi-sentient Rococo are capable of handling the mining."

She let that settle in for a moment and then said, "If the Kalazecis behave themselves, we should have nothing to fear. If not, we'll blow them to hell."

"And bring down their entire fleet on our heads," Grabel moaned.

"You could be right, Martin. However, it seems the Pagmok have warned the Kalazecis never to try to go around them and attack the Rococo bug-lemurs. It would appear things are not as rosy between the three as we first thought."

Someone quipped, "The Pagmok don't like the idea of having to work the mines."

"Not only that," Ann said, "The Pagmok vastly outnumber the Kalazecis. Like forty-to-one, even on their home world. Seems the Kalazecis have invited large numbers of Pagmok to do their work. At least the manual labor. Like farms and factories."

Macon said, "A revolt on the Kalazecis home world could mean their annihilation."

"Exactly" said Maria. "But we hope it never comes to that. If we can resolve this diplomatically, it's to our benefit. Remember it's either that or we may have to move on."

What went unsaid was that the humans had no other place to go.

Having had a taste of a world other than a space ship, staying and fighting was a sentiment that seemed to be gaining strength.

Erik's voice over the com cut the silence like a razor. "Fighter launched."

All heads turned as David entered the wardroom. Unsteadily, he headed for a seat. Maria quickly pulled one from the table and for the first time in more years than she could remember, he grinned and nodded to the group.

In a frail voice, he said to the startled gathering, "I can put together a few cannon, both energy and projectile, if that would help."

Maria had to contain her enthusiasm. "Do we have the materials on board that would stand up to the heat and forces?"

"No, but the planet has. And we can process it ourselves."

Maria paused for a moment. How would Martin take this? Right now, she didn't need to add to that problem but the prospect of having meaningful weapons ranked high on her need list. The temptation was too great to resist.

"Martin, you and Ann see to it that David has whatever he needs to get the job done. Spare nothing. This has priority over everything." She stared directly at Grabel as she spelled out what would happen. He sat rigid in the chair. Not a good sign.

"Who's in charge," fired back Martin.

Maria walked around the table and stopped at Grabel's chair. She sat against the table's edge; her feet crossed and eyes locked on Martin. Matters were reaching a point that she felt she couldn't spend time wet-nursing Martin—far more than his vanity was at stake. "It is utterly essential we be able to defend ourselves. If David can help, don't you think it's wise to move with absolute purpose to get this done?"

Martin didn't answer immediately and refused to look at Maria when he finally spoke. "Someone else should work with Ann. I have other things that need doing."

Maria didn't question him about the other work but said to Ann, "You're in charge. Make it happen. Whatever you need."

"People?" Ann asked.

Maria looked directly at Martin, "Whatever you need." Obviously, Martin's ego had gotten the better of him. And she'd have to deal with it. She turned to David. Every fiber in her body wanted to hold him but this wasn't the time or place. "Are you sure you're up to it?"

Again, the smile that stirred her soul touched his lips. He followed it with a nod.

Geologic analysis showed Cancri D had an ample supply of rare isotopes that can produce new and exotic materials, resources needed to process super-strength hulls and weapons. Kalazecis had a legitimate interest in the Rococo, maybe a different one for the Pagmok.

Over the next four days, the two shuttles made dozens of trips to the surface returning with ores mined as David directed. Pagmok data provided him with the specifications for processing the minerals.

Everything seemed to be going well—so well, Maria knew she should have suspected something bad was going to happen.

"Hey." Alarm edged the astrogator's voice. "One of our shuttles made an unscheduled departure and is headed toward the Pagmok ship."

Maria had just stepped onto the bridge. "O.D., hail the shuttle to return."

The Officer-of-the-Deck had only to motion the com operator.

Fingers flew over the consol. "Orion shuttle, you have no authorization to leave base. Return immediately."

David's quiet voice came quickly. "Don't worry. Be back shortly."

A cold shudder raced up and own Maria's spine. She had no way to stop him and could only wonder what possessed David. Why now? She had just gotten him back and… she had this dreaded fear control might slip from her grasp if it hadn't already.

Erik's voice came across the com. "Sorry Captain. I was busy in the other hanger when David took the shuttle."

"Any idea what he's up to?" She dreaded the answer.

"You're not going to believe this but he took soy mix and soy beans."

A puzzled look crossed Maria's face then she smothered a burst of laughter slightly tinged with fear. "David, you wonderful man. Always thinking. And so far ahead of the rest of us."

Puzzled looks appeared across the bridge as Erik commed, "Mind letting us in on the joke?"

Holding one hand against her chest, the other hand's fingers touched her lips as she said, "Erik, it's not a joke. David is going to try soy substitute meat on the Pagmok. He must be going to explain to the Rococo how to cultivate soybeans as a crop. He's showing both there may be a way out of their dilemma. Can you imagine the Pagmok eating tofu hot dogs, soy sausages, and soy bacon bits? My beautiful David."

One by one, laughter erupted on the bridge and one voice expressed the hopes of them all, "Let's hope this wins us some friends."

Even if the Pagmok favored ending their reliance on the Kalazecis, Maria didn't expect David's actions to change their habits any time soon. But it was an act of good faith. Of course, the Kalazecis most likely wouldn't see it that way. And rightfully so. That would be a problem.

* * * *

First Contact

Two days later, the huge Kalazecis ship took up orbit fifty thousand klicks from the Pagmok. Orion's lidar showed a vessel, most likely a shuttle, leaving the Pagmok Tusgan for the new arrival. Everyone on Orion knew their fighter would be in the shuttles electronic shadow and hopefully undetected. Orion could only wait.

Martin stayed busy translating communications between the Pagmok and Kalazecis vessels. The Kalazecis, apparently satisfied with their superiority, had shown little concern and no panic with the newcomers' arrival. But they weren't complacent either, having set battle conditions long before entering orbit. This ship outsized the Pagmok with three times the tonnage and armament—over ten times what Orion carried.

What ability Orion had to defend itself was minimal, but with the armaments David had developed and Erik's nukes, the human ship was quickly becoming more deadly.

CHAPTER TWENTY-THREE
The Face Off

Maria pushed David's trek to the Pagmok ship to the back of her mind. For the moment, she could do nothing to help him even if he needed her. She brought her attention back to the thirty or so assembled bodies.

Her command staff and the civilian hierarchy, plus anyone wandering by, crowded the conference room.

"Well, I didn't expect everyone to go dumb on me," she said with a trace of humor. I'll ask again, culturally, who are we? We are getting a very good glimpse of three races and I've never given a second thought to how we must look to these beings.

"Who are we? We came from Earth. We are long-lived, at least for the time being and by the standards of our kind. We don't really know if this aging is sustainable over repeated generations. We have no idea of our visitors' life spans. We may not be unusual in that regard."

Bhani finally broke the silence, "Captain," she too had taken to using the military title since the Pagmok had arrived—maybe a sign Orion's people were rallying around her in case shooting started. Or maybe it just meant they were frightened and turning to her for some kind of assurance. "I can only speak for myself. But I need a little time to think about this. Like you, I've not given a moment of thought to who we are. I might suggest we hold gab sessions to kick this a few times and see what materializes."

Maria nodded. "Excellent idea. Bhani, would you coordinate these get-to-gathers? Try to sum up your conclusions, if any, following each session."

The group broke and Maria headed for her day cabin. As she neared the door, her com squawked to life. "Captain, David's shuttle is on the way back."

He'd only been gone slightly over an hour.

Maria detoured to the hangar.

A few minutes later, the shuttle and David anchored safely in the cavernous bay.

A nod greeted her as David stepped from the shuttle. "Permission to come aboard," he said.

She cocked her head. "Even though you left without it, you're welcome back." The two hugged.

He gently pushed her back. Haltingly, David said, "You need to understand that my memories of you and everyone are nonexistent. I have no recollection of anything, our marriage, how I got here, nothing, only my engineering. I guess I don't know who I am. Doctor Macon has been very helpful and of course, my nurses never stopped telling me more stuff than I could absorb. Some of it feelings, relationships and I don't have any for anyone. I have met my son whom I don't know at all."

Maria stepped back and silently admonished herself. She should have thought this through. Of course, he had no recollection of his past. She quickly realized as much as it hurt, she had to let him go. Both would have to start over. In that instant she also grasped that the results might turn out entirely differently than they had when they'd been two people on Earth.

As they walked toward the passageway she said, "Yes, you have a son, we have a son. He's a grown man now and a very good botanist. Maybe the best I've seen. And a pretty darn good military strategist."

At this point in his recovery, that meant nothing to David. He smiled. "The Pagmok really like the soy meat. Don't think they'd want a steady diet of nothing but, but as a staple it appears to suit their taste."

She hugged him and he seemed pleased. "Let's put this on ship-wide intercom and dirtside as well so you tell everyone. I think they could use some good news. And coming from you, it will mean a great deal."

* * * *

Two hours later, com alerted. "Audio signal from the Kalazecis," the operator said.

"Martin, can you translate?" Maria asked.

"Just a moment. The message is in Pagmok. That will help."

"Thoughtful of them," Maria mused.

Martin said in a bored voice, "Here it is."

As the electronic voice of Orion's translator increased in volume, Maria strained to make sense of the strange arrangement of words. Translation with accuracy remained a problem. Interpretation required input that remained mostly trial and error.

"Alien ship, this is Hcsic, first lord of his majesty Emperor Djuc's ship Omklik. Prepare to be boarded. Any effort to resist will be met with deadly force."

A smirk crossed Eric's face as he glanced at Maria. "Everyone wants to board us. I'd say things just got a lot tougher."

She left the bridge and returned shortly in full uniform. "I want this message sent in Kalazecis—audio and video. Let them know we have mastered their language."

She pretty much repeated the message sent earlier to the Pagmok when they entered the system hoping it would have the same affect. And maybe the Rococo/Pagmok shuttle that had arrived on the Kalazecis ship could help.

Erik stepped onto the bridge as soon as she'd completed her transmission. "Captain. Looks like we may have to demonstrate our seriousness about staying here."

She nodded. "Not yet. Hopefully, we're a long way from needing a show of force. We have made some influential friends and we certainly don't want to alienate them if we can avoid it."

"Whatever you say, but we're ready if and when you give the order."

Maria nodded as everyone waited for the Kalazecis response.

Over an hour went by before the answer came and it wasn't what anyone wanted. The transmission, audio only, demanded immediate surrender of both the ship and installations on Usgac or they would be fired upon.

"Well, well, well, no boarding. Sounds like our new Pagmok and Rococo friends pushed back. If anyone boarded Orion it would be the Pagmok. They're the warriors." Maria believed the Rococo and Pagmok must have put up a strong argument. How she framed her response could well decide what happened next.

Maria glanced down at the bridge deck, then at those around her. "Erik, talk with David. See what weapons we have available that give us some offense." She pointed at him. "I know it won't be much but I'm betting the Kalazecis are without Pagmok help right now, and they have no army, just the armed ships. Maybe, between a little show of force, some deception, and what we've done for the Pagmok and Rococo, the Kalazecis can be convinced of a more rational course of action."

Erik laughed as he left the bridge.

No one else saw any humor with what they faced.

A few minutes later, Erik and David came through the hatch. If Erik knew something, his face hid it well. Finally, a grin appeared. "Captain, I believe we have the best engineer in this part of the galaxy, maybe in the entire galaxy." He'd apparently give no thought to Martin's presence and how he would react to the accolade. Martin had never mastered hiding his feelings and clearly David's recovery only added to the man's personal problem.

David, standing behind him showed no emotion as he spoke. "Start two Casimir engines and we can have enough power to operate at least four energy canons."

Maria asked, "And that means?"

Erik's grin widened. "I can modulate their frequency. We'll be able to penetrate the Kalazecis electronic shield and blow the ship to hell."

Mathew Hammond said, "Have you considered the chances of capturing the Kalazecis ship?"

Reflexively, Maria said, "How?" She mulled whether to try to drive a wedge further between the Kalazecis and Pagmok or confront Orion's antagonist directly. If she did the latter, she felt certain Orion would win in the short term. After all, exploding the bomb clamped to the Kalazecis ship before the enemy could react, in less than a second, ended the matter immediately. Using the energy canons might not be necessary. But the bomb might be a matter of winning a battle and losing a war, particularly if it resulted in more Kalazecis warships joining the fight. And it wouldn't take many more. Orion simply could not withstand any kind of attack. On the other hand, if she tried and failed to convince the Pagmok to expand their minor revolt, it could just as easily backfire and bring the two sides back together. If that happened, detonation of the nuclear bombs on the hulls of the three ships would most likely be her only option. And no captured ship.

"Start the engines," Maria ordered. "When they're powered up, send the following to the Kalazecis ship."

She dictated the message, blunt and forthright. "Kalazecis Lord Hcsic, if you insist on a fight, in one minute a bomb will explode off your stern.

144

Attached to the hull of your ship, Pagmok, and Rococo vessels, you'll find similar devices. They are located just forward of the engine compartments. You are invited to inspect these weapons but do not attempt to remove or disarm them. Any effort to do so will cause detonation."

Erik said, "If we blow the bomb off the Kalazecis stern, they will feel the blast. There's nothing to attenuate it. They will know we mean business.

"Send the message," Maria ordered.

"Wait," Martin Grabel screamed. Directly behind him Roberto Macon made the same objection. "This is stupid. It's suicide. This is insane. We're no better than what we left behind on Earth."

Maria walked toward the diminutive mathematician, looked down at him, and calmly said, "Martin, you may be right. What would you suggest? As you know, we've been ordered to surrender or die. Do you suggest we surrender? Before you answer, remember most likely as far as the Kalazecis are concerned they'll be better off if we end up as dinner for the Pagmok."

Both Martin and Roberto stepped back. Roberto's expression changed from anger to fear and then mixed with humiliation. Martin momentarily remained determined then fear took its rightful place. Neither said a word.

Maria said, "Erik, assemble gunnery crews. As soon as the weapons are operational, let me know."

A little over three hours later, the message went out to the Kalazecis. Orion had no *general quarters* command. Until now, they'd needed it.

CHAPTER TWENTY-FOUR
The Future

Four nervous hours passed before the answer came. Almost noon on the planet, Orion's shuttle left the hanger for New Earth and arrived minutes before the Kalazecis.

Colonel Jabari ordered his troops to disarm and prepare for hand-to-hand combat if the need arose. They formed two ranks as an honor guard, providing the Kalazecis a corridor to the meeting site. This wasn't a pure formality—if a fight started, he wanted the Kalazecis to have to defend from two sides.

The shuttle landed and the dignitaries disembarked at the New Earth landing field.

Amazed at the size of Jabari, the Kalazecis, who at their best reached five feet and one or two inches, stood gawking at the six foot four Marine. More human like in appearance than either the Rococo or Pagmok, and obviously omnivores, the Kalazecis strode toward the meeting area with the arrogance of beings accustomed to exercising control. Short and slender, skin not unlike that of the earthlings, noses not as prominent, as were the ears, with eyes that favored oriental, maybe Thai, the Kalazecis walked with assurance of who they were. Hair covered almost all their visible body and the four aides' color varied from blonde to black. Apparently, these beings had a problem with the nitrogen-rich air. The breathing apparatus certainly suggested that.

The apparent delegation leader's eyes swept the assembled group repeatedly. Whether it had the effect of sizing them up Erik couldn't tell.

Neither the Rococo nor Pagmok seemed to take his actions with any concern. Apparently, Kalazecis posturing came across as normal to them.

Almost five minutes, quiet minutes passed before he spoke. The delay caused by the translator was almost imperceptible, and he raised what went for an eyebrow.

"I am Momn. First Lord Hcsic's representative. In the name of Emperor Djuc, Lord Hcsic demands your immediate evacuation of Usgac."

A litany of who they were and why their claim to Usgac took priority included the number of years the Kalazecis had peacefully ruled, gave them dominion over the planet.

Pagmok and Rococo heads bobbed as Momn stressed that because of Kalazecis intervention, intellect, and persistence, peace had been the norm for over thirty passages (years). Momn didn't restrict his comments to the earthlings. He reminded the Pagmok they were no more than meat-eating naked animals living a very harsh life until rescued by the Kalazecis. He was less callous toward the Rococo whom, if the computer had made the correct interpretation, were treated as children. Perhaps he had a liking for bug-lemurs. Perhaps he was simply trying to keep their confidence before allowing the Pagmok to imprison the Rococo, use them for forced labor in the mines, and breed them as a food source.

Erik didn't buy into the boasting Momn had put out. Intimidation never worked for long. Maria had called their hand once—it appeared he'd have to do the same. But this time, he'd leave them some diplomatic wiggle room. Maybe the underling Rococo and Pagmok only needed a little prompting to set the Kalazecis straight. But that decision he couldn't make on his own.

Momn stared past Erik, a smug look on his face.

The translation didn't surprise Orion's XO—he'd expected just this attitude.

"This area of space is Kalazecis. You must leave. Find another planet." Momn repeated himself.

Erik agreed the humans were the intruders. The Kalazecis had a nice little package here and if it were his, he would probably react the same way.

One Rococo stood and spoke into the translator. "I speak for Cslic (Selic), Prime of the ship Msimic." The translator still didn't have a firm grasp on the Rococo's ship's name and translated it as Majestic. "We owe a great debt to the humans. Their medical technology has solved our problem; we are no longer a dying race. They are our friends and deserve to stay on Usgac (New Earth). We can withdraw our forbearers if they wish and leave Usgac to them."

Erik silently gave a *hooray*. Yet he knew the Kalazecis would not look favorably on that tidbit so he waited for Momn's response.

Before the Kalazecis could answer, Jabari's com unit broke the silence, "Three ships approaching at high speed directly for this system."

Not wanting to make known Orion's early warning satellites, Erik said, "Must have picked up a transmission." Then asked Momn, "Your ships?"

He wasn't lying—just not telling the entire story.

Momn didn't answer for a moment, just stood, staring at the Rococo and Pagmok. Finally, he jerked to attention. "We must leave now."

Followed by his attendants, he strode from the meeting.

Neither the Rococo nor the Pagmok delegation moved.

Momn spun on his heels and barked an order the translator couldn't handle.

From the expressions on the normally expressionless Rococo and Pagmok faces, it wasn't complimentary.

Momn wasted little time in getting off New Earth and heading for the Kalazecis ship leaving the three groups wondering if events ended any discussion.

Rococo and Pagmok withdrew some distance from the meeting site and conferred.

Erik didn't interfere as the two groups boarded their launches.

* * * *

Seated in the wardroom where most of the crew had just finished lunch, Maria asked, "What else do we know about the Kalazecis hierarchy? Who governs? Do they have legislative councils?"

Ann opened a folder and thumbed through the pages. "Emperor, hereditary. Current family has ruled for at least three hundred passages or years.

Actually, their years are just thirteen days short of an Earth year. The race prides itself on intellectual prowess and from what I've seen, rightfully so. There are twenty-five legislative districts with the Emperor appointing six delegates, or deputies, from each. Women are not eligible to sit in the Chamber of Deputies, as the parliament's called. Obviously, our leader being a woman is just another strike against our staying. We appear to represent everything the Kalazecis are against politically and socially. They have imported many Pagmok to their home planet, which is by the way called, the best translation is from Greek god, *Coeus*. In Greek mythology, Coeus is the Titan of Intelligence. The actual spelling is Chzzis. No real idea how it's pronounced. By the way, Pagmok cannot serve in any governmental roll."

Erik stood and headed through the door into the passageway. "I've got a few things to take care of."

After he left, Maria said, "Our first officer has a little surprise for the arriving Kalazecis ships."

The dozen people waited.

"In case any of you have ever wondered where our ten nuclear bombs are, I will tell you. As you know, the Rococo, Pagmok, and first arriving Kalazecis ship each have a nuclear device attached to their hulls. Every one of our three early warning satellites has, as part of its make-up, a nuclear device. Of course, we had the one orbiting off the first Kalazecis ship. That leaves three in our arsenal.

"Our first officer will shortly initiate a preprogrammed command that will put our satellites on the hulls of the arriving Kalazecis ships. These bombs will be our insurance the newly arriving guests don't get out of hand."

"Insanity. Pure insanity," said Macon. "We just keep escalating the situation and we have no idea if they mean us harm."

Com interrupted, "Shuttle's leaving the Pagmok and headed for the Kalazecis."

Martin Grabel sat silent. Bhani's talk with him appeared to quell his temper but Maria doubted it.

Roberto's ranting had gained him a small following and that ignoring that wasn't an option.

Maria turned toward him. "Roberto you and Martin are both right about the danger. But as commander, I have to consider alternatives. The way I see it, I'd rather be ready for a fight and not have one than not be ready if something develops."

Doctor Macon said, "You haven't even attempted to communicate with these new arrivals. Erik has at least talked with Momn, Rococo, and Pagmok. And we know the Pagmok were very persuasive earlier on."

Maria's com squawked.

"Oh shit! Captain—you need to see this." The voice rang with alarm.

Maria sprang from her chair and sprinted for the bridge.

"What is it?" She no more than got the words out than something rocked Orion, shaking everyone and everything. She grabbed the rail separating the

Captain and com areas steadying herself. "What was that?" she quietly asked.

Calmed by Maria's manner, the com officer said, "All four of the Kalazecis ships fired on the Pagmok and destroyed it. They put enough energy into that ship to destroy half a dozen at that range. Those," he paused, "beings didn't stand a chance."

"What about the Rococo?" the Captain asked. Martin and Roberto quietly left the bridge.

"So far, no action against them."

She stepped back to her chair and keyed the intercom. "Erik, what's the status of our satellites?"

"Twenty minutes for the first to attach, at least an hour for the second and almost four until the third reaches location."

Most likely, the first Kalazecis told the others about the bomb attached to their hull. The new arrivals would be on the lookout for anything like that.

Emissions were coming from the Kalazecis ships but so far, it wasn't directed toward the satellites.

"Rococo shuttle leaving for the Kalazecis fleet," the com officer said. "Arrival in one hundred minutes."

"Open a channel to the shuttle," the Captain said.

The com queried the small ship but got no answer. Apparently, they realized talking to the humans would only further antagonize their masters.

"Looks like we're in for a wait and see," Ann said. "Actually, Captain, that works in our favor. Wonder if the Rococo thought it out that way?"

Maria had no idea. Maybe they had. Maybe not. But it bought Orion time. She hit the com key, "Erik."

"Yes, Captain."

"Can you arrange it so that all the satellites arrive at the same time?"

"Yes sir." His reply was almost strident. "Wish I'd thought of that. What about attaching? You didn't mention that."

"Let's sit on that one for the moment."

* * * *

For almost sixteen hours, Orion and New Earth waited for the next Kalazecis move. It would be their first response as they'd ignored Maria's earlier attempts to talk with them.

David stepped through the door and approached Maria. "I have an idea."

Still grappling with the who's and what's of dealing with people, he stood waiting for an answer.

"Please David, what have you got?"

He seemed to mull over something, maybe how to present his thoughts. He'd not shown any reluctance to speak out regardless of the consequences, even if it meant offending someone. It wasn't that he didn't care, just that in his recovery, he'd not experienced enough situations for most interpersonal relationship matters to have that much affect on his behavior.

Quietly but with great intensity he said, "I've studied the engineering information on the Kalazecis ship we downloaded. I can tune our energy cannons to a specified frequency and fry every electrical and electronic circuit on all those ships."

It seemed the human inherent will to survive had stayed healthy and strong in David.

"This changes everything." Maria keyed Erik to make sure the satellites were not attached to the Kalazecis hulls.

Again, she keyed the com, "Colonel Jabari, can you come to the bridge please?"

"Yes Ma'am. On my way," the Marine quickly responded.

A few minutes later, Jabari stood before the Captain. In answer to her question, he said, "Yes ma'am. I think we can board one ship. Maybe two. With only eleven Marines in each shuttle, we couldn't take them without one hell of a fight and more than our share of luck."

"Maybe. David tells me he can neutralize virtually everything on those ships." She repeated the engineer's comment and watched the Colonel's reaction.

A coy smile touched the Marine's lips. "Does that include environment? Like air and heat?"

David nodded without hesitation.

Jabari turned to the Captain. "Is there any chance we can supply enough air to keep the Kalazecis alive if their systems are killed?"

"David?" Maria asked.

He knew approximately the crew size on each ship, four hundred eighty. That meant over seventeen hundred converted oxygen rebreathers.

That, Orion could accommodate.

So far, no one knew that much about the Kalazecis anatomy and physiology.

"I need to talk with Roberto," David said. Macon answered the com from his laboratory. Between he, David, and what information their database had on the subject, they figured out the air mixture could be altered enough to keep the Kalazecis alive. They would, however, suffer from what humans called altitude sickness until their systems starting functioning again.

Roberto indicated a strong concern about what he called HACE or High Altitude Cerebral Edema. "If their brains start to swell, there's no recovery."

Maria turned to the assembled crew and said, "I think we've found our answer. Let's get the shuttles loaded with everything needed to make this happen. David, can you target only the environmental systems? I mean not destroy propulsion, navigation and so on."

"Risky," he answered. "It might give them time to get a shot off and that's more than we could take. One shot and we're done for.

"What I can do, is target the environment and weapons systems. They feed off the same circuits."

Maria almost jumped with joy. "Do it," she ordered. "Now I'm ready to talk to the Kalazecis."

CHAPTER TWENTY-FIVE
The future

Maria stepped onto the bridge in full uniform. Everything that had happened to the people of Orion over the last one hundred seventy years came down to this. They had endured years of struggle, boredom, and innovation to survive in the face of terrific odds. Orion represented some of the best Earth had to offer. Despite leaving behind everything familiar and dear, they had built a new life. She would do everything possible to make sure it hadn't been in vain.

A quick glance at the faces surrounding her told her all she needed to know. The people of New Earth depended on her.

"Transmit in Kalazecis and Rococo, audio and video," she directed the com officer.

"To the four Kalazecis ships on orbit around Usgac, New Earth and the Rococo ship, Msimic. I am Maria Presk, Captain of the ship Orion and New Earth. We, the people of Orion and New Earth left our world many years ago. We came here looking for a new life and that hope has remained strong. Part of that better life is knowing we can get along with any beings willing to meet us and resolve differences. We recognize something new can appear a threat. That certainly isn't our intention. We come in peace with a desire to live with whoever our neighbors might be. We hoped our finding a cure for the Rococo and the First illness might be proof of that. We could have left them to die. But this is not our way.

"Do not mistake what I am saying for weakness. Your destruction of the Pagmok ship was the act of a coward. That too is not our way. What I am saying is we will warn you before destroying all four of your ships and anymore that your Emperor might send. We don't enjoy this but you seem to have a need to pick on those weaker than yourselves. I want to assure you we are quite capable of delivering on my threat. Our technology is beyond your comprehension and you have no way to protect yourselves. I am ordering you to stand down and surrender. This is the only warning you will get. A contingent of Marines will arrive to take command of your vessels. They will treat you with dignity and respect as long as you obey my orders. Do otherwise and you will feel the full force of our might. It is your decision." She signaled the com to end the transmission.

"They're powering up their engines and weapons." The com officer spoke maybe a little too fast.

"David, are you ready?"

She got the acknowledgement and issued the order, "Fire." Four light green beams sped forth from Orion. Instants later, allowing for light-speed delay, the Kalazecis ships started to die. "Launch the fighters and shuttles," she ordered.

* * * *

Colonel Jabari had the lead in shuttle one and followed one fighter. The same formation held for the second. The remaining two shuttles had no fighter

151

cover so were ordered to attach to the Kalazecis hulls and await orders. He had selected a circuitous route to the Kalazecis ships, leaving David with a clear field of fire—just in case.

Marines hated tackling a fight wearing bulky space suits and no body armor to protect them. For this job, though, it was necessary. Any tear or hole in the spacesuit ended the argument. Packed in the rear of both shuttles were rebreathers to keep the Kalazecis alive until repairs could be made to their air supply.

The first ship showed no light, external, or internal as the Marines approached. In fact, it showed no signs of life. Maybe David's solution had been a bit more final than anticipated.

Maybe, but the experienced Marine commander wasn't about to get careless or sloppy. Years before Orion left Earth, he'd been in far too many fights to let his guard down.

True to his nature and reputation, Jabari exited the shuttle first, followed by the entire squad. They expected to either blow a hatch or cut the Kalazecis ship's hull—something that would be time consuming in a situation where seconds mattered. David had estimated over an hour to torch-penetrate the hull.

From the starboard side, the Marines approached the largest Kalazecis ship, some thirty meters ahead. To the Colonel's amazement, the forward main hatch stood open to space. That wasn't by accident or by itself. It was either a trap or the Kalazecis had surrendered.

Cautiously, using jet packs, one marine moved toward the hatch's rear side. Jabari took the front, providing cover for each other. That left ten Marines for support.

Jabari dug a stun grenade from his beggars pack, signaled the Marine to get a handhold, pulled the pin, and tossed it through the opening. The small flash laced from the hatch but the vacuum of space transmitted no sound and the hull shielded both men from the blast. Secured with safety cables, the two burst through the opening to an empty room and air lock.

Ten more Marines piled in. The weightlessness of space, no tether lines and no handholds, made it impossible to stop. It also made coordinated movement impossible.

Jabari tried not to get exasperated working with inexperienced fighters. They often let their gung-ho attitude cloud their judgment.

He motioned for them to clear the airlock. Again alone with one Marine, he closed the open external hatch.

Using helmet lights, the interior gave way to virtual daylight. He looked around, found the control to restore normal atmospheric pressure, and punched the button. That's when he remembered David had killed every electronic system on the ship.

Virtually every space faring ship is equipped for these kinds of situations and the Colonel returned to the bulkhead next to the hatch and found the manual valve.

Within seconds, the atmosphere stabilized.

With a stun grenade ready, the Marine unhurriedly tried the hatch handle. Slowly it moved and the small door opened far enough for the grenade to make it into the passageway or whatever was on the other side. This time they heard and felt the explosion. In one motion, Jabari twisted the handle and followed by the Marine, weapons ready, burst onto the bridge.

Jabari held up his hand. The astonished look on his face didn't begin to register the concern he felt in his gut. A piece of white cloth hung in place, held there by the closed hatch. He puzzled for a moment, wondered how this enemy knew to offer a flag recognized for talks, truce, or surrender.

Two Kalazecis emerged from behind a partition, scared from what Jabari could judge but unharmed.

Both marines swung their weapons toward the two.

The Kalazecis stood at attention, but neither moved again.

Jabari assumed they were the Captain and his first officer. He reached into his beggars pack and extracted a portable translator. He didn't need it, the Kalazecis had taken, or copied one Orion had given the Pagmok and spoke.

At first, the officers seemed overwhelmed at the size of the human confronting them. Jabari still in his space suit reached a foot taller than he really was and loomed over his much smaller adversary. It was, apparently, the first time they'd seen anyone that large.

"I am Gnacislas, the Emperor's command officer for this ship; the Emperor's second officer is Rnadslas. We are your prisoners."

Jabari signaled the remaining ten Marines to make entry and ordered the bridge hatch closed. He then called Orion and advised them of their status.

Hand signals dispersed the Marines as they made their way down the passageway and set up a perimeter guard. He turned back to the two officers. "I am the military commandant of the New Earth and Orion Marines. I accept your surrender. Where are the rest of your crew and how many are there?

"Crew numbers one hundred thirty. And—"

Jabari cut him off, pulled his sidearm, and put it to the Captain's head. "You lying son of a bitch. I'll blow your fucking brains out if you lie to me again. Now the goddammed truth. How many," he didn't know whether to ask how many beings, souls or what; they damned sure weren't humans—he finally settled on beings, "beings are there on this ship?" In fact, he wondered how his vulgarity might translate.

It took a few seconds for the translator to come alive but there could be little doubt the Kalazecis officer had a good idea of what he'd better do. "Four hundred eighteen," he answered both eyes closed as if expecting the bullet.

"That's better. You and I just might be able to do business. Where are they?" Jabari's eyes remained fixed on the two officers; the delay imposed by the translator didn't distract the Marine.

"I ordered them to their bunks. They will use up less breathable air. I do have a crew working to restore the air systems. Twenty-five workers."

"Excellent." Jabari complemented the officer. The guy did have a decent head on his shoulders.

The Colonel continued. "Are you the Commander of this fleet?"

"I am."

"Order your other vessels to surrender immediately. If they resist, we will destroy them without hesitation. Is that understood?"

The Kalazecis nodded. Using Jabari's relay through Orion, the Kalazecis Commander issued the order. When finished he added, "We will not resist you. If you are unable to help us restore life support to our ships within an hour, we will all be dead. You have effectively killed us."

"Perhaps," said Jabari. "We do have a number of rebreathers on the shuttle that could make a difference. You are welcome to them." Actually, between the two shuttles, they had enough of the nitrogen extraction generators for all four Kalazecis ships and he transferred them to the Kalazecis. After all, over nine hundred souls had inhabited Orion so he had claimed plenty of rebreathers for the Kalazecis.

"Captain, let me remind you. If anyone resists us, we will shoot without warning. We are few in number so will brook no opposition. Is that understood?"

"Yes, conqueror."

Jabari reined in his temper, upset at the way the Kalazecis had addressed him.

The Kalazecis officer said, "You have not told me your name or rank. Otherwise I would have addressed you appropriately."

Only Jabari's black skin kept the blush from showing that he knew had to be there. "I am Colonel Jabari."

* * * *

"Works for me," said Erik. "In fact, I think it's one hell of an idea.

Generally, there were nods around the conference room.

Maria continued, "That will give us four heavily armed ships, all capable of FTL, along with at least some time to prepare to defend ourselves from a Kalazecis attack that I'm sure will come." As aggressive as the Kalazecis had been, she had every reason to assume they would return with enough firepower to mount an attack.

For the next three months after that agreement, Maria directed the stripping of Orion; removing labs, shops and virtually everything that made life and travel possible and moved it dirtside. They left only the necessities to sustain life and propel the ship. In fact, Orion's engineering and maintenance crews overhauled the engines and life support systems, putting everything remaining in perfect working order. After all, the Kalazecis would need it to survive the sub-light trip to their home world.

At three tenth's c, the trip would take about thirty-five years—although everyone expected the Kalazecis home world to send rescue ships long before that. Humanity had laid claim to this piece of the universe under duress. But they were willing to share or defend it.

* * * *

First Contact

There were few misgivings about trading Orion for the four Kalazecis ships. In general, sentiments favored the decision to swap the space ships regardless of the inequity or consequences. To the victor belonged the spoils. Besides, the humans hadn't started the fight and had done their best to avoid casualties during the fight and treat the Kalazecis prisoners with dignity afterwards. If you can call it dignity, capturing their battle cruisers, sending them packing in second rate ship barely space-worthy and not FTL capable. Most agreed doing their best would still bring retribution when the Kalazecis returned. But, most everyone agreed to do anything less or differently would border on criminal. Maria had most of New Earth's population solidly behind her.

Naming the four ships brought a feisty exchange. Finally, George Washington, Simon Bolivar, Nelson Mandela, and Mahatmas Gandhi emerged from the spirited wrangling.

* * * *

Orion had been under new management and underway for almost a week. It would be another month before they could use the Casimir engines, and accelerate out of system.

In her new day cabin aboard the George Washington, Maria examined the results of a software program. "Where's Martin? I need him."

"Haven't seen him," Erik responded. The mathematician could have been any one of the four ships or dirtside. Since David's near miraculous recovery, the volatile mathematician had taken to secluding himself even from Bhani and his sons, sometimes disappearing for days at a time. Increasingly, his behavior had become erratic even for Martin Grabel.

She keyed his com unit. No response. She keyed Bhani just as the lady stepped into the conference room.

Her eyes flooded with tears, Bhani handed Maria a note.

"My dearest Bhani, by the time you read this I will be well on my way to the Kalazecis home world. I can no longer stay on Orion or New Earth and submit to humiliation after humiliation. Just as I gained some respect, David had to make a miracle recovery, robbing me of what I had rightfully earned. You are the only woman I ever loved. The children are, of course, grown men and women and I'm sorry for any embarrassment I may have caused you or them. I shall miss you all."

Maria her voice calm but full of steel said, "We could not have lost a more dangerous person. He knows more about us than any one else. New Earth is in jeopardy."

CHAPTER TWENTY-SIX
Making a life

Maria slowly settled into her form-fit chair—one of the last items removed from Orion and installed in her day cabin aboard the Washington. David, Erik, Ann Bartlett, Roberto and Gramina Macon, Jimmy John Jabari, and Mathew Hammond had all taken seats, waiting for her to say what was on her mind. To a person they knew it would be about Grabel's desertion.

She began the meeting, her voice steady, unrelenting, but still showing disappointment. "There was no way anyone could have anticipated Martin's defection to the Kalazecis. No one should feel he or she could have done anything to prevent this. One of the noblest things we as humans do is trust others. When that trust is betrayed, we have little or no defense and we are at our most vulnerable. Martin knows every aspect of our computer systems. He knows its strengths and weaknesses. Most of it, he designed. And there's little or nothing we can do about it. It would take years to make enough software changes to impact significantly any intrusion he might make. And of course, the Kalazecis know the operating systems in place on these four ships. The advantage lies with them."

Almost mid sentence Maria stopped turned toward Bhani who had just entered and said, "Bhani, how sorry I feel for you." She stood and hugged the still sobbing woman who broke loose and ran from the cabin.

A long sigh escaped Maria as she sat. Time without end seemed to pass and no one spoke.

David broke the silence. "Maybe we'd all have been better off if I hadn't recovered." He didn't seem to be feeling sorry for himself, just stating what he deemed the obvious.

Maria quelled an instant urge to lash out instead her voice became calmer. "No David, we're better off with you running engineering. Martin may have learned virtually everything about how things worked on Orion, and that accrues to the Kalazecis for the time being. But he's not the pure engineer you are. I doubt seriously that he could lead us through the learning we have to do on theses new ships. No, your return may be all that can and will save us."

She continued to force calmness she didn't feel but a slight sigh still managed to escape. "Let's all take a break for the evening. I would like all of you to spend some time thinking through what has happened. I need cool calm deliberation from all of you. Meet back here at oh seven hundred tomorrow."

* * * *

The next morning, Erik arrived first, pouring his own coffee as David stepped through the open hatch. Maria strode from her private quarters and greeted both men with a smile that lingered on her husband. "Good morning. Sleep okay?"

Erik said, "Yep," and David nodded.

Ann Bartlett entered next along with Roberto and Gramina. To Maria's amazement, Bhani soon came in, obviously having slept little.

Maria walked to the woman and took her hands in hers. "You up to this?"

She nodded but no emotion showed.

The Captain wasn't all that sure. Had it been her in Bhani's position, she wasn't sure she'd want to hear the decision of the crew. It could well be more of a sentence.

Bhani nodded again and then said without waiting for any invitation to speak, "Martin has betrayed us all—even his children. I have spent most of last night with them and we are of one mind."

Maria motioned everyone into seats around the long Kalazecis table. Kalazecis built for smaller physiques than humans.

Colonel Jabari appeared at the hatch and Maria motioned him in. His presence made the table seem even smaller.

She sat at the far end of the polished slab and said, "Suggestions?" Then she leaned back in the chair.

For the next few minutes, mostly meaningless chatter filled the room. Maria, David, and Erik stayed out of the sometimes-heated exchanges. As people ran out of suggestions, and anger finally vented allowed the mini debates to subside.

Bhani, her voice steady, face cast in stone, spoke first. "I say we go after them and force Martin to return with us. We cannot permit the Kalazecis to make use of what he knows. I think most of us feel they will return and when they do, they'll be our enemies."

Startled looks crossed the room. Some seemed to doubt what they had just heard and some questioned Bhani.

She didn't back down or falter under their stares.

Erik flashed a broad smile. "She's got my vote."

Maria met everyone's eyes in the cabin. David nodded and by then everyone joined the chorus of approval.

"David," she said. "Can you drive this ship?"

During the three months refitting Orion, David had taken the Mandela *out for a spin*, as Erik put it, a number of times including FTL flight, but that only twice. The Washington wasn't all that different.

A slight sigh escaped him. Pensively David said, "Maximum crew is four hundred eighteen, normal is just over three hundred, recommended minimum skeleton is one hundred ten. We can put at the most around sixteen. Three on the bridge, four in the engine room on twelve hour shifts. And two cooks. Bridge crew can handle the astrogation and forward gun positions, cooks, one overhead or top turret, and engineers side and aft weapons stations. That ought to about do it."

Abject silence settled over the room following his precise dissertation. To a person, disbelief seemed to settle over the group. The immensity of what confronted them finally gripped them all.

Maria said, "*Can* you do it?"

David didn't seem dissuaded. "The engineering crew is by no means

157

proficient. But Orion is still on ion engines and will be for another ten days or so before they can start the Casimir engines. She hasn't been gone long enough that we would need trans-light speed. We could catch up with them. Probably take a week or two. But we can do it." His voice seemed reassuring and the faces around the table reflected it.

"That will have to do," Maria said. Then added, "Back to Martin."

David said, "Not yet Captain. How we locate them is another matter."

Every head in the room turned toward him. He seemed startled and a little taken aback after the kindly response he'd just gotten for solving the manpower problem.

Maria said, "David?"

"Orion is stealthy to Kalazecis and our radar."

You could almost feel all the air suck from the room as David brought everyone back to reality. What had been a huge asset for Orion was now New Earth inhabitants' nemesis.

Breaking the deadly quiet Maria asked, "Is there any way to get around this problem? What about the emissions from the Casimir engines? Are they detectable?"

David reflected for a minute and then almost thinking out loud said, "If the Casimirs were running, their emissions are easily picked up. If not, I'm afraid we have no way of locating them. It may prove impossible for us to sneak up on them."

Maria pressed her hands against the table. "There has to be some way. With all this," her hand swept the cabin signifying the Kalazecis technology, "there just has to be some way," she repeated herself in frustration.

"Maybe there is," said Erik. There was no doubt he had the entire groups attention. "Calculate where we think they are, go FTL, pass them, then back to normal space and lay dogo, dormant waiting for them."

Without a word spoken, all eyes turned back toward the engineer. In a rare show that the old David was back, at least to some extent, he got that old devilish smile that characterized him. With his usual conservation of words said, "Should work."

David leaned over a plot table. "My calculations show the jump to hyperspace will last only one second. That will put us about two million kilometers beyond Orion. It's based on our best estimates, so we could be off considerably."

Maria breathed a silent sigh. "When can you be ready to go?"

David reflected for a minute or so and said, "Probably a week. Maybe two. Who'll be at the helm?"

Maria avoided her first officer knowing he expected the captaincy. "I will. Sorry, Erik."

Her XO shook his head. "I did bring him back once. He'll listen to me. Maybe I can do it again without bloodshed."

A quick glance around the cabin told her Erik wasn't alone in his thinking. She stood, her resolve evident. "I know these aren't the streets of New York, but this is something I have to do myself."

Roberto Macon nervously cleared his voice, most likely recalling the last time he spoke, the entire staff and command almost handed him his head. "I think we may be overlooking something." He hesitated.

"Roberto, please," urged Maria no hint of the past conflicts evident.

"Now that the Kalazecis know about Earth, what if they decide to attack it? Our fellow humans have no way to protect themselves. Not against ships and weapons like these. The planet would be defenseless."

Maria stifled a gasp. Her worries about what Martin might do to New Earth had trapped her. "My god you're right, Roberto. And what we didn't tell them, Martin surely can and..." she paused, as all eyes in the group fell on Martin's wife, "Bhani, would Martin sell out Earth?"

The small Indian seemed to become even smaller. She had no defense against what her husband had done and yet still had to bear his burden. "I," she stuttered, hesitated, regained her composure and said, "I don't know. But, my opinion is that he would not."

Erik quietly spoke, "Just a few minutes ago, we were all sure Martin would be back with the Kalazecis again and him leading the pack. Why us and not Earth? It's a bigger prize."

"I don't believe Martin would help them to destroy us or Earth—"

Erik interrupted Bhani, "Earlier you said—"

The petite Bhani cut him off, "Earlier I only said the Kalazecis would be back. After seeing them blow the Pagmok to hell—" that put all eyes on the Indian, no one had ever heard her swear before, "—I just can't see them trusting Martin. If they come our way, it will be to destroy us. I haven't changed my mind on that. But I never said I thought Martin would be a part of it. I think they will use him to learn all then can and cast him aside—most likely killed."

For the longest time, no one spoke. Finally, Maria said, "We have to send two ships to Earth. The sooner the better."

"Why two?" Someone asked.

Maria continued, "We'll leave one ship, a complete set of plans and," looking at David, "your next best engineer and as many tech's to support him, all volunteers of course, that you can spare. Once Earth's made the primary decisions, like who's going to control this technology, the second ship will leave a shuttle for your engineer and tech team to return to New Earth. Your crew can come back when Earth's engineers have the basics in hand. We can't do much to help with strategic planning to handle an attack since we don't know that much about Kalazecis thinking ourselves."

Erik said, "From what you didn't say, all of our people will stay on Earth orbit. Never go dirtside. Right?"

Maria nodded. "There's still the long life matter and its effect on Earth's population. Deciding who's going to control this technology might be the toughest problem to solve." That was perhaps the most important question and she didn't have the answer. At last word, the troika the US, China and Russia tried to form had never materialized.

* * * *

Maria nodded almost absentmindedly. "Mathew Hammond will assume the full powers of the presidency. Erik Svern will serve as his deputy and have control of the two remaining ships." Turning to Hammond, she added, "What you do to begin preparations for a Kalazecis attack, I leave in your hands. Neither David nor I have any strategic knowledge to offer.

"According to David, it will take us about three weeks to transit and I've no idea how long we'll be there. But rest assured, we'll prod them into action. We'll take the George Washington and Nelson Mandela. We leave in two weeks."

* * * *

President Arthur Robertson put the finishing touches to the memorandum of understanding and handed it to Marge Summers, his secretary. He leaned back in his chair. "Well, that takes care of the meeting with Premier Cho Chin Wha and President Choninko." As far as he was concerned, it had taken far too long just to agree on an agenda with the Chinese and Russian leaders. In only two days, he would meet both men for the first time.

It had been six years since the leaders of three super powers had met. Years, during which the world came to the brink of war far too many times. He shook his head thinking about how many millions of people had died just fighting the Muslim jihadists before finally beating them into submission. The only good thing to emerge from that—the moderate Muslims had led the battle.

It hadn't taken Robertson long to become accustomed to the oval office and its many nuances. Some he considered perks and others nuisances. He couldn't imagine what had the NSA Director and Secretary of Defense so stirred up. It was his first emergency meeting since taking office ten days earlier. In fact, it would be the first time he'd met the NSA guy. Ross Deverman sat across in one armchair, purposely distanced to keep off the presidential seal so expertly woven into the rug.

Ross, his long time friend and now press advisor, looked at his nails before chuckling. "Wonder what these two are up to? Be careful with this NSA dude. He's so straight laced and hard nosed you can never tell when he's lying."

Robertson tolerated Ross's oblique comparisons, knowing the man had his best interests at heart. They'd been friends since teenagers, served together in the Marine reserves, seen combat together, went to the same college, and married sisters. By high school, it was evident Arthur had more on the ball than Ross, smarter, much quicker, and more resources to bring to any problem he had to face. Ross wasn't without skills, however. He'd waded in to help when a street gang jumped his friend. It changed the odds enough to make the difference. And of course, he'd saved Arthur's life in the Kurdistan war when an ambush caught the entire squad in a devastating trap. He was also someone the President could count on for the unvarnished truth. Often, people would say things to Ross meant to get to the President when the author lacked either the guts or venue for delivering a message. But beyond that, his usefulness to the President was questionable. Washington power brokers had a distinct dislike for the man, most likely because he had the President's ear.

Marge Summers gently knocked on the door, opening it simultaneously, stuck in her head and said, "DOD and NSA are here Mr. President."

"Of course, show them in." Robertson, tall, lanky, thin, had Lincolnesk, almost rough-hewn features, and was known for sharp penetrating political skills. He stepped from behind the desk and met them halfway warmly greeting the shorter and slight overweight Secretary. He turned to NSA, equal his height but heavier and said, "I've been looking forward to meeting you General."

Austin Methune had been NSA director for nearly two years and was highly regarded for his leadership skills and intellect. Maybe, in all of Washington he was the second man you didn't want to try to screw, the President being the first.

DOD said, "Thank you for seeing us Mr. President. I'm sorry this was on such short notice but it's of the utmost urgency."

"Of course," a wearisome turn of phrase the President overused, "but what's so damned important?"

Both the guests looked at Ross. "Mr. President," NSA said, "Until you've heard what I have to say, I'm must insist that it be in private."

"Of course. Ross you'll excuse us."

As the door shut, the president took his chair, folded his hands across his stomach, and said, "Okay, you have my private and undivided attention." For those who knew this man, that was a warning that what you had to say had better be goddammed important.

Two minutes into NSA'S presentation, Robertson held up his hands. Ashen white he said, "Preposterous! How do you know this isn't a hoax?"

"Our deep space telescopes have taken pictures of the ships. It's in the brief. Add to that, these people have information no one else could have. Mr. President, I think you have to hear me out."

Robertson leaned back in his chair anything but relaxed. Twenty minutes later, NSA finished, "Their problem, the New Earth people, is who gets this technology. They may pass it to China and Russia. If they decide to, there's nothing we can do to stop them. They have made it clear the UN is welcome to participate but will not have jurisdiction unless that is the will of the three major powers."

Robertson leaned forward, his mouth open as if to speak, but no sound came out. Finally he managed to speak. "This could have least waited until I found out where all the toilets are." There was no humor in his voice. He stood, walked to the window, and peered out at the sun now well into the otherwise clear sky. After a minute, he turned and asked, "Where do we stand with our visitors? Are they expecting an immediate reply?"

"No, Mr. President," answered NSA. "They've told us to take all the time necessary. They want to help, not hinder."

"Of course. Otherwise why would they be here?"

The President returned to his chair. He still hadn't looked at either man. He folded one arm across his chest cupping the elbow of the other, his free hand alternately stroking his chin and pulling at his nose. "Is there anything else?

Anything you wish to add?"

He obviously wasn't asking either man for their opinion. "No, Mr. President," they answered in chorus.

He picked up the folder and said, "I want to study this in depth. When I've finished, you can have it back."

Robertson stood, extended his hand, and said, "Gentlemen, you have handled this quite properly. Under no circumstance is this information to go any further until you hear from me."

CHAPTER TWENTY-SEVEN
The Troika

His decision made, hesitant, not knowing for sure it was the right one, President Robertson thumbed through the NSA folder, pressed the intercom, and asked Marge to summon the Security Council and leaders of both houses.

* * * *

As host, Robertson stood in the middle of the large UN room and greeted the Prime Minister of the Republic of China and the President of the Russian Federation. After some minor fussing among the staffs and delegations about who was to sit where, things finally settled down.

Robertson had seen press reports and, as a voracious reader, knew of numerous meetings that took days to get underway hung up on who sat where. Even seat assignment at formal dinners could be a serious point of contention. Strength and never giving in to even the minutest point remained important in some parts of the world. Sometimes, just the table arrangement could make all the difference.

President Robertson steered the two leaders out of the streaming courtiers each had in tow. "Gentlemen, I realize we have an approved agenda. However, a matter of the utmost importance has come up that we must discuss. Is it possible the three of us, along with our interpreters, could move to an adjacent room for a talk?"

Apparently, the other two leaders had dreaded the general session meeting as much as Robertson. Their acquiescence to an ad hoc session took only seconds to arrange when under normal conditions, months were the norm.

A few minutes later, in another room, the three sat in a small circle, their interpreters at their elbows.

Robertson said, "Gentlemen, what I'm about to tell you will be world news. Everyone will know as soon as we can agree on a course of action."

The two leaders listened in stark silence for the few minutes it took the president to brief them. Finished, he handed each a folder, written in their respective language, containing much of the data NSA had given him two days earlier.

He waited a brief period for either man to speak before he added, "Since this information you have in your hands was assembled, the United States has had additional communication with the two space ships. They have offered to bring an Earth delegation onboard but only if it is representative of the final authority over the ship and technology."

The Chinese prime minister, his stoic nature betraying him, made a determined effort to hide the alarm that seemed to consume him. "I must have discussions with my government. This is too sudden, the decision monumental. In order to move with certainty, I must involve many people on my central committee. But I make you no promises."

The Russian President, a giant of a man, his face normally masked with a perpetual frown said much the same. Robertson told them he understood—it was require of him also.

As the meeting appeared to be over, he said, "I know this astounding information is coming hard and fast. We are under no time edict to provide an answer to the orbiting ships. I would point out that the fate of Earth is in our hands and we should make the best use of what time we have."

* * * *

Maria watched the HD intently. Simulcasts from all over Earth flashed on the dozen monitors surrounding the Washington's bridge. She had had no illusions about the reception and conflicts her arrival had sparked. Every range of emotion would be unleashed—from the deprived to those fearing Armageddon. It remained to be seen when order would prevail.

She had prepared a chip for worldwide broadcast and forwarded it to the UN. World leaders had yet to release it. Concern had been expressed that it would only inflame a situation approaching desperate.

She would leave that decision to them. She had flatly rejected calls for her two ships immediate surrender to UN officials and advised them not to send any spacecraft or try anything stupid.

* * * *

Maria Presk stood on the Nelson Mandela's raised sideboard platform, waiting for the shuttle to dock. This first delegation put together by the troika, under the auspices of the United Nations, would set the tone for future meetings. She had no reservations or illusions; in fact, she'd given a lot of thought to forcing some form of government on Earth. She saw no way they could confront any enemy with the killing power of the Kalazecis short of a massive concerted effort on the part of all nations.

The seriousness of what faced them had the entire world's attention. The press, HD, and Internet were having perhaps their most glorious day. Her return to Earth was in itself cause for streams of oration, hypothesis, and speculation. However, those vanished with the news of a potential invasion. The news and the fact she refused to set foot on Earth or allow any New Earth personnel to disembark had galvanized world leaders as nothing had—perhaps in the history of mankind. Her return brought not only news about Orion, which had been relegated to history and conspiracy theories, but faster than light starships. The space age had truly arrived on Earth and they were no more ready for it than they had been when Maria and her band left for the Cancer system and 55 Cancri.

Perhaps the threat now facing mankind would bring the political and social stability that had so long eluded this world. Newspaper banners and HD's heralded her return as a double-edged sword. Some got it right: space is a dangerous place. She did harbor some concerns about the radical groups. They had changed little in the one hundred forty eight years since Orion left Earth. Perhaps it was no more than human nature that those kinds of people manage to thrive no matter the social, political, or economic condition. Some group or cause always had a claim that their voices be heard above all others.

Bringing events to this point hadn't come without stiff opposition. India felt it should be included in the initial group making the trip to the Nelson Mandela. Pakistan said it would declare war on India if it was included and Pakistan left out. There were riots throughout the world, some out of fear, others out of denial of opportunity. Some sought to destabilize the situation, others used it as an opportunity to impose their will.

Finally, the troika set everyone straight. All countries of the world would be included in talks, negotiations, and any benefits realized from Presk's visit. Internal affairs would remain the prerogative of each nation unless any troubles reached across boarders. In other words, keep your problems to yourselves. However, the troika realized it had to maintain a stable world to prepare for an attack. Any country warring with its neighbor, or starting any conflict would feel the wrath of the troika. It would be swift and sure. Peace between nations would be defined as the absence of war. Maria was sure someone or nation would test the troika but she believed it had the strength, and determination to see this through.

Latches locked, securing the shuttle to the rails as the 'boson's whistle piped the delegation's arrival. An honor guard stood on each side of the hatch— honor guard in name only, these Marines were armed.

Maria, dressed in traditional navy white with gold braid, her short cropped hair neatly trimmed under a visor cap, held her position, posture erect, and expression as neutral as she could make it awaiting the arrival of Doctor Gerhardt Vinson, head of the Earth delegation. The personnel on the George Washington had been hand picked and closely screened. It was imperative there be no physical contact between the New Earth peoples and Earth's. The long life gene must not be reintroduced on Earth, at least until Earth was ready for the massive changes it represented.

The hatched opened and one Marine entered the shuttle.

One by one, the delegation stepped onto the hanger deck of the Mandela to the recorded strains of 'This is a New Day'.

The twelfth member and Marine did not appear in the hatchway. Maria maintained her stoic posture.

Looks of anticipation seemed to worry the eleven as they mounted the platform. All eyes moved to the shuttle awaiting the last member of the group.

A gasp went up as the Marine emerged with the man in handcuffs.

Maria grimaced and stared hard at Dr. Vinson.

"Dr. Vinson. Can you explain how an armed person got aboard my shuttle? You were given very specific instructions that no weapons were allowed." Both her face and voice showed intense anger.

Gerhardt Vinson winced under the stare, recovered enough to nod. "Yes, Captain. These people are my responsibility. I cannot tell you how this man got on board with a weapon." He knew his words were on simulcast and HD all over the world. He could just imagine the storm this would unleash. Confidence in the UN was about normal, almost non-existent, and this certainly wasn't going to enhance the image.

Even Vinson's Prussian upbringing wasn't enough to withstand Maria's anger. Vinson had to explain something he knew nothing about and it left him stammering. Diplomatic skills just were not enough. "Rest assured Captain, we'll deal with this matter appropriately."

"*We* have custody of this man. He is our prisoner and we will deal with him in our own way. It is apparent he violated our rules and laws, not yours. I shouldn't have to point out this ship is sovereign." The man was ultimately returned to UN custody.

Maria had no desire to ridicule the man, in fact, just the opposite. She could do nothing about the embarrassment he had already suffered. Maybe she thought Earth would take heed that she and her crews were not to be trifled with.

Ambassador Vinson could only shake his head. "We are at your mercy. What do you want us to do?"

"A poor way to start anything that required trust on the part of everyone," Maria muttered to no one.

She stepped to the microphone and as if nothing had happened said, "Ladies and gentlemen. I am Maria Presk, Captain of the George Washington. May I present David Rohm, Captain of the Nelson Mandela and your host. Welcome aboard."

She and David took the time to shake each hand of the remaining eleven-member delegation and personally introduce themselves.

To a person, events had clearly overtaken their guests. For all but three, the space flight was a first. All were overwhelmed with the size of the Mandela. Even Maria had to admit, the three vessels, including the pinnance, were an awesome sight. Mandela, weighing in at over one million tons, its hanger alone capable of holding ten shuttles or six pinnances dwarfed everything and everyone.

A Marine stepped forward and asked the guests to follow him to the wardroom. Shortly, a steward seated them.

In front of each, a brochure showed interior and exterior pictures of the great ship. An electronic notepad, carafe of water, and glass, neatly arrayed on a napkin made of a material they had not seen before.

Maria, followed by David and three stewards, strode into the wardroom. Her demeanor was completely relaxed, as if the earlier confrontation had never occurred.

She took the seat at the head of the table. "Captain Rohm will conduct this meeting," she said. "When he has concluded, we will endeavor to answer you questions. Unfortunately, there will not be sufficient time to give you a tour. That will have to be reserved for another date."

Relaxed and mustering a smile, David extended a warm welcome. "We'll proceed with our original agenda."

He picked up his notepad, flashed it, "These are electronic recording devices. Everything said in this meeting will be transcribed onto your pads in real time." He held up his pad to show his inscribed remarks. "If you wish to

166

add your own notations, the stencil located inside will permit you to do so. Our computer does not record whatever you add to your pad, it is your private information. These are your pads and you may take them with you at the conclusion of these meetings."

David sat next to Maria and punched up the consol to start the meeting.

Almost in unison, the guests flinched seeing an image of the agenda flashed on a holoscreen above and off to one side, distracting them from their discussion about the form fitting chairs.

David's casual manner did little to end the awe most faces reflected. Exchanged protocols prompted some lively discussions.

"We are pleased to have representing the United Nations, Deputy Secretary General, Doctor Gerhardt Vinson, and his aides." He introduced the aides, for the record noting this was an historic moment. After he introduced the engineers, and astronauts from each of the sponsoring nations, Republic of China, Russian Federation, and United States, David said. "The twelfth member of your delegation was the head of the technical group." He faced the engineers and astronauts, "and selected by the three major nations. I understand he is a citizen of the Republic of China."

The Chinese engineer started to speak but David brushed him aside.

"I hope this isn't a reflection of the cooperation you can expect from each other. Notice, I said from each other. I'll tell you now, and I'm not given to repeat myself, we will stay with you long enough that your technical people have as good a grasp of Mandela's systems as we do. Then we are leaving. Our home world expects an attack from the Kalazecis and we have much to prepare. If you cannot get along and use this technology for what we firmly believe will be an invasion of Earth, so be it. It will not be on our heads."

He turned to the Chinese engineer, and said, "Do you have something to add?"

The man gave a wave that indicted acquiescence.

"Good," David said.

An understanding was reached on subsequent delegations. David only restricted the size, to make sure he had enough people to provide adequate training although he and Maria agreed their task was one of familiarization, not detailed instruction. David had yet to figure out how some of the systems worked, let alone the technology required to build some components. His greatest fear was that some would remain unknown to him. Discovery and development of new and previously unheard of materials would be perhaps the most important chore facing Earth and would tax Earth's research labs. Without these materials and basic elements, hyperspace travel simply would not happen.

Worse, Earth didn't have long to prepare itself. He and Maria suspected the Kalazecis would need a few months to prepare the Pagmok battle fleet. Earth, being at the far end of Kalazecis present haunts, probably bought them time. Kalazecis loses suffered at New Earth would not be taken lightly. They would learn from their mistakes. And knowing the Pagmok were warriors and not given to terrific cerebral power, preparations would be very thorough. How much time until the attack came remained anyone and everyone's guess.

Maria, aboard the George Washington, made plans to return to New Earth leaving her pinnance behind. She'd relented on demanding David return with her. It was evident that his expertise was essential if Earth was to have any chance at understanding such advanced technology. It was equally evident that she was concerned whether David could emotionally handle the responsibility. She made it emphatically clear that, at the end of the designated training period, he and his crew were to return to New Earth—no exceptions.

Accommodations aboard the pinnance in no way approached those on a starship. It would most likely be the most boring transit anyone on board had ever made. In fact, she was sure of it. It only took a few days longer to make the hyperspace flight in the pinnance than the George Washington, just over four weeks, GMT. She chuckled at how easy it had been to pick up again on the standard time. While the celestial clock kept the two systems comparative time, she, and the others were firmly in sync with New Earth.

As the day of departure approached, dignitaries had a change of heart. Overcoming reluctance or fear they lined up to take a pinnance ride to the Mandela.

Maria pressed the Washington's shuttle and pinnance into service to accommodate the increasing number of trips. The UN employee who had spent his time in Mandela's brig would return to Earth for trial. She keyed the consol and the images of the four leaders appeared.

Maria spent as much time as possible on the Mandela as the departure date approached. She and David had established something beyond a working relationship. She wasn't sure what that meant. But he did seem to want to spend time with her. She thought, *maybe*, and hoped she wasn't wishing with her heart and that what she sensed was real.

Earth personnel voiced complaints that they were never allowed to visit the Washington. But from the beginning, that ship had been off limits. Had anyone desired to capture one or both ships, they would have needed access to both. So, no earthlings ever sat foot on the George Washington.

Before the George Washington left orbit, the three heads of state and UN Secretary General joined Maria in a closed circuit teleconference.

"Gentlemen," she said. "This is the last time we will have such a meeting. I've done all I could to help you prepare to meet your commitment and defend Earth."

UN Secretary General said, "We'll do whatever is necessary to be ready. You've no idea how appreciative the people of Earth are for your assistance. You didn't have to make this trip, give us such a magnificent ship and all the technology. You very well may be our savior. I believe with all the nations of Earth pulling together, we will meet and overcome this threat."

Maria recalled some of the eloquent speeches she'd heard from Earth leaders but kept her thoughts to herself. In turn, Russian, China, and United States express their thanks.

First Contact

As she prepared to sign off, Maria added an admonition. "Gentlemen. I am leaving eleven people behind to assist you in understanding this technology. To a degree, their well-being is in your hands. I trust there will not be a repeat of the earlier armed incursion. If anything untold happens to my people, I will return and you will feel the brunt of my wrath."

Assurances poured in, specifically from the troika and UN, that anyone making such an attempt would be harshly dealt with. Apparently, the UN Secretary General hadn't read up on the history of Orion when he asked what happened to the mutineers who tried to take over the ship. Maria merely answered they'd been properly dealt with. David stretched the truth somewhat when he answered coldly and calmly that they'd been put out an airlock.

The silence from the four men, gave David the response he felt she wanted.

"Well gentlemen, we will be leaving orbit within the hour. Once we've settled this matter with the Kalazecis, perhaps our two worlds can discuss a long-term relationship. I wish you God Speed if the Kalazecis turn their attention toward you. Goodbye." She kept the communication open until each had responded and then cut the signal.

Over the next month, experts from every conceivable technical field from Earth's best and brightest made the trip to the Nelson Mandela. David spent considerable time with his counterparts developing the idea of using stealth nuclear mines scattered across the most likely entry points into the Sol system. Fortunately, for Earth, David knew the vectors available to the Kalazecis and the limits they imposed. That advantage went to Earth.

CHAPTER TWENTY-EIGHT
In Whose Interests

Cho Chin Wha ended the communication, and turned to his small select audience. The Chinese prime minister started to address the group but Gin Gee Din, secretary of the Communist party rose and interrupted. "What makes that woman think her little settlement is anything but a satellite of Earth? She actually believes we will negotiate with their trifling 'New Earth' as if it is a worthy partner. It's not big enough or important enough to merit further discussion."

"Do you think the other members feel the same way," asked one man? "After all, this little group, as you so disrespectfully put it, has given Earth the means to try to protect itself and have a chance to survive what is sure to be a most devastating attack."

"Who cares? The Chinese Republic will dominate this as we have everything for the last fifty years," Gin responded harshly.

Another voice asked, "How do you propose to do that with the troika firmly in control of the technology? Take it away from them?"

"Your caustic attitude is not welcome. I propose nothing of the sort. We all understand that political solutions are the only answer. War only destroys the wealth we have built. In addition to contributing to the technical and manufacturing organizations the UN, US, and Russia establish, we will set up something quite secretly in the interior. The mountain caves of Liang gave sanctuary to our great leader Mao over three hundred years ago. It can give sanctuary to our great efforts now. For every ship the troika builds, the Republic of China will build two. We will dominate every government on Earth, defeat these little aliens, and then annex New Earth—if there's anything left of it."

Prime Minister Cho said, "We must not exclude the Army-Navy from sharing in this great idea. It is time to remind everyone that without the Army-Navy, none of this would be possible." He smiled at the party secretary. He smiled at his political enemy of over forty years.

Cho continued, "You are a fool. You and what you represent is no more than a bureaucracy. Agreed, one that keeps the wheels of government functioning. But you have contributed little beyond paper shuffling to the real strength of the new China. You will continue to do as told as you have for the last twenty years."

His smile turned to a near snarl but the diminutive communist leader would not back down. "The Peoples Party of the Republic of China will not be talked to in this manner. We have earned a place at the center of the New China and you will not deny us."

Premier Cho looked past the little man. His concern, or lack of, quickly changed as his eyes swept the audience. His elevation to the premiership had come largely through the power the members of this gathering could and did ruthlessly use. It had won him the confirmation and could as easily strip him of that position. He had to pick his response carefully. The party had in fact, played an insignificant role in the development of the new China. If anything, it had been a hindrance mainly because it contributed little except political payoffs. And the Army-Navy was not immune, having perhaps contributing more to graft than all the rest combined. But he didn't need to open that wound now. Not when he could sense the time had arrived for world dominance.

"Of course the party has an important role to play." Cho felt confident that as long as he didn't publicly embarrass the party, he was relatively safe. After all, he did have the military behind him. As political commissar over the entire armed force, he had ensured their political power. His maneuvering over the last few years had made their place in the hierarchy secure. The generals owed him and he never hesitated to remind them of that.

Most estimates indicated it would take fifteen to twenty years to master the necessary technology to build these advanced ships and weapons. A lot could happen during that time. In his pocket, he wadded the note Maria had sent to him just before her departure for New Earth. How had she known about them building their own fleet? Her admonition that she would be watching nettled him. Who was the traitor among his own?

* * * *

Maria warmly greeted President Hammond. "Mathew, I see someone has been diligently working on a defensive plan against the Kalazecis. How's it looking?"

"Perhaps, in a manner of speaking, very well, even if I do say so myself. I asked Colonel Jabari to get his thinking down on paper. What was most pleasing was his inclusion of the scientists. Jabari knows we'll never be able to match the Kalazecis in numbers, so his strategy is to outsmart them. I like his thinking and most certainly agree with his strategic assessment. Now if we can only come up with the tactical plan to get the job done."

Maria sensed Mathew had struggled to overcome his natural tendency toward pacifism—a sentiment that would have been bolstered by most of his scientists. War was against his and their natures. But perhaps more than that, he did not understand that a good strategic plan could take them only so far. The same thing could be said for a good tactical plan. Without either, one had little chance. With both, you still had to have the men and women willing to make the sacrifices. Even then, you could still lose. There simply were no assurances in a war—other than that a good many people would die. And New Earth could not afford that. They simply didn't have the people to lose. Life was their most precious commodity. Whatever they came up with, they had to minimize casualties.

"I certainly agree," she responded thoughtfully absorbed by the battle plan. "Might work. Just might work" she heard herself say. "Have any of these ideas been tested. Any dry runs?" The one drawback, they only had plans to defend New Earth from dirtside. Maria knew if the battle ever got that far, it was lost.

"Not yet. Jimmy John and his advisors have scheduled a thirteen hundred meeting today. You're invited—of course." Both laughed. "In the conference room, he added."

New Earth's facilities were changing daily. The application of anti-grav to construction had cut concept to finished project by years. New Earths standard of living had gone up phenomenally along with the birth rate. That would all mean nothing if they couldn't stop the Kalazecis before they could get in range to attack New Earth.

Maria was the last to arrive at the conference room. Everyone stood as she entered. Technically, Mathew Hammond was the leader of New Earth. But, it was obvious the people looked to her leadership—a trust she wasn't sure was well placed. After all, she'd never fought a war. But then she'd been their leader through every crisis since leaving old Earth. And for some, not turning to her now would have been unthinkable.

Hammond moved from the head of the conference table offering his chair to Maria. When she hesitated, he said, "Please."

Maria sat and motioned the others to do the same, Hammond to her immediate right. If she'd learned anything about leading a group under stress, and particularly when you're outgunned, outmanned and on the short end of the technology curve, you had to show confidence. If she didn't, how could she expect the others to believe they could win?

"I appreciate your trust. I'll try not to let you down." She spent a few minutes briefing them on her trip to old Earth. She didn't try to hide her fears that Earth would implode before the Kalazecis ever got there.

"We've done what we could to help them. It is now up to Earth. They must put their differences aside if they are successfully to defend their world.

David and his people should be back here in two and one half months." She fully expected David to overstay his allotted time of two months. It would be just like him to want to pass on that last extra bit of technical information and instruction.

"Colonel Jabari." She motioned with a sweep of her hand. "Let's see what you've got for us."

For the next few minutes, the Marine took them step-by-step through the preparations for an invasion of New Earth.

Without any outward sign of concern, Maria sensed the fear that permeated the room. It was obvious these people knew they were planning their own death struggle.

She said, keeping her voice as light as possible, "Okay. What about before they get here?'

"Just started on that," Jabari said.

"Good," Maria quipped. "That means I won't have to argue so hard for my ideas." That brought a laugh and the tensions seemed to leave the room. She laid out how she saw the battle, and the only way New Earth could win. The enemy had to be stopped or so severely hurt it couldn't afford to engage New Earth. She defined winning as not losing as opposed to defeating the Kalazecis or Pagmok, depending on which group came at them. She suspected it would be Pagmok ships, manned by Pagmok with the Kalazecis on the bridge.

"I can tell you David has made the most of the time teaching our Earth brothers what this equipment can do and how the technology works. Without a doubt, the old adage, 'if you want to know how something works, teach it to someone else' has paid off in spades. But, for the time being, it's up to Colonel Jabari."

The Marine grimaced but took the floor. "During your absence, we've managed to learn a great deal. We've become very good at maneuvers and putting firepower on a specified target. A lot of it. We know our limitations but more importantly, how to play to our strengths. Maria has brought some changes David suggested and we are eager to incorporate them. It is my understanding Maria made some of the suggestions and has become an accomplished engineer in her own right."

Maria flipped the collar of her jumper, signifying she acknowledged the tribute laid at her feet.

Over the next two hours, she coaxed, urged and cajoled the plan until she had what she thought was something workable. And it wasn't too far off what she had originally thought out. But a lot of work remained, most of it manufacturing the hardware that would give them their chance, their only one. Science might be on their side, and with Martin Grabel in the Kalazecis camp, even that was not a sure thing, the numbers were not. Stop the Kalazecis or be overrun. She had no doubt Kalazecis would willingly sacrifice Pagmok ships and crews would be willingly sacrificed to gain their objective. Deceit and stealth would play a major role. Particularly since they'd have the Orion, with its stealth capabilities, as well as Martin to warn them of what had been New Earth's primary advantage..

* * * *

Martin stepped into his cabin and removed his rebreather. It hadn't taken much of an adjustment to change the nitrogen and oxygen mix to levels acceptable for him. Desiccants had reduced the moisture to a comfortable level. The emotional adjustments had been a struggle for him, one that had made him doubt the wisdom of leaving New Earth and joining the Kalazecis. Their distrust of him at times verged on overwhelming. The maneuver he'd given them to avoid Maria's trap had eased tensions somewhat. Well, that and the fact he knew more about Orion than all of them ever would. His many years handling the engineering while David was incapable of leading had uniquely prepared him. And that was an edge the Kalazecis would never match. He'd already decided someone other than the Kalazecis had developed their high tech science. What they knew about FTL, they'd learned from someone else.

Still, that didn't keep them from shunning him or jumping on a good put-down when it presented itself. The humane treatment the Kalazecis received while captives of the humans made little if any difference in their attitudes.

In some circles, this might have been understandable. Gnacislas, fleet admiral, was going home minus his four-ship armada, beaten by an inferior opponent. And now the earthlings had FTL capability, energy weapons, and all the other technology the Kalazecis had brought. Not only that, the humans had gained the respect and maybe the loyalty of the Rococo and the First. Since he had personally ordered the destruction of a Pagmok ship and its one-hundred eight crewmembers, the Pagmok were even less to be trusted than normally.

Martin's review of Kalazecis records suggested this commander might not have long to live once Orion reached the Kalazecis home world. And even that arrival remained problematic. How long would they be out there, moving at three tenths' c before a Kalazecis ship came to their rescue?

Martin jumped as the com buzzed. "Earthman, report to engineering."

This Kalazecis had made no effort to hide his contempt toward him. To his own surprise, Martin's response had been one of controlled aggression. And for him, that was a major accomplishment. He keyed his translator.

Martin had tried to get his tongue around the Kalazecis language but found it impossible. He'd gained some proficiency at reading with the result that more and more documents were kept out of his sight and video screens were customarily blocked from his view. His hosts wanted to isolate him as much as possible. But without his knowledge and technical ability, Orion and their prospects of reaching home were considerably diminished *and they knew it.*

"I'm tired. What is the problem? Maybe it can wait until I've had some sleep," he responded curtly. Martin shook his head in resignation as the hatch opened.

A guard, only a centimeter or two shorter than he, leaned in and motioned him to follow.

Martin obeyed, being dragged through the passageway once was enough.

It took almost an hour to fix a problem that could have waited until he'd had some sleep. Still, the supposed emergency gave him the opportunity to make a few unheeded adjustments that could benefit him if and when the time for his confrontation came. And he was sure it would. Most importantly, the Kalazecis often left him alone when he was working and did so this time. He took the chance to access their mainframe computer and worked some algorithms that would ensure him having some control over his destiny. Once at the Kalazecis home world, the Emperor just might see things a little more clearly than Gnacislas—but he couldn't count on that.

* * * *

Hours later, Martin awoke as the claxon sounded the Kalazecis equivalent of battle stations. Whatever was happening, no one had summoned him.

Deliberately, he dressed and headed in the passageway toward the galley. He stopped long enough to grab some sandwiches from the cache prepared solely for him before heading on to the engine room.

Keeping any semblance of circadian time had proved impossible. Martin managed to keep track of the passing hours through the computer. By that reckoning, Orion had been underway for sixty-seven earth days or T-days, for terra days as he now accounted for time.

Crews hustled around the engine room doing little more than making sure everything was as he'd told them it had to be. Kalazecis attention to detail lacked the persistence of humans but he'd managed to convince them Orion would explode if they didn't maintain the engines as he said.

On the engineering control consol, he saw an image transmitted from the bridge. A ship was approaching.

Must be Kalazecis he realized as the *all clear* sounded.

Three crewmembers joined him. So far, his ability to understand them had gone undetected. Yet they spoke cautiously.

From what he picked up, the Emperor was not particularly the forgiving type and that this would be the last time, they'd see their Captain.

Martin watched as the Casimir engines were throttled back to idle, something that required a degree of finesse and only the fourth or fifth time this crew had performed the maneuver.

After completing the task, Martin followed orders and retreated to his cabin. He no idea what would happen next or to him.

Sitting forlornly on his bunk, he looked up as the hatch opened and the Kalazecis first officer stepped in.

Standing next to the opening the Kalazecis said, "You may have fooled some of the crew but I know you understand a great deal of our language. You are to transfer everything in this ship's computer to the vessel standing alongside, the Cccrcjola. A crew will be here shortly to assist in the transfer."

He turned to leave. Through the translator, Martin said, "And then what happens?"

Without passion he answered, "This ship will be destroyed."

Martin's carefully laid plans would evaporate with Orion's destruction.

"That isn't a good idea," he said. "There is technology here you can use but we need time. We need to strip Orion and take the hardware with us. To destroy it along with the ship would be foolhardy. There's information here that could be invaluable. You must talk to your superiors."

CHAPTER TWENTY-NINE
Kalazecis Home World

Martin Grabel waited in the outer chamber, alone in a crowd. That wasn't new to him. Up until Erik found him on the streets of New York, he'd spent most of his life alone. Even when working with others, Martin remained isolated—mostly due to his choice.

Kalazecis didn't lack understanding of what grandeur and pomp were all about. Gilded stone colonnades six meters tall fronted the throne room entrance, embracing four-meter solid ebony colored wooden doors inlaid with ivory. White marble floors, intricately patterned with precious and semiprecious stones smoothly polished to a mirror finish, reflected light from numerous small glass covered domes overhead. The effect gave a surrealistic look to the entire antechamber.

The wealth, the extravaganza was beyond anything Martin had ever seen. It didn't say much for the benevolent side of this ruler, or maybe all Kalazecis. But what knowledge he'd gained over the last few months about their civilization, left him with the definite impression the majority of the population didn't share in the wealth. And in this case, the majority was Pagmok.

He waited, flanked by Kalazecis guards. Even with his rebreather on, the nitrous reducing atmosphere left a tangy taste. Since arriving three months earlier on Myslac, he'd been totally isolated from other beings except for technicians assigned to learn what they could from the equipment stripped from Orion.

Most coveted by him and unknown to his hosts, Orion's computer data downloaded into the Kalazecis computer base included some key program he'd written and the algorithms to protect them. They could make the difference in whether he lived or died.

He knew he was smarter than the Kalazecis, his science more advanced than what they fully understood if not always as advanced as what they had access to, but was that enough?

And where did the Kalazecis technology come from?

Wherever or whoever provided it, remained a closely guarded secret. They never spoke of it, nor had the people of Myslac. Still, Martin was convinced Erik had been right—these beings were not bright enough to have developed everything he'd seen.

Responding to some silent signal Martin hadn't seen, the guards surrounding him came to attention.

Slowly, unattended, the great doors swung open.

In a rhythmic cadence, his guards moved forward, with Martin in the middle. Entering the throne room must have been an event few Kalazecis experienced. The look on his guards' faces showed a mixture of fear and marvel.

A few meters into the room, the guards stopped.

First Contact

A Kalazecis approached and said, "New Earth Human Martin Grabel, I will escort you to the throne and be at your side throughout your audience. If the Emperor speaks to you or asks a question, look directly at him and answer forthrightly." Maybe a hundred people, Martin had decided long ago to think of the Kalazecis as people, lined the walls watching his entrance.

Martin nodded and asked, "What is your name?"

No answer came. All attention focused on the Emperor as he entered from behind the dais.

A person dressed in a deep purple robe stepped from behind the throne. Martin's guide said he was what amounted to an oracle, a prophesier of good to come of whatever he spoke.

The oracle declared in a tenor voice, "All gather to hear Djuc, Emperor of Myslac, the Pagmok, Rococo and the entire universe."

The Emperor seated himself on a very common looking wooden throne, silencing everyone in the room as they bowed.

Martin's attendant took two steps forward and joined the communal raking. The entire entourage seemed to do so with one eye open, watching to see how he reacted to the Emperor's presence.

Not to be outdone, Martin took a step forward and gave a bow, really more of genuflect that would have made Shakespeare proud. As he returned to his spot, he eyed his attendant and saw a most approving countenance. A collective gentle sigh echoed across the room.

Emperor Djuc motioned Martin forward.

Both he and his escort walked to within three meters of the throne and stopped.

"Human," said the Emperor as he brushed long flaming red hair off his shoulder, "Tell me of your world, and of your role there. From what my people tell me, you must have been a human of great importance."

Martin waited for the translator to finish. Apparently, the Emperor had been told of Orion's journey and other information the Kalazecis had picked up from their encounters during their three-month incarceration at New Earth.

Slowly and with much deference, Martin gave a succinct as possible interpretation of Earth and the people without seeming to run on forever.

The Emperor leaned forward, "Your people are warriors."

Martin stuttered and offered a denial to the remark.

"Since learning of your planet, we pointed our radio and HD receivers toward that segment of space. My scientists tell me it is a hodgepodge of systematized clutter with much war and talk of war. Many languages and just as many leaders add to the confusion. How do you accomplish anything?"

In a quiet almost retiring voice, Martin said, "Earth is primarily made up of nation states. Most of the nations have democratically elected governments. The people select who will be their leader."

Djuc brought his hand to his mouth in a show of surprise. "What a novel idea. I don't think it would work here on Myslac."

Martin couldn't tell if the Emperor mocked him. He responded with deference, "Some nations are led by monarchs." He wanted no argument with the Emperor, public or private although he did acknowledge that any transmissions coming from Earth would certainly leave a confused impression.

"What would we gain by an alliance with Earth?"

Martin didn't hesitate. He'd worried about how to point this audience in a positive direction, one that could lead to a dialog that would beneficial to the two worlds. "Both cultures are rich in customs, knowledge, and history. Establishing diplomatic relations could lead to trade that would be of great benefit to all."

"What if they fear and do not welcome us? What if your Earth brethren see us as a threat? They do not have FTL capability. And obviously do not possess the energy sources the Kalazecis own."

"I believe they would welcome opening a meaningful relationship with the Kalazecis world," your highness.

"Really?" Suddenly, the Emperor turned dower. Eyebrows bunched, lips pursed he took on a look that Martin could only interpret as menacing, deadly.

"I think you are lying. Your world is a cauldron of hypocrisy, deceit, and treachery. I think we should take our great ships to Earth and annihilate all opposition. Subdue the people and impose our leadership. Our science, our technology, in particular our ability to lead, are much advanced over your species. Therefore, we should rule."

Martin tried unsuccessfully to hold in a gasp. "Surely your highness, you cannot countenance war without first making the effort to establish a peaceful relationship."

Djuc held up his hand in a truculent gesture, signaling Martin to stop.

The Emperor stood. "You will provide us with all the knowledge and information we require to make our invasion a success." With that, the Emperor left the room.

Martin was dumbfounded. He'd betrayed his own people when they'd idiotically decided on war without giving the alternatives proper attention. But the Kalazecis were worse. He couldn't make his feet move when his attendant took his arm to lead him away.

* * * *

Martin was surprised that the Kalazecis made no effort to keep their order of battle information from him—information he would put to good use given the opportunity. Nightly, his soul wretched at the terrible situation he'd placed Earth and ultimately New Earth. Any time he could steal from his Kalazecis tasks, he worked on his own plan—one that he hoped would disrupt if not destroy the premeditated invasion of Earth.

The Kalazecis intended to do what was necessary to conquer Earth; they'd take New Earth when they got around to it. Earth was the immediate prize.

According to the *great plan* put forth, the Kalazecis needed at least five T-years (the Kalazecis had followed Martin's suggestion for calibrating time) for the fleet to build up the strength necessary to take Earth with one decisive blow. They wanted no protracted fight and knew that overwhelming power was the way to achieve victory.

Martin made no effort to push the plan one way or the other. In fact, he'd eagerly endorsed it. If asked to comment, he made his suggestions as truthful and forthright as possible. They got his very best thinking. But it was always in line with the great plan. In order to make his *own* plan work, the Kalazecis had to have complete faith in what he was telling them. At every opportunity to check his work or advice, the Kalazecis never found it wrong or lacking. He had their grudging confidence. He was giving them sound advice.

Occasionally, the Kalazecis sent a pinnance out to launch probes to Earth. Their primary mission was solely to collect information and return to Myslac, the home world. Occasionally, a probe was lost but that was acceptable for the information they got in return. Earth, from their minds, clearly had no way to detect these probes or interfere in their information gathering. It was this attitude that Martin Grabel encouraged.

No one on Myslac could match Martin's skills in developing computer systems. They simply had no one that could compete with his intellect. It hadn't taken him long to learn the Kalazecis system and how to defeat it. More evidence the Kalazecis had not developed their own technology. His fellow scientists had no idea they were almost daily being manipulate by their traitor scientific colleague.

* * * *

Almost one year to the day after arrival on Myslac, Martin sat at his desk watching a HD of a Kalazecis warship leaving home world with twenty drones on board and a pinnance in its belly. Fifteen drones were planned for Earth with the warship monitoring and five for New Earth, launched and monitored from the pinnance. Martin had no assurance he would ever have another chance to alert both Earth and New Earth. No matter what he did, neither Earth nor New Earth would receive his efforts as an act of contrition. He wasn't doing it for forgiveness—he would never forgive himself.

It would be almost a year before the warship returned to Myslac. So even if the Kalazecis discovered his treachery, he had at least that much time to move forward on his plan to thwart the attack. He had been so wrong to turn on his own and besides, his new masters had not given him the honor he was due. He would make it right.

* * * *

"Captain, were receiving a signal from just beyond the hyper limit."

Maria stepped to the consol. Since Martin's defection, she spent most of her time on board her flagship the George Washington, anticipating an attack at any moment. She and David had become an engineering force to be reckoned with. Daily, new ideas and solutions to problems flowed from their group. And she couldn't have been happier. Some of the earlier feelings the two had had for each other were beginning to show. David had taken particular interest in getting acquainted with his son.

In her quiet command voice she asked, "What is it?"

"Can't tell for sure. It's on an old frequency. We don't have anything out there. Can't be ours."

"Can you read it?" She forced herself to remain calm in spite of what she was thinking and feeling.

"Yes."

"Put it on my plot board."

Maria jolted almost as if someone had struck her as the words scrolled across her screen. "Are you recording this?"

"Yes Ma'am."

Her first reaction. "Is this believable or is it a trick? Assemble my staff in the wardroom immediately. Pipe this reception in there."

"Aye sir."

Maria was first in the wardroom and continued reading the message.

Within minutes, her staff seated themselves around the table and stared at the screen. Not having benefit of the opening statement, no one was sure what they were reading.

Finally, Maria stood. "I'll start this from the beginning. As you will see, it is a Kalazecis probe and the message seems to be from Martin."

Exclamations, some derisive, others of unbelief erupted. Maria made no effort to refute or encourage any of the remarks.

For the next twenty minutes, the group sat spellbound. Martin had sent the Kalazecis Order of Battle. But that wasn't all. In detail, he outlined what he'd done to disrupt the planned attack on Earth and subsequent launch against New Earth.

Maria let out a short pent up breath. "Do we believe it?"

CHAPTER THIRTY
Response

Maria watched from her plot board aboard the George Washington as the fleet assembled. With this as her flagship, she would lead them into battle. Everyone understood this war to save Earth was necessary. Particularly since New Earth was responsible for everything that had happened. Earth had had no part in the conflict, yet the Kalazecis designated it as their first target.

"Wait until Old Earth finds out we went to war on their behalf and never told them," said Erik.

"I can wait," said David.

Maria shook her head, her smile border on a grin. Here she was, leading her people into war and asking no one for help. Did she really trust her judgment over anyone else's? Was she being arrogant? Could she be setting everything they'd accomplished up for failure? She decided that could be the outcome but she wasn't about to submit New Earth's future to people who had yet to prove they could, let alone would, work together for their own good. She was satisfied with her decision. She would apologize to old Earth later; *when she knew the outcome.*

Data extracted from the Kalazecis computers gave the location of the Kalazecis home world and provided Washington's astrogators the precise location where the enemy would come out of hyperspace to transition to its new course to Earth. Time to the intercept point at Praesepe or the Beehive Cluster less than two FTL T-days. It was here New Earth would lay its trap for the Pagmok fleet soon to be en route to Earth. If Martin's warning was correct, the enemy fleet would leave Myslac in three T-days.

"Everything set?" she asked.

"As ready as we can be. Any more practice and I think the entire fleet will go stark raving mad," Erik said. David chimed in with a chuckle echoing Svern's wearied beleaguer voice.

New Earth could not build warships the size and complexity of the Washington in they time they had. They lacked the people either to man them or even to build facilities capable of handling something of that size.

Instead, they designed and built FTL fighters faster, more maneuverable, thanks to the development of inertial dampeners, and armed with technologies that could kill Kalazecis and Pagmok long before they were within range to use their own weapons. That was thanks to David's engineering skills. Even if the enemy stumbled onto this technology, their fleet was just too large to accomplish any significant modification that might influence the outcome of the engagement. The launch date they'd set was a good indication they had no new technologies to deploy.

Most of New Earth's fabrication took place on the processing and assembly station orbiting at almost half a million klicks above the planet. Mining of the minerals necessary for hull FTL fabrication was done on New Earth. To keep the Rococo from becoming dinner for the Pagmok or earning the wrath of the Kalazecis, Maria had not used them in the mining or processing of the vital ore.

Each space fighter was a self-contained unit, carried a crew of three, and was capable of staying out at least four months.

In most navies, these would have been described as pickets but not here. These ships were deadly and size-for-size more lethal than anything the enemy had. Two supply vessels equipped to extend this time to eight months had joined the armada.

"We needed the practice with these new weapons," Maria said. "Hopefully, they won't be necessary but with the Pagmok leading the enemy charge, we have to expect an all out frontal assault once they know we mean to stop them."

The folderol stopped as Mathew Hammond stepped through the hatch.

"Mr. President," Maria said. "Have a good night's sleep?"

"Yes, indeed Captain. It seems the fleet is about ready to leave. I need to make my goodbye's and get the hell out of here or end up in some spot out there." He waved at the overhead. Hammond didn't understand the science or mechanics involved in space or space travel. And he made no bones about it. He left little doubt of his high regard for everything the scientific and engineering groups had done to prepare New Earth for the assault that would eventually come. Maria had to agree it was far removed form the coziness of academia and cloistered courtrooms.

Colonel Jabari stuck his head through the hatch. "Mr. President, your shuttle is ready when you are."

Hammond walked to Maria and extended his hand. Then quite un-Hammond like, he embraced her. "God speed Captain." Tears welled in his eyes. He knew the perils these people were about to face and for him, it hurt.

Maria returned the hug. "We'll be back shortly." She knew some of them would not return and she hurt also. Buried deep in her mind laid the inevitable questions. Who armed the Kalazecis? And would they stand by and see their surrogate interests destroyed by the rag tag bunch of upstarts from New Earth?

She walked down the passageway to David's quarters and knocked at the open hatch. "May I come in?"

"Of course. You didn't have to come down here. I planned on seeing you off from the bridge."

"Thank you. But I really prefer it this way."

It didn't seem to make much difference to David whether he went or stayed. But he was needed on New Earth. Much equipment from Orion was beginning to show the ravages of time and use and New Earth was in a race to replace or update most of its technical infrastructure. She did want something functional to come back to.

"I know Michael is looking forward to working with you."

"Me too. He's shown a talent for engineering. Actually, he's applied good principles in basic research. We'll get along fine."

"He did want to accompany us. But Colonel Jabari convinced him he was needed dirtside. So, it's done."

First Contact

Maria had waited fifty years to marry David the first time. His near miraculous recovery had been only seven years prior. She could wait again. And a lot longer if necessary.

"I shall miss you and Michael." She gave David a peck on the cheek.

"You can do better than that." He pulled her close and softly kissed her lips.

At that instant, she hated the Pagmok, Kalazecis, and Martin Grabel more that anyone could know. She could only guess what David thought or felt about her. As far as his own mores were concerned, he was starting with a clean slate. One that events would mold afresh beyond her control, one that might not include her. Of course, she had changed. He would see a woman quite capable of ordering the death of another person or being. One who could and would order her own people to their deaths protecting some reasoned philosophy and maybe not his, maybe one mired in a past that he could not understand. She ached as never before.

David waved as he walked toward the hanger.

Three T-days later, Maria stood in the ready room just off the hanger deck, surrounded by the fighter pilots and their crews.

Erik Svern stood at her side.

Somberly she said, "Mr. Svern, take command of your squadrons." She knew she was ordering some of these young people to their deaths. And they knew it too. But she saw it as their best hope. There was always the chance the Pagmok might see the desperation in their situation and surrender or withdraw. She just couldn't believe the Pagmok adoration for the Kalazecis was all that great.

"Aye, sir." Erik responded. He looked out across the assembled crews. "You all have the order of battle. Once the Pagmok commit, we will open fire at least five hundred thousand klicks before the enemy can bring their weapons to bear. We have that much advantage and must make the best of it. They have, by our last count, at least one hundred fifty ships, mostly over one million tons each, much like the Washington. Against that, we bring our forty—thirty-seven fighters, the George Washington and two supply ships, unarmed. Your fighters are faster and more maneuverable, your weaponry almost twice as effective in range and destructive force as anything the Pagmok have. They do have long-range torpedoes. However, their fighters are no match for you. As long as we can, we'll stand off and pound them. If we're lucky, we'll get enough of them that they might withdraw. Most likely, they will try to overwhelm us, run us down. If we have to engage at close quarters, I hope to sow enough confusion that we can get in amongst them and really raise havoc. In close, they won't be able to shoot without hitting their own. We have to count on that. Also, once you close, target their engines and flight hangers. Their fighter's mission time is less than thirty minutes. Destroy their landing and takeoff platform and they die. It's our only way to succeed. First squadron designation, Arthur; second squadron Guinevere. Any comments?"

* * * *

Gnacislas, the highest-ranking Kalazecis on board the Pagmok fleet and therefore the Emperor's official representative said, "How long to shed all delta v?"

"Six periods at our current decel," answered the Pagmok astrogator. Almost twenty cycles would be saved on the Earth transit by stopping dead still to affect the course change. Normally, a warship would never allow itself to be dead in space but the Kalazecis were confident no enemy was within striking distance so the dead stop and course adjustment shouldn't be a problem. With an armada approaching one hundred ships, their exposure was minimal. Besides, there wasn't anyone within two hundred light years capable of bringing sufficient force to challenge the Kalazecis.

"Continue the decel. When you reach one half light speed, launch twenty fighters," ordered the Pagmok Captain.

Gnacislas's derisive laugh irritated the Pagmok.

"You waste our resources. Have you seen a threat? I see no enemy?"

Slowly, the Pagmok Captain turned to the astrogator. "Make sure we don't out run the fighters. They can stay aloft for only one half period. He then turned toward the Emperor's representative. His voice sounded like acid. "I am a warrior, you are a politician. Do not try to tell me my business."

This was probably as close to a threat as the Kalazecis had ever had directed at him. As he considered his response, the astrogator, his voice at a high pitch, said, "Sir," but before he could finish a Pagmok voice spilling through the com demanding they stand down. The Kalazecis visibly shook as the woman's voice stopped all talk on the bridge.

* * * *

Quiet settled over the group.

Maria walked among the pilots and their crewmembers occasionally calling one by name—she knew them all. To each, she said a variant of these words. "You are the best of the best. You've trained for hours in the simulators, and logged over one thousand hours of actual flight time. Your enemy cannot match your skills or your equipment. Still, do not underestimate the Pagmok. They are formidable warriors. They are warriors by their very nature. Humans have never experienced any one like them. I have no illusions about their willingness to fight. I'm not that sure about their willingness to die for the Kalazecis. But, we can't count on any reticence on their part. Kill them before they kill you. Good hunting."

Erik stepped beside Maria and said, "Man your fighters at eighteen sixteen; launch at eighteen thirty-one. Any questions?"

Maria saluted the squadrons and left the ready room.

Contemplatively, she said to Erik, "Why the sixteen and thirty-one?"

"Give them something to think about. Make it fifteen and thirty and it can mean anything. Sixteen and Thirty-one means just that. I want them to think precisely. It could make the difference in whether they return or not."

"I like that, particularly if it brings one more back."

Once on the bridge, Maria positioned the Washington behind a small planetoid. From there she watched Erik direct each squadron on the tight beam transmitter.

Arthur moved behind a similar rock one million klicks ahead off Washington's starboard. Ten fighters, each with a pilot and two crewmembers disappeared from the screen, securely in place, out of sight. Her gaze never faltered as she watched Eric address the pilots in a calm command voice.

Guinevere squadron took up position behind a slow moving-asteroid off the port side. It would only be in position for them for about twenty hours. But that should be more than enough. The Pagmok were in system and less than five T-hours away. "Call signs 'Alpha one' for Arthur, Alpha two for Guinevere, Omega for Washington to join the fight," Erik said.

Maria said, "Whoever would have thought you a romantic? You romance them with Arthur and Guinevere then settle the matter with the alpha and omega. The beginning and the end."

He nodded. "See, you thought you knew me."

"Why not Romeo and Juliet?"

"They killed themselves. Not quite what I had in mind."

She laughed and added, "Let's hope we have a good plan."

"It is. We have surprise working for us in every maneuver. Coupled with superior firepower and better trained pilots, we'll win this."

Almost aside and for the bridge crew to hear he added, "If it doesn't work, it's your idea."

She ignored the macabre remark, understanding he meant to relive tension. "It was just a suggestion. You didn't have to follow it and besides, you fleshed it out."

Com announced, "Pagmok fleet within two million klicks."

Erik issued the opening order, his voice firm and commanding, "Alpha One, move into position and hold."

The ten fighters slid from behind their cover and stopped twenty degrees off the Pagmok fleet's current heading, just under two million klicks distant.

Maria spoke calmly to com. "Open a channel to the Pagmok fleet, wide beam and transmit in Pagmok.

"Pagmok fleet commander. This is Captain Maria Presk, commander of the New Earth force. We do not want a fight with you but cannot permit your passage to Earth. Reverse your course and return to the Kalazecis home world. You will not receive another warning."

A few minutes passed.

As expected, the enemy launched over fifty fighters and altered its course, taking it on a heading skirting the conflict.

"Sir," com announced in a surprised voice, "Enemy fleet has slowed. To half light speed."

"Don't want to run away from their fighters. Remember, those small ships have only thirty minutes of flight time and have to refuel. They've launch too early. Couldn't be better for us."

Erik waited until they had a definitive bearing on the hostiles that confirmed they were coming for Arthur. The Pagmok fleet's new heading would take it further into the trap.

He punched the com icon, "Guinevere, take position Alpha two and hold."

The next few minutes would decide the day—fight, or no fight. All eyes on Washington's bridge stayed glued to their plot boards, all chatter had stopped. No one moved.

An additional fifty enemy fighters launched in response to Alpha two. As anticipated and hoped, the Pagmok had taken the bait. Their fighters went after Arthur and Guinevere while the main fleet again altered its course. Its escape from the trap had become impossible without devastating losses.

Maria, her voice calm, ordered Washington from behind its cover and launched the remaining fighters, then waited.

At seven hundred thousand klicks, Maria, with a touch of sadness in her otherwise iron voice ordered, "Com issue orders to open fire."

Systematically, the twenty fighters of squadrons Arthur and Guinevere closed to within two hundred fifty kilometers and blasted the Pagmok fighters into nothing. In less than fifteen minutes, all the enemy fighters were dead. None had even fired a shot.

There was profound silence on Washington's bridge. They'd hope for this result but were subdued at the total devastation they'd caused on the enemy. Even Erik seemed awed.

As Maria had said, the Pagmok were warriors. The enemy fleet increased to military speed without altering their heading. As much as Erik hated it, his fighters would have to close. All he was sure of was the Pagmok ships would take one hell of a beating—as would his fighters as the two groups engaged.

He ordered continuous firing as his outnumbered little squadrons attacked the massive ships. New Earth's more devastating firepower may not be enough. They would soon know.

Maria flinched as two bright spots appeared on her screen and as quickly disappeared. Com announced, trying unsuccessfully to remain calm, "Two lead enemy ships have disappeared."

Maria, Erik at her side intently watched the plot. The range between fleets was too great for the Pagmok weapons. They had yet to score a hit despite firing far more salvos than the New Earth fighters. David's design changes made the basic Kalazecis weapons more lethal by a factor of two and his own designed targeting system was everything they had all hoped for. In fact, his changes turned the head on attack against the Pagmok from a suicide run to one of devastation for the enemy.

But that was changing rapidly. Erik turned to com, "Signal the squadrons to start evasive maneuvers." In another ten seconds, Pagmok weapons would start killing his people.

Both squadrons accelerated toward the Pagmok fleet.

Within Pagmok range, Erik ordered twenty fighters to execute a starburst; inertial dampeners cancelled any g-forces. Reaching the top of their arc, the fighters swung parallel to the Pagmok fleet and raced to get behind them, raking

186

the great ships as they passed with devastating laser fire. No enemy fighters rose to challenge the New Earth attack. In addition, little or no effort had been made by the Pagmok to arm their laser cannons. Almost thirty minutes were required to bring them to battle readiness. Time they never had. Apparently, the enemy hadn't anticipated the need and had prepped only the one hundred fighters previously launched and destroyed. Potentially, over four thousand could be in reserve.

Both Arthur and Guinevere squadrons raced to get beyond the range of the enemy energy canons. Once inside the effective range of the enemy, blasting the hangers beyond anything usable became almost a casual event. But it meant the death knell for the Pagmok fleet.

Getting there wasn't without pain. Seven fighters had fallen to Pagmok weapons.

The enemy, unable to shed delta v fast enough, unable to accelerate because heavily damage ships blocked their passage, unable to maneuver in close quarters without inertial dampeners, unable to kill its enemy, could only die. And Marie made sure they did.

Four more spots blossomed on the plot—four more Washington class ships were dead. At least forty more severely damaged—some no more than floating hulks, others with repair, serviceable.

Eric recited the statistics, "The count, Pagmok losses, Ships: forty-six; crew: eighteen thousand either casualties or at the least unable to fight."

New Earth, seven fighters, twenty-one dead crewmen. The Pagmok were clearly at the mercies of New Earth.

"Open a channel." She remained standing at her command consol. "This is Captain Maria Presk. As you can see, you are no match for us. Stand down and the death of your fellow warriors will end. Your alternative is total destruction."

Pensively, she walked toward the captain's chair and sat. Almost twenty minutes passed when they had an answer.

"New Earth Captain, what are your terms?"

An explosion of pent up anticipation seemed to burst forth from every member of the bridge crew. Yet, in the back of Maria's mind nagged the question, would New Earth get away with this victory or would a Kalazecis benefactor show up and make its displeasure known.

CHAPTER THIRTY-ONE
The Aftermath

Seated, Maria faced Gnacislas, the Kalazecis imperial representative. "I would think you would have learned a lesson after we defeated you at New Earth." She shook her head. "Apparently not."

Gnacislas had led the four ships captured by New Earth forces almost five years earlier.

"So, what do I do with you? It would appear while the Pagmok are willing to fight for your Emperor; they are not as anxious to die for him. That must mean you only pick on the weak and those smaller that you. Not a very good resume." She paused, watching the Pagmok carefully. "You will return to your foster world and tell your Emperor we wish to have peace between our peoples. Tell him we can destroy him and all Kalazecis if he forces us to."

The George Washington's conference room was eerily quiet as the dozen or so people waited for his response.

Gnacislas looked around the room with interest. It had changed much since he'd called it his and the Emperor's crest hung on the wall. Now, a New Earth's emblem hung in its place.

"You have signed my death warrant. You would have done my family a greater favor had you killed me in battle."

Maria laid her hand flat on the table, her lips pursed into a thin slit. "So. That tells us a great deal about your civilization. If your leader kills the messenger, and in your case, the loser, how did you survive the debacle five years earlier?"

"Martin Grabel saved my life," Gnacislas quietly said. "He intervened on my behalf before the Emperor."

Maria couldn't hide her startled look try as she might. "Martin?"

"It has not always been this way on my world. Djuc's grandfather ruled with kindness. The people much revered him. As the old Emperor lay dying, Djuc killed his father and took the throne for himself. He kills for pleasure." He looked hard at his Kalazecis compatriots. Apparently, he'd given them a visual reprimand that what was said here went no further. His life was in their hands.

Maria stood. "That's all for now. We'll meet again in the morning."

After the Kalazecis left, she ordered the Pagmok leaders brought before her.

She didn't stand as the three ranking prisoners entered the conference room and aides motioned them into seats. "Who is the senior officer?"

One Pagmok stood.

His move misinterpreted, the two marines stationed at the door moved forward, leveling their rifles at him.

Quickly the Pagmok sat, realizing his mistake. No fear showed in his eyes and the face remained a mask of stoicism.

That's the warrior in him, Maria thought.

He gave the names and ranks of the three-member group.

Maria asked, "What are we going to do with you? Will the Emperor have you killed if you go back to Myslac? That's a lot of your kind to sacrifice. Do the Kalazecis mean that much to you?" She eyed the Pagmok leader looking for any indication her words had some resonance.

Back stiff as a board, commanding all his dignity he answered, "We were no more than cannibals when the Kalazecis came among us. Whatever we are today, it is because of them. We owe them much."

"You didn't answer my question. Will the Emperor execute all of you if you go back to Myslac?"

"No, just the leaders."

"You and your staff? How many more?"

"The Captain of each ship and his staff." Still the Pagmok, none of them, showed any emotion. Death or the prospect of death seemingly held no fear for them.

"Is that all right with you?" Maria almost felt personal shame for asking what she considered a ridiculous question.

"It spares our families. That is sufficient."

"Really? We could settle you somewhere else. Do you have a home world? Maybe we could take you there."

"No." His emphatic answer startled Maria. "Then our families would die. That is not acceptable. We will return to the Kalazecis home world and whatever fate Djuc commands."

Maria stood and the Pagmok followed suit. "I will give you my answer soon. You may return to your vessels. But," she sternly warned them, "tell your warriors if anyone on board any Pagmok ship does anything that harms even one of my people, we will resume firing on your ships. We will destroy all of them and every member of their crews. Is that understood?"

Somberly, in what she interpreted as sadness, the Pagmok commander nodded.

With that, the Marines escorted the Pagmok to the hanger bay.

Maria had given no indication what might be in store for the Pagmok or Kalazecis prisoners or their ships.

Erik was the first to speak, "Seems our options are limited."

"Maybe," she said.

Erik asked, "Why do I have the feeling you're about to overreach?"

"You know me too well. I'm not sure I like that." Her smile suggested the comment was a joke.

"Okay, Captain. Out with it. I know and you know you've got something in mind and I can tell already that I don't like it."

"Erik, Erik, Erik." She shook her head. "Okay, you win. Maybe we need to look into a different government for Myslac."

"Regime change? Oh, shit. Excuse me Captain but this is too much."

"Relax. Not regime change but a change in governance. What happens if there's a parliamentary form of government? Djuc is still Emperor, but all the

189

power is vested in parliament.""

"The old British system."

"Why not? The Kalazecis in the House of Lords and Pagmok in the House of Commons."

"Oh, shit. I can't help repeating myself. That seems the only expression that fits." He shook his head and looked at the overhead. "I wonder what life would have been like had I met some nice lady who wanted to cook for me, grow gardenias and my weekly highlight was going to an Elks club meeting?"

Maria couldn't hold back the laugh. "No Mr. Svern. That is one scene that mankind would never see. Now tell me. What do you think of the idea?"

Erik grew serious, "Captain, you have some reason for going to all this trouble. Want to let me in on it?"

She cupped her hands and rested her chin on them. "I can't stop worrying about where the Kalazecis got this technology. Out there, somewhere is someone who could most likely knock us off as easily as we have the Kalazecis. If we can demonstrate our ability to govern, even showing the Kalazecis and Pagmok how they can co-exist in a well-governed society, it may help us when these beings finally show their faces. And I have no doubt they will. "If we are to have a place in the part of space, we have to stop the Kalazecis from using the Pagmok as if they were conquerors."

"You may be right. I'm not much of a prognosticator and sure no philosopher. What happens next?"

"Prepare a pinnance to return to New Earth. They need to know what I have in mind since it will affect them as well."

Five days later, Maria had New Earth's answer. *Do whatever you think necessary to secure our existence.*

* * * *

Maria summoned an orderly to her day cabin. "Have the Kalazecis and Pagmok commander here for a fourteen hundred meeting." Then she called Erik.

Svern stepped in to her cabin. "Yes, Captain."

"We're alone. Drop the Captain. I need to talk to you as a friend."

Erik nodded and took a chair. He'd never seen her quite so alone.

Maria seemed to be sorting out her thoughts and feelings. "It's very easy to get the idea that you can solve everyone's problems. At least it seems that way for me." She stopped and was quiet for some time.

Erik didn't press her.

"I firmly believe that the Kalazecis must be neutralized in order for us to survive. Question is, should it be us who take on that chore? Am I getting us in deeper than we can handle? A past U.S. president said, "if not now, when. If not us, who?

"I need some honest feedback. You're a practical person. As long as I've known you Erik, you've dealt with the possible. I need all of that now."

"Turn the Pagmok loose on the Kalazecis. That solves our problem." Lurking in the back of his mind was the concern Maria had voiced for the unknown race that had armed the Kalazecis. Pagmok informers indicated Djuc had the backing of these benefactors. They, in fact, had stood by when he killed his father, and seized the throne. It almost seemed their interference was anything but magnanimous or high-minded.

He started to speak again and she held up her hand. "Erik, we could turn the Pagmok loose and you're right. They'd have them for dinner before the sun rose again. The problem with that, it seems to me, is that it really solves nothing. The Pagmok are not capable of self-governing. It wouldn't be long before their society collapsed and they reverted to cannibalism. I suspect they'd keep the Kalazecis and breed them like cattle for food. I won't sanction that.

"If we do it my way, it forces whoever armed the damned Kalazecis front and center to protect what they've got going here in this system. And who knows, maybe the Kalazecis benefactors armed the Kalazecis because they aren't capable of carrying the fight themselves. They might be no more than bright cowards. Something we might do well to consider."

"Or..." she nodded in thought, "...they may be every bit capable of pulling the trigger themselves. And I fear that they may show up and take their displeasure out on us. Whether they're fighters or not, I certainly don't know. However, it may be more difficult for them to persuade the Kalazecis to help them if a bona fide government is up and functioning since the Pagmok will have become a political factor. If we can get some form of legitimate government established there, it should help us, I believe that. I realize the Pagmok may be reluctant to do this but it seems we must persuade them; the Kalazecis we'll have to hold their heads down while all this happens and we can help there also."

"Not only reluctant but the Pagmok can't think that far ahead. Maria, the Pagmok require someone to satisfy their basic needs. The Kalazecis figured that out and made it work for both groups. The Kalazecis feed them and the Pagmok fight for them. Pretty damned simple and straightforward."

"Except the last two times the Pagmok have been called on to do their masters' bidding they got their heads handed to them. The Kalazecis have to be asking themselves how they straighten this out. They have to be worried that we might attack their home world. They must realize they are vulnerable."

Quiet settle over the cabin. Maria punched a button on the control consol. "Yes, Ma'am."

"Jimmy, would you bring us a fresh pot of coffee?"

"On the way, Captain."

A few seconds later, the door buzzer sounded and Maria called the orderly in. He sat the pot and a tray of snacks on the side bar and left.

"Good man. Brought us some treats." She tossed Erik an empty cup and poured her own.

He grinned, stepped over, poured his full and placed the tray of tidbits on a table between their chairs.

She broke the silence. "If we turn the Pagmok loose on the Kalazecis, what happens when the Kalazecis' benefactor arrives at New Earth? I don't think it will be a social call."

"Maria, I don't disagree with anything you've said. And I certainly don't minimize your concerns. I share them as well. But—we're out here ricocheting around, obviously, in over our heads with no clear idea of what we're doing, where we're going, or what we're going to do when we get there. And that's assuming we recognize *there* when we see it. What happens if we get a government in place and the bogeymen show up and dislikes what we've done? How are we any better off? All we will have done is waste valuable time that could have been spent preparing our own defenses, feeble or inadequate as they might be."

"I know we're new to this game. But remember, all the bogyman knows is we've defeated the Kalazecis-Pagmok twice. Our victories were overwhelming. What do you think the bogyman feels about his chances against us? After all, it was his ships, his technology and weapons, and probably his tactics that got stuffed in the can."

Quiet again found its place. Finally, Erik asked, "What did Hammond have to say about it?"

"Mathew thinks it's a good idea. He expressed about the same sentiment as you did but still concluded it's worth the effort."

"Okay. What and how do you want it done?"

She knew Erik wasn't convinced. But she also knew her XO would give it his best and accept no less from his subordinates. "You give up easy."

"I know a losing hand when it's dealt. No sense drawing dead to a stacked deck."

"Stacked. I'm shocked that you would accuse me of treachery."

"Ha! You shocked? You knew Hammond's answer before the meeting started. I didn't stand a chance."

"Yes, you did. Hammond also said if the arguments against getting further involved were strong enough, he would gladly accede to them."

"You didn't tell me that. That's a stacked deck and you know it." He grinned and munched a frosted bagel.

CHAPTER THIRTY-TWO
A New Beginning

Maria decided to start with the Pagmok and had the orderly show in the three delegates. She greeted Momn.

"We didn't meet when you visited New Earth a few years ago, but I did watch the proceedings on the video screen. Welcome aboard the George Washington." She motioned them into the chairs.

A Pagmok Maria had never met seemed to be the delegation head. Dressed in their finery—gray coverall-looking uniforms trimmed in black—they did look elegant.

They took their seats and accepted the refreshments provided.

They seemed impressed that they were being treated with dignity.

Maria hadn't been able to fathom their psyche. The Kalazecis clearly has some sense of security allowing the Pagmok to control ships that could destroy their world. Yet the Pagmok didn't see this as giving them stature.

She switched on her translator. Over the next few minutes, she explained to the three what she had in mind.

The Pagmok listened without questions or interruption.

When she finished, she asked Erik if he had anything to add. That brought a no and she turned to the Pagmok leader.

"I am Momn. *First* among the Pagmok on Myslac. Not believe it will work," he said forthrightly.

Maria almost jumped from her chair. "You speak our language." It wasn't a question. "You learn very quickly." Then she realized Martin Grabel had had quite enough time to teach them. Yet she had to admire his style. Ask him a question and get a straight answer even if it was in broken English.

"Some."

"Oh," she quietly said. "What's wrong with the plan. Where does it fall short?"

"Nothing wrong with self governing. Do different way."

Maria perked up. "Give us your thoughts, please."

Apparently, the Pagmok had given considerable thought to the idea of having their own leaders. "Pagmok need Kalazecis. Kalazecis need Pagmok, *Rshcococ and the First* need both."

Maria blinked. It was the first time either the Pagmok or Kalazecis had mentioned the Rococo, and he used the formal pronunciation. While that could be significant, that they recognized a symbiotic relationship was necessary stunned her. She looked at Erik.

His eyebrows raised Eric said, "Seems both races had it figured out." He didn't say *I told you so* but then he didn't have to. It was exactly what he'd said only a day earlier.

Puzzled she asked, "If the three races have such a dependence on each other, why do you tolerate Djuc's murdering you or your people?"

"Did not say it worked. But could. Few changes." He paused then corrected himself, "Many changes."

Maria leaned back in her chair. "Momn, tell me what changes you'd like to see."

Over the next hour, the five of them huddled around the table.

The Pagmok had a clear perspective of what they thought could work. That didn't mean the Kalazecis would buy into the idea. In fact, the odds were against it. But with New Earth's presence, that dynamic could change.

After listening, Maria sat for some time, mulling over the discussion. On Myslac, the Pagmok inhabited one of the two continents that made up the landmasses, the Kalazecis the other. "You want your own leaders over the territory you now inhabit. The Kalazecis would rule their current continent. You will continue to provide protection, work the factories, and do the domestic chores much as you have been for over two hundred years, except now it would be under a treaty between two equal nations, two equal peoples."

"Pagmok paid for all work."

A large smile broke across Maria's face. "Of course." That had to be the hand of Martin Grabel. A secret smile touched her lips.

She turned to Erik, "Well, XO, what do you think?"

"There are a few things I'd like to kick around—in private."

"Chief," she said, "Let's adjourn until tomorrow. You come back at the same time. Bring the Kalazecis with you."

He nodded. With the other two behind, Momn left the conference room.

"Aren't you going to talk to the Kalazecis today?"

"What am I going to say? We just divided your planet and took away your dominion over the Pagmok? Besides, I think what we've just heard was the political fix authored by Martin Grabel."

Erik shook his head and said with a chuckle, "You're a hard woman, Maria."

She ignored the remark.

Erik looked hard at her. "I have a problem with this solution. What's to keep the Kalazecis from attacking the Pagmok and again subjugating them?

Maria just smiled.

* * * *

The remnants of Kalazecis/Pagmok armada, on orbit around Myslac, prepared for Djuc's Pinnance now headed for the George Washington.

Maria had ordered no repairs be made to the ships, other than what was required for life support, until political decisions were finalized.

It was the first time the Emperor had ever ventured into space. Maria regretted it had taken a show of force to convince him he had no other choice. The Pagmok were already rebuilding his summer palace after she ordered its evacuation and destruction from space. Something his ships could never have done.

Standing as each dignitary arrived, she questioned how she'd react when Martin came aboard.

Her first response was to have him arrested. But the Pagmok had virtually put him on a pedestal eliminating that possibility.

When he emerged from the pinnance, he looked at her then Erik, nodded, and then took his place at the table.

"Have you had a chance to talk to Martin," she whispered to Erik.

Erik shook his head. "No, and I think it was planned that way. He doesn't want to confront us."

"I'm surprised he hasn't at least asked about Bhani and his children."

"The Pagmok delivered a package addressed to Bhani. I suspect it's from Martin." He paused and then added, "We had it checked. Nothing dangerous."

Both looked up as the Emperor's pinnance locked to the hanger deck.

The Pagmok had set up a small throne on the hanger deck a few meters away from the conference table. Djuc emerged from the pinnance after two courtiers to the normal boson's pipe, and drum roll.

Regal training and plumage on display, he strode to the throne. Both Kalazecis and Pagmok bowed, Martin included. Maria's first impression of the Emperor was mousey. No, more of a ferret. He even acted like one.

Dressed in the white uniform of supreme commander, properly embroidered with what she assumed was gold, and a lot of it, he made a gesture of acknowledgement toward Maria who stood at the opposite end of the long table.

She nodded in reply, motioned for Erik to join her and signaled them all to be seated. She'd let Erik talk her into this proceeding, mostly to let everyone see that real change was taking place.

Over the three months it had taken to bring this to reality, Eric had gained a measure of tolerance from the Emperor although his distrust remained. He was convinced that once the New Earth fleet had departed, Djuc would quickly subvert the entire process and regain his former stature. Erik made sure Maria understood his thinking.

Maria was comfortable with the assembled leaders although she had to admit the prospects for a lasting peaceful arrangement was very much in doubt. Only time would tell.

Mukluk, First of the *Rococo and the First*, didn't hesitate to sign.

Maria was particularly proud as the Rococoan strode forward to the pedestal where the document resided.

Martin Grabel, the newly elected leader of the Pagmok signed next, amid what passed for Pagmok grins from his followers.

She didn't share their apparent triumph. Maybe it would work. Martin was certainly smart enough to handle the job. But emotionally, she had grievous doubts. Did he have what it took to make tough decisions?

Erik reminded her that they now knew Martin would outlive his counterparts by a factor of three. Maybe with a little skill and a lot of luck, he might make the difference.

Finally, Djuc motioned for the document to be brought to him

Maria's orderly never moved a muscle. Standing at attention as he had for the others, pen in hand, he remained fixed.

All eyes locked on Djuc.

Finally, the diminutive Emperor stood. As he walked the twenty paces toward the documents, Maria joined him. Each signed, to the applause of the entire assembly.

Maria turned to the Emperor, towering over him by at least fifteen centimeters. She extended her hand, which he less than graciously took.

She leaned forward and whispered something that left the man ashen. Then she turned and walked to the podium. "These proceedings are closed."

With Erik at her side, Maria saw all the dignitaries off, Martin Grabel having already left, and headed for her day cabin.

"Captain," Erik asked. "What did you say to Djuc after the signing?"

She shrugged.

"Captain. I will keep after you until—"

"Quite simple. I told him I knew he gained the throne by murdering his father. I said, if things got out of hand and I had to come back, I'd kill him."

She was at least three strides up the passageway when she turned to the moribund looking, dumbstruck XO. "Come on. Let's go home. We've still got a lot of work to do."

EPILOG

The technology the Kalazecis possessed still haunted her. It came from somewhere else. But where?

Despite her questions, they had refused any comment.

Only there was no smugness in their response, in fact, Maria detected concern. What was going on? Where did these weapons and FTL drives come from? Maria knew her little band could never let its guard down.

EXHIBIT

(Reprinted with permission)

From: Jordan Maclay
Sent: Thursday, April 28, 2005
Subject: ZpvSF

Dear Ken,

Thanks for the inquiry about ZPV engineering. I will write about a vacuum drive as an engineer in the future might write a description:

In order to use vacuum energy in propulsion, the chaos, or randomness of the vacuum needs to be reduced, thereby allowing us to organize and utilize the tremendous energy and momentum in the vacuum. The success of the Casimir drive lies in the discovery of how to initiate the process of cohering the vacuum energy and momentum. Actually, only a very small fraction of the total vacuum energy is cohered: about 1 photon in 10^{40} is cohered, resulting a theoretical energy density of about 10^{55} grams/cc, which is still about 10^{30} greater than any the energy density of nuclear matter [I need to check these units and values when I get home.] The factor of 10^{40} arises because of ..... If a much higher degree of coherence were obtained, there would be the possibility that the process would become unstable, and, in the worst scenario, cause the collapse of the universe... Fortunately, no one knows how to obtain higher levels of coherence. Higher levels could cause the creation of black holes. The actual energy density obtained is smaller by a factor of about 10^5, due to limitations in the materials available. The coherence level is controlled electrically in the Casimir space drive, but if the coherence drops below a critical level, it dies out. This is a design issue, because it can be inconvenient or difficult to dissipate the energy at low conversions when the spacecraft is stationary. Most craft utilize a small idling Casimir drive during operation to maintain a coherent vacuum region.

Enormous energy density with the proper geometrical configuration and materials is required to initiate the coherence. The seed energy is equivalent to about the amount of vacuum energy cohered in 10^{-30} second in the idler drive. This energy is usually obtained by the discharge of electrical energy or from small nuclear explosions. The latter method is dying out because of radiation issues. The coherence process begins in a very small region, but the coherence can be extended to nearby regions by means of the proper guiding surfaces of high-density superconducting materials and electromagnetic fields. With the AR250 quantum vacuum jet, which uses the Casimir Drive, the coherence starts in the center of a region about the size of a proton, and is extended and guided to the entire thruster region, which occupies an area of about 1000 sq meters for a craft 50 meters in diameter, weighting 3 million tons. The coherence is controlled over this area to obtain different thrust from different regions, thereby permitting the spacecraft to turn.

The thruster size is limited by the strength of materials to sustain the forces of accelerations. Namely, it must disperse the thrust from the regions of cohered vacuum over a large area, to reduce the forces.

The engines used in passenger ships are often designed with energy capacity that results in a gravitational field about the same as that of the earth or any home planet.

Best to you,
Jordan Maclay

Made in the USA
Charleston, SC
26 January 2011